D0092255

ROCK CRITIC MURDERS

Jesse Sublett

A DELL BOOK

Published by
Dell Publishing
a division of
Bantam Doubleday Dell Publishing Group, Inc.
666 Fifth Avenue
New York, New York 10103

ISBN: 0-440-20703-7

Reprinted by arrangement with Viking

Printed in the United States of America

Published simultaneously in Canada

May 1990

10 9 8 7 6 5 4 3 2 1

OPM

To Lois

A big, warm thank you to Abigail Thomas, Lisa Kaufman, Louis Black, and Ed Ward. Passionate gratitude to my wife and *chief inspiration*, Lois Richwine. And a heartfelt toast to all the musicians and fans who make Austin, Texas a great place to be, especially at night.

ROCK CRITIC MURDERS

1

Austin, Texas, 1984. It was a dull, hot, mid-July Monday with nothing going for it. I was holed up in the small room in my apartment that I used as an office and storeroom for my music gear. Sometimes when I had nothing else to do I just sat in there and stared at my things instead of watching TV.

My bass guitar leaned against an amplifier, ready to play the blues. Maybe I'd get around to changing its strings later, since I'd decided to take the afternoon off from the collection agency where I'd been working part-time as a skiptracer. When gigs got too few and far between, I took it out on people who'd moved without paying their bills, and that was how I paid my own.

I was good at it, but I was better at playing bass and that was what I preferred. I sat there, blowing smoke rings at the instrument, admiring its curves, its hard mystery, watching the smoke fall into lazy tendrils around the body. Knowing that it was an idle beauty, and idle beauties can't stay that way long.

I'd been thinking about True Love. The band I used to play with, not the emotion. I'd heard they were getting back together.

The phone sat there on the corner of the desk, squat, black, and ugly. There was something malignant about it and its silence, just as there was something magical about my musical instruments. Gradually I realized that I was sitting there staring at the machinery of my fate, getting the same feeling you get when you stare at a clock long enough to see the hands move.

I knew that if they hadn't gotten in touch with me by now, I wasn't their first choice. I wasn't the original bass player, and I had no right to expect anything from the old band. And I'd almost talked myself into expecting nothing but a phone call letting me know that I'd be on the guest list. It was a few minutes later, after I'd decided how I would take the news—cordial but coolly distant—when he called.

"Is this Martin Fender, semi-legendary Austin rock and R & B bassist?" asked a voice that was calm and sober. "Fender, as in . . ."

"As in the guitar," I said. "Post-Bogart and pre-synth pop, this is he. Hello, KC." A gig review in a local rag had said all those things about me. I was surprised that anyone would remember, especially the bourbon-chugging guitar player. "It's barely after noon. I'm a little shocked to hear from you so early in the day."

"The day starts a little bit earlier when you stop drinking, Martin. I'm just down the street, having some migas at Dos Hermanos. I was wondering if you could use a gig this weekend."

"Odds are I could," I said.

"It'll be easy money, Martin. You already know the songs . . ."

I looked at the clock again, and the calendar too. I hadn't worked with a guitar player half as good as KC in a long time, but what were the odds he'd still be on the wagon by the weekend?

". . . and this seems to be the year for reunions. I know they might seem corny, but we got a damn good offer. It'll be the grand opening of a new club."

"Those kind of gigs can be loose with things besides cash, KC. They flash a lot of dollars at you and then it turns out they haven't built the stage yet or remembered to get their ad in the paper. Remember when we drove all the way to Brownsville for that rock festival and came back with nothing but a couple of switchblades from Matamoros?"

"Sure do. Nothing like a night in Boystown to take the sting out of getting stiffed by a promoter."

"But as I recall, you woke up in a motel room and she'd only left you a garter belt to remember her by."

"No goodbye note, no wallet, and no shoes. Had to walk two miles to find a pay phone to call you guys to pick me up. Barefoot, in the middle of June."

"August, I believe."

"Probably right, Martin. Anyway, this one's in town. And I'm sitting on a certified check. Your cut would be two grand."

Ten weeks of afternoons at the collection agency. My cut of a dozen fraternity mixers or debutante balls. More than I'd see after thirty or forty midweek one-nighters at the Continental Club or the Black Cat Saloon. And it was the old band.

"What do you say, Martin?"

"What time is sound check?"

He suggested that he come by so he could give me the rest of the details and then I could give him a ride by the Tavern and then home. I said that would be fine.

While I still had the phone in my hand I almost called Ladonna. She would probably be at work, though. The guys she worked with would go, "Was that Martin?" and they would know I hadn't called in over a week, so they'd ask if I was on the road. She would have to say no, and there you go.

"Has it really been five years?" asked the guitarist as we rolled down South 1st with the top down on my banana yellow 1970 Karmann Ghia, caught in the flow of traffic that would sweep us from laid-back South Austin across the Colorado River and on into the heart of the boomtown, if we let it.

"Close enough," I said. He had put on a little weight. He wasn't fat, but the trademark black leather jeans—which had always been tight—and black sleeveless shirt were carrying an extra twenty to thirty pounds. The tiger in the tattoo on his arm looked less likely to spring, and there was an extra fold of skin under the eyes behind the Ray Ban Wayfarers. But he hadn't lost any of the defiant shock of hair that stuck up like stiff black flames, tousled enough to have that look of ambivalent neglect. Nor the ragged fingernails, the hoarse cough, the three-day beard.

"Think you'll remember the songs?" I asked.

"How could I forget? Never stopped playing them. You know that. People never get tired of hearing Al Green, Wilson Pickett, Stax, and Motown. The originals might take a little time, but I can fake what doesn't come back straight away. And the way I remember it, so can you."

When I'd been called in to replace the original bass player, True Love already had a large following throughout the Southwest and a couple of albums on small independent labels, making them enough money to make payments on a van and keep it running. Which was good, since it was on the road the better part of the year. True Love would be pick of the week when we played New York or LA, but the band was never snatched up by a major label and therefore had never, as most people would say, "made it."

"We were the biggest band around here for a good six years," said the guitar operator.

"Legends," I said.

"Ex-legends," he said, lighting another cigarette, "who are going to look like clowns if we don't sound good. I admit I took the gig because of the money, but it's gotta be right. I hope you don't feel too put out by having to spend a week in the country rehearsing—"

"It's got to be right," I agreed, cutting him off. We'd already been through that. He'd given me his scribbled directions out to the ranch house we'd rehearse at all week. Only a beat later, he told me which new club we'd be playing at. I knew the clubowner well enough to almost change my mind about taking the gig.

"I know how you feel about Ward, too. He's stiffed me a couple of times and pulled dates out from under me more times than I can count, but like I said, I got the certified check. The money's enough so that I don't mind playing his little game. I guess he figures I'll be less likely to backslide and start guzzling Jack Daniels if we're stuck out in the hills, and you can't blame him for wanting us to do the interview. You could use the publicity just as much as the club can, and I told them we could only give them a half hour since we need to get going."

"We do?"

"Relax, Martin. We'll make it fun."

There must be an interview school somewhere where all prospective music journalists must go before they can practice their trade, and at that school they ingrain upon young impressionable minds the necessity of asking the ten stupidest questions a musician can be asked. When our cub reporter started out with the time-worn "What are your influences?" and then proceeded to stupid questions number two, three, and four, I decided to cut things short and try to sum it all up for the record.

"True Love was a helluva band, one of those bands that believed that the blues is all there is. But we played the blues loud and hard, our own way. Somebody once said that the blues are sad and lonely and kind of raw, the way that freight trains always seem raw and sad and lonely. Well, True Love was raw and sad and lonely as a freight train doing 90 miles an hour. So, one more time, for a couple of hours this weekend, the blues will be all there is, because we'll be firing up that old train. The 123 Club will have state-of-the-art sound and lights and free champagne and *everyone* will be there, including this guitar mangler here, KC, along with Frankie Day on lead vocals and Billy Ludwig on the drums."

"But aren't you looking at this as the start of a new career for the band? A chance to really go for it this time?"

I looked at KC. There was no life in the novocaine face. He could have been a killer, sitting in a windowless room, talking to a hack lawyer about a no-hope appeal. The interviewer fidgeted nervously as the tape rolled in the cassette recorder, preserving the methodical sounds KC made as he dropped another Gitanes out of the box and struck a match for it. He inhaled and deliberately let the smoke roll out across the table after he'd had a lungful.

"We'll see," he said finally.

I had a pretty good idea of how the story would run. It would say something about how it seemed like only yesterday when True Love kept the town's feet tapping and ears ringing. It would wax nostalgic, associating the reunion of the band with better, or, at least, more carefree times. Typical Baby Boom stuff. And it would mention that the original bass player, a guy named Dan Gabriel, had left the band after five years, and that was when they asked me to join. Now Dan Gabriel was a successful real estate hustler with a downtown office, Armani suits, and a secretary who had dutifully taken the messages that KC had left about getting the band back together for one night, messages that could just as well have been dropped in the middle of Town Lake.

The story would have a smattering of song titles, mostly re-workings of R & B classics that sounded good in smoky bars and trendy dives. It probably wouldn't mention KC's drinking and it probably wouldn't mention my hassle with the law last year. Which was OK with me. That kind of publicity we could do without.

When the reporter was gone and it was just the two of us again, the sounds of the restaurant seemed to envelop us, reminding me that we were in the Tavern, one of the loudest places in town. Dishes clattered together in cold greasy bus trays, wait-resses threw orders at the guy flying the deep fryer vats, beepers beeped, voices at other tables talked software and real estate. And all of it was mashed together into one big din.

But the Tavern's abrasive atmosphere went down easy as a frost-covered longneck at a patio barbecue. There was a cool blue neon sign in the window that said something about air conditioning, and a '50s deco clock the size of a truck tire over the bar that made time seem like a friendly thing.

KC had both elbows resting on the checkered oilcloth and seemed to be watching the cars skate by on Lamar Boulevard.

The journalist had left a print of a photo with us that was supposed to run with the story. I looked at it.

KC had changed, but I hadn't, not really. I was thinner than he was even then, and, at six feet, a bit taller. My hair was still, at just under thirty, a dark brown that was just this side of black, and the front bit of it still fell over my right eyebrow no matter how often I combed it back. I even had on the same clothes—black Converse All-Stars, skin-tight black jeans, black cotton shirt cinched up with a bolo tie, and the same black, blocky, unvented, thrift-shop jacket with notched lapels that was draped over the back of my chair.

KC noticed me looking at the photo and frowned. "Some of us have changed a bit," he said.

I shrugged. "Why don't we seal the deal with a—"

"Water will be fine, or maybe one more cup of coffee," he said. "Go ahead, have a drink, I can take it. I ain't that much of a wimp."

"Just trying to be sensitive."

"Go ahead, have one. I know you could use two or three fingers of Scotch after that bullshit," he said, signalling our waitress. She came, coffee pot in hand, serviced KC's cup and scratched my drink order on our ticket.

"Salud," he said, tipping the cup. "I just want you to know, Martin, I'm glad it all came down the way it did. As much as I can't stand the prick, Ward is the only guy in town who can come up with the cash."

"That may be true, KC. But he needs us, too. He's buying nostalgia. He's gotta have a gimmick, and we're it."

"I know. Screw it. It's gonna be mighty trendy, you know, with video monitors everywhere, big screens, multiple levels, after-hours disco, and that New York trip where they make you wait on the wrong side of the velvet rope before they decide if you're cool enough to get in. Not the kinda place I'd hang out."

"It'll need some gimmicks to compete with all the other clubs on 6th Street. Might even run one of his other clubs out of business. What's this one make, four?"

"Yeah," said the guitarist. "But I just want you to know I'm glad it came down this way, even if it means you might have to shake hands with the sonuvabitch afterward. I really wanted you for the gig, even though I was sorta obligated for authenticity's sake to give Gabe a call."

"No big deal," I said, downing my Scotch seconds after it was placed in front of me.

"You're a better bass player, anyway."

"Thanks."

"Too damn loud, though."

"Got to be to compete with your shit," I said. I looked for some life in the whiskery mask. There was a little. It was jaded, and it was hoarse, but it would pass for a laugh.

"Ready to give me a ride?"

We walked to my car, and as we got in—careful not to get burned from the door handles or seat belt buckles—I suppose both of us gave a nod or a squinty wink to the object slowly turning on its sixteen-foot pedestal across the street. It was a red and blue and green steel insect almost as big as a VW Beetle, with glass wings and blinking eyes. The bug had been the figurehead for Texterminators Pest Control for more than twenty years. But it was more than just a mascot. It was an old friend that stayed the same in a sea of change, a reminder of the often quirky personality of a town that was prospering and metamorphosing but that still, in many ways, refused to grow up.

We lit up cigarettes as we pulled out. Up the 12th Street hill going into Clarksville, KC went into a coughing fit. Having seen him go through half a pack in less than two hours, I wasn't surprised. Being around him proved that if you wanted to keep your smoking in check you shouldn't give up drinking. Nature abhors a vacuum.

"How'd you quit drinking?" I asked.

"Lorraine. You've met her, haven't you?"

I nodded. I'd met the redhead all right. I'd met her over at their house years before when I'd dropped by to loan him a Howlin' Wolf album. I reminded him.

"Oh yeah. Remind me to give that back. I still have it, don't

I. Anyway, it was her idea. She paid for a detox deal. Here we go."

We were in front of his house, a run-down white frame thing with a porch and untended yard, a not uncommon sight in the funky but trendy neighborhood. Lots of musicians, hip professionals, and, as everywhere in Austin, college students, lived there and paid the inflated price for hardwood floors and relaxed atmosphere on the near west side of town. A cedar stood a little too close to the sunset side of the house. That would be the tree that was outside the window of the bedroom, the room with the door I'd opened when I was looking for the bathroom that night.

"Think you can figure out the map?" he asked.

"Yeah. I just need to pack some things and cash a check. You really think it'll take all week?"

"Hell no," he replied, leaning one hand on the open door. "And I wouldn't bother cashing a check unless you need some gas money. You won't need any cash out there. Ward's paying for the groceries."

"All right," I said.

He got out and shut the door. "She's coming, too. It's a big old house, there's plenty of room out there and . . ."

"KC," I interrupted. It was too hot to listen to explanations.

"What?"

"Thanks."

He nodded, flipped his cigarette butt into the street, turned and went inside. I let out the clutch and turned the car around in the narrow road, only once glancing in the rear view mirror at the house where I'd accidentally walked in on the guitar player's girlfriend. I still remember the sight of that tree outside the window on the night of a full moon, framing the standing figure of the girl who looked up at me with those big blue eyes that showed no sign of being startled. Even though she was as naked as you can get.

I set the controls for downtown. Somewhere a dog was barking.

2

So I had a gig. I hauled my watch, a missile-shaped circa 1955 Louvic, over to the jeweler on Congress Avenue and dropped it off. By the time it was repaired, I'd have the money to pay for it. The jeweler loaned me a digital watch. It was as plain and ugly as any digital watch ever was. I doubled back and took the tree-lined drive around the state capitol, nodding at the cranky old men who sat in lawn chairs guarding the bureaucrats' parking and feeding the squirrels that scampered around the elm and pecan trees.

The double-domed granite building was five feet taller than its Washington, D.C. counterpart. Atop it stood a zinc goddess of liberty with a foul expression on a face even a zinc mother couldn't love. Maybe she was unhappy about the pigeon's nest in her right armpit, or about the crack in her shoulder blade. There had been some discussion about giving the lady a make-over, maybe even giving her a new face and slimming down those nineteenth-century thighs, but no one knew how she got up there in the first place eighty years ago and no one knew how to get her down.

I took the avenue back toward the river, keeping an eye out for buildings that might have gone up since the night before. Construction cranes towered over the avenue like surgeons giving it a quadruple by-pass. New post-modern monuments were shooting up all over, loud and tall and squeaky clean.

Did the town need any more of these new buildings? Did it need another rock and roll reunion?

Normally I shied away from funerals and reunions and I

couldn't figure out which was sadder or more shot through with hypocrisy. Funerals were ostensibly about confronting death and celebrating life. But in the center of the whole thing was a dead body, cold proof that Death had won again.

Reunions were supposed to bring people together, to show that the old war horses were still alive and kicking, still vital. But did they? Reunions brought out the seedy side of rock and roll, as bloated caricatures waddled onstage with roots that had been nurtured in Memphis or the south side of Chicago now slanted towards Vegas. Showing what rock and roll can do *to* you, when it hasn't done enough *for* you. Half the time the music was so lame you wondered if it had been any good the first time. Bad examples came to mind—the Grass Roots; Crosby, Stills, and Nash; Steppenwolf; the Guess Who.

Reunions. I cringed at being associated with the word, much less the groups that had been doing it. But True Love wasn't like that. We were tough local boys and we were still—all of us except maybe Billy—under thirty. And we played the blues. You could play the blues forever. We weren't going to be a side show.

Also, it would be good to see the old crowd of regulars out in force again, wearing the essential Transylvanian black and gravity-defying hairstyles. They were night creatures, people whose days started where other people's days ended, who lived in dumpy houses without central air so they could spend their money on *important* things: records, leather jackets, custom guitars, cool cars, Harley-Davidsons, and sometimes drugs. Lots of times drugs. Some worked day jobs, considering them only temporary, while others got by doing things that were somewhat illegal. These were people with an advanced degree of cool. Many of them had no last names. They weren't in any of the lines of cars idling at the drive-in banks. They weren't wearing hard hats, tying steel on any of the new skyscrapers. They hadn't succumbed to condo fever. Thinking of them brought warmth to my jaded heart. Too bad they'd have to come to one of Ward's clubs to see us.

Maybe the reunion was a good thing. The scene needed a

big shot in the arm. Live music was down—more people were staying home, watching their VCRs, playing with their home computers. Spending their disposable income on the back catalogs of old favorites that had just been released on CD. Having babies.

Live music was also down on account of the real estate boom. Because in a city with more live music venues than either L.A. or Manhattan, things had always centered around a downtown area no more than a couple of miles in diameter. And in that area, skyrocketing land value called for maximum use for maximum profit. Hi-rises were in and clubs were out. Venues were closing left and right.

Things had always been tough for local live music, though, and it was hard to feel sorry for clubowners. Down at the street level, the clubs—as well as booking agencies, studios, and bands—often survived only by bending laws and cutting corners and using money that someone needed to lose. Sometimes the money came from drugs, sometimes it came from someone just trying to avoid a tax bite. I remember one club that was run by men who had connections with a string of sex-oriented clubs out of Houston. When you went downstairs to get paid, they took the cash from a big steel trunk the size of a coffin. There would be four or five guys down there and at least that many guns. You didn't ask where that money had been.

Not that everyone got by with transfusions of illegitimate cash. Some of the clubs were like the town's Old Money—it seemed like they'd always been there and always would be. There were clubs that stayed open even if no one liked them, while some popular spots closed no matter what was done to keep them going. Also, every six months or so a club or a band came up with the right idea and it was a big success. You saw glitter and flash and lines around the block. Bartenders saw their tip jars overflow and clubowners saw themselves get fat and happy. It never made sense.

The slippery economy gave the whole business a surreal aura. It made the musicians embarrassingly subservient to the clubowners because it made the clubowners look like the real magicians. Pulling a club through hard times appeared to be a lot harder than pulling a rabbit out of a hat, maybe even harder than whipping out a blistering lead on a Stratocaster. It wasn't as glamorous, but it was essential, and it certainly held an air of mystery. Mystery can be power and once you have both, look out.

Even if a band was hot, a clubowner could make them feel like he was doing them a favor by giving them a gig. And if he cancelled it two days before the date, or didn't pay them after they played, he could shrug and say, Hey, that's the way it goes, isn't it? That's rock and roll.

It didn't help that musicians have a natural tendency to be laid back and naive about business. In Austin, you could generally count on that tendency being doubled or tripled. You don't see many Austin musicians at motivational seminars. To a musician, motivation is a simple thing. Love of music, respect for the icons of the genre. Wishes for fame. The desire to be wanted, loved, adored.

But what motivated a person to be a clubowner? The desire to emulate Rick Blaine in *Casablanca*—smart, amoral, and in control? I doubted that. Clubowners didn't generally have that kind of class. Nor did the curious assortment of misanthropic bouncers, anti-social bartenders, deaf sound engineers, and mercenary agents who only used pencils, never ink, on their booking calendars. They were a whole sub-class of people with a subterranean bottom line. They made things work by being there and running things, but they were in the music business the way cheap hookers were in the love business.

Yeah, they were.

But that was the way it was, and it worked.

Music and the music business. If you only knew one and not the other, you weren't a professional. You were just a fan.

I loved it. I hated it. It was screwed up enough that it could put you off music, and it was run by people that couldn't be put off because they were too weird to do anything else. Those people paid you, or didn't pay you, and even if you didn't care for them, you had to live with them, or you didn't work.

And that was how Ward fit in.

I was packing my bag when he called.

"Well it's all set then, Martin. I'm really relieved that it's all been worked out. It'll be twenty-four hours a day of chaos down here, but the grand opening is going to happen this weekend if it kills me and a couple dozen other people too."

Shrill screams from electric saws and the sounds of things being slapped together were irritating, especially when amplified by the speaker phone the club owner was using. I could just see him, pacing around a desk in an office above all the work, waving invoices, picking out carpet samples, and dispatching foremen with a nod of his head, all the while keeping his bony hands off the actual work. He probably hadn't even dialed the phone himself.

"If you're expecting that kind of bloodshed," I said, "maybe I should get an advance on my $2,000."

"Oh, Martin, don't you worry about a thing. Everything's happening. You've got the easy job. Just get out there and get it tight, OK? And don't get lost on the way. You've got the directions?"

"I'm afraid I do," I said.

"You'll love it, Martin. Just give it a chance. I picked up the lease on that place for a song, too. You'd die if I told you how I got it. Beautiful hill country out there, lots of deer and fresh air. My man Pedro has my dog out there and he just loves it. A great chance to get away from it all for a week."

"Just what I was about to do when you called."

"Right. You better get going. The rest of the gang should be there already getting set up. Your old roadie chum, Johnny, is taking care of the equipment. Anything you need, any amps or guitars you need repaired, just tell him—he can fix it. But you know that, you've worked with him more than anybody in town. Just one little thing, Martin, I'd appreciate on a personal level, OK. It's the reason I called."

"Bring my bass?"

"No, it's something I don't want you to take."

"What?"

"Your gun."

"My gun."

"Leave it at home. We know you think you're some kind of detective but there will be people out there who don't appreciate firearms and then there's KC and we know he's had some problems. I don't need any extra headaches, OK?"

"I hadn't planned on bringing it." Just like I hadn't planned on seeing bandmates of mine blown away for our Saturday night earnings in Houston. Both times, walking from the club to the van, approached by men in the dark. *Some kind of a detective.* . . . Now I had a gun, and it wasn't going to happen again, not like that. Sometimes the law seems written for the wrong people, and sometimes the cops don't come at all. I had never fired the 9mm Beretta, but it and the fifteen-round clip in my dresser were there, just in case a person might need a little edge against something dark and unforeseen . . .

". . . snakes, for example."

"Snakes are easy to avoid, Martin. Just don't step on anything that looks like a garden hose."

"Except it's covered in snakeskin."

"Just pack your Precision."

"Gotcha."

I threw some things in an overnight bag, grabbed the bass and some spare strings, set the answering machine, asked my neighbor to feed the cat for a couple of days, locked up, and drove until there was no more city.

3

They were talking heat wave on the car radio. Past Westlake Hills you could follow the winding curves of Bee Cave Road out to the lakes or you could join up with 290 West and, if you weren't careful, find yourself in Dust Creek, a spot on the road with one red light and a high proportion of necks to match. I popped a cassette of the Fabulous Thunderbirds into the Walkman and that made the miles go a lot smoother.

Following KC's directions once I left the main road was a little easier than transcribing one of his solos, but not much. The hill country land was harsh and dry, rocky and not only not green, but hardly any color at all. Dark birds glided out of colonies of thick shrubbery that stretched for miles.

The car and I bumped along a couple more miles before rounding the curve on the edge of a small canyon. It was picturesque and evidently someone had thought the rugged banks made an ideal setting for a hacienda-style ranch house. Terra cotta roof, saltillo tiled steps, wrought iron burglar bars. A few yards from the house, the road forked. Weeds had overtaken the bend to the left, the hurricane fence around the yard, and the sidewalk leading up to the front door. To the right, the road led to a covered side entrance where the sight of two humans and a dog clashed with the dead landscape.

I pumped the brakes so I wouldn't run over the German shepherd with the blue Frisbee in its teeth. It bounded back to the girl, who patted him on the head and slung the disc out among the rocks and weeds again before she acknowledged the cloud of dust I had arrived in. Wearing mirrored Sportsman shades, she was upwards of five ten or eleven, taller than KC, almost as tall as me. A big girl, too, with big, broad shoulders, fleshy arms, plump breasts. Not to where you'd think of her as being fat, but fleshy and not ashamed of it.

She didn't wear clothes as much as she spilled out of them, and there was a color to her cheeks that had nothing to do with sun or shyness. Then there was the hair. It was a burnished red, long and voluminous. She wasn't my type at all, and maybe that was why I didn't feel guilty about looking at her the way I probably did.

"Better get used to the dust," she said, leaning back on a stucco column, ordering the dog to sit after it returned again and gave up the plastic disc, wet with dog spit. "It gets on and in everything. You just can't get away from it."

Her feet were bare, the troublesome limestone powder clinging to the tanned skin of them. The cut-off jeans were short and tight and the T-shirt big and loose, the sleeves ripped out, a black bra underneath. Shiny things dangled from her earlobes.

An elderly Mexican man with high flat Indian cheekbones and a cheerful, sleepy face shuffled over to me, palm outstretched. "Hell-oh. I wach car," he said.

I gave him the keys. "You're going to watch the car? Seems like you'd only have horse thieves out here, not car thieves." I looked over at the redhead, lighting a cigarette.

"No, going to *wach* car," he corrected, making circles with his free hand. "Get off dirt." He pointed to a barn half a country block away, opposite the canyon road and the house. There were empty livestock pens and a drive leading up to the big red building with the rusty roof. Apparently it was being used as a garage.

I pulled the bass and my bag out of the back. The old man pointed at himself and said, "Pedro." I shook his hand, a working man's hand, and introduced myself. He smiled and got in the car, and drove it off toward the barn. The dog loped happily after him, barking the whole way.

"His name's Diablo," said Lorraine. She held the screen door open and motioned me inside.

We passed through a foyer of rifle racks, hat racks, coat hooks and boot jacks, into a kitchen that smelled of lemons and bacon grease, on through a long narrow hall with cool saltillo tile floor and deer trophies along the walls.

"We call this the motel," she said, and it was easy to see why. As we walked, I counted five doors on the right and left, most of them open, revealing small rooms with double beds.

My room was at the end of the hall. Covering the floor was a sad shag carpet that had possibly at one time been orange. There was a twin bed in one corner, an old Zenith black and white set on cinderblocks by the window, and a box fan.

"Nice," I said, dropping my bag on the bed. At least it was on the side with windows.

"Since you were last to get here," she shrugged. "Bathroom's across the hall. Jiggle the lever on the toilet to get it to flush. The guys are in the main room getting started." She crushed her cigarette in a Night Hawk Steakhouse ashtray on the TV and walked out.

I checked my bag to see if the Walkman, paperbacks, and Scotch were in good condition. I left them on the bed, went across the hall to the bathroom, splashed some water on my face and knocked some dust off my clothes.

Back in my room, I was picking up my bass when the noise began in earnest. A snare cracked several times and then a four count propelled the whole drum kit into action. A loud guitar fell in with big ragged chords that rattled the window panes.

The source of all the sound was in a room on the other side of the house. In fact, the room was most of the other half of the house. The ceiling was high and vaulted. More clay tile floor, stucco walls, and a fireplace of rough-hewn rock. At one end, a chandelier was jittering nervously over a long heavy oak dinner table.

Jungle rhythm. Billy Ludwig, the drummer, had already worked up a sweat. The relaxed shoulders underneath the loose green rayon thrift shop shirt contrasted with the muscles sticking out in his arms and the maniacal scowl on his face.

Leaning against the fireplace, microphone cradled in one

hand, was a guy with the pale skin and slicked-back hair of a vampire, the negative cheeks and bony frame that earned him some modelling money between gigs, and a wide, flat chin he kept tucked in his upturned collar when there wasn't a microphone around. That was Frankie Day.

The little red light was flickering on a big tube amp hooked up to two road-scarred bass bins. I plugged in, cranked up the treble, cut back on the mid-range, and the place began to rumble. The song was "I've Got to Use My Imagination," made popular by Gladys Knight and the Pips a long time ago. We thundered through it.

KC segued into the Temptations' "Just My Imagination," then, "Standing on Shaky Ground." We roared through them like the pros we were, barely looking at each other, except for occasional almost imperceptible cues. Billy kept the rhythm going with a confident kick drum, adding an edge if not just a little speed to KC's guitar solos, then settling back when the vocals came in.

Frankie had a tendency to flatten out melodies and had the weirdest sense of timing this side of Al Green. But people said Mick Jagger couldn't sing and he managed to get by, and Frankie had a world-weary slouch—dangling on the mike stand like a tarantula on morphine—that looked good in front of a rock band.

But when people talked about us, the talk was nearly always about KC's guitar playing. Critics may have carped about it, but people in bars were mad for it. He could say more with five seconds of feedback than most could with a double album. The paying public regarded KC's playing the way they regarded '57 T-birds and leather jackets and James Dean. Cool. The art of it, the state of being it, neither questioned nor taken for granted. Not even discussed in great detail. Just—

—That KC is *cool*, man.

—Damn right.

—*Plays* that guitar.

—Cool.

From the first chords that afternoon, he still worked out of the same basic style, the one he had in True Love and the one he'd still had when I'd last played with him at a regular Monday night jam session on 6th Street. He had the same stance, and the guitar looked familiar. But his timing was a little off, he clammed a few more notes than usual, and mostly he just seemed to have trouble getting *comfortable* with the music.

Once, during an old Muddy Waters song, he actually played the solo in the wrong key. But musicians are cruel. No one stopped playing, no one even looked at him. I was no exception. What was I supposed to do?

Maybe he was nervous, which I doubted, or his guitar was a little out of shape, needing some adjustments. Or maybe the years of not enough success and the recent drying out had taken a toll. But people would like that, the brave, wounded artist look, thinking that validated his playing even more.

Soon I was out of cigarettes and KC's guitar was hopelessly out of tune. Except for the humming amps and a ringing in my ears, everything got real quiet.

Lorraine walked in with a tray—four Heinekens and a Coke. The drinkers grabbed the green bottles, KC lit another Gitanes while she set the Coke on his amp. He shook his head and moved the bottle to a coffee table.

"Oh I'm sorry," she shrugged, giving him a goose on the arm, just below the tiger tattoo, "I forgot. That would blow up your tubes if it got knocked over, wouldn't it?"

KC nodded, twin plumes of smoke running out his nostrils. "Why don't you take a break, boys?" she said. "It sounds just like old times. Ward called. He just bought some new video cameras and he wants Johnny to videotape the gig. He asked if he should send a hairdresser out."

Sighs all around. No response except cigarettes being lit by those who hadn't yet. Lorraine didn't seem to get it. Billy broke the silence and changed the subject.

"I can't believe I still know these songs. Of course the originals may take more time, and I've got to get these drums in shape but hey . . ." punctuating his sentence with a whack on his snare drum, twisting a tuning peg, then whacking it again.

Each stroke reverberated through the room like a slap, making everyone wince.

"You know," he continued, "all the sessions I've done in the last five years . . . I've learned hundreds of songs. Maybe thousands. Seems like my brain would overload and lose these old ones."

"Be-*cause* you never learned *any* of them right," said Frankie with an affected lisp.

Smiles. It was OK to kid the drummer. Good drummers were like beautiful girls—never without a date on Saturday night. And they were the mechanics, too. They rarely got songwriting credit or the big checks the center stage stars made, but they got steady work and they got respect.

Billy puffed thoughtfully on his Kool, a pack of them showing through the pocket of the rayon shirt. "You know," he said, through a cloud of menthol, "this room's got great reverb, better than the new five thousand dollar digital unit they got at the studio." He crossed his arms just above his beer gut and leaned back on the drum stool, craning his neck to survey the room from floor to ceiling, corner to corner. Then he whacked the snare again.

"Do you have to do that?" asked Lorraine.

"I got an idea," he said, looking pleased with himself, ignoring the redhead. "I could take this drum track I've been working on—got a tape of it in my suitcase—play it in this room, loud, and record the room echo with my portable four-track here. Then I'd use that track for the echo track on the song, giving it that Led Zeppelin drum sound everybody's so crazy about now, only better."

He chuckled and scratched his stomach with the hand holding the cigarette. "And nobody'd be able to duplicate it."

"Unless they hire you for a producer," I added.

"Don't give him ideas, Martin," vamped Frankie, using the admonition as an exit line.

KC and Lorraine also drifted away from the tangled cords and buzzing amps towards the dining room. The door to the kitchen was propped open, treating the hot room to a dose of air we hadn't used yet. Billy, rummaging around in a road case, pulling out sticks, tape, and other odds and ends, chuckled: "You notice how he talks, prancing out a room with his eye on the mirror? Like he's trying out for a movie or something."

He held on to the smile as he bent over the case, but I knew that neither of us was really thinking about Frankie. There were some bad notes still reverberating around the room.

I had taken off the ugly digital watch sometime during the session, so I wasn't sure about the time. It felt like we had played about an hour, which probably meant it had been several. I unbuttoned a couple of buttons on my sweat-drenched shirt and unpeeled it a bit in front and back. It was getting dark out there but wouldn't get far below 90° for a long time. Texas.

KC and Lorraine stood together by the window and they weren't talking. KC looked solid and self-contained, a tough, no-frills artist. He could have been a general looking out over a battlefield, or a cow puncher looking over his herd, keeping an eye out for coyotes. They weren't touching. It was too hot for touching. She was too big for him anyway. I couldn't imagine him putting his arms around her.

I wondered if she had ever told him about me walking in on her.

"They been together for six and a half years," said Billy, taking a long pull from his beer. He wiped his mouth on his shirt sleeve and stuck a Kool with an inch of ash on the end of it into his mouth.

"Have you been counting the days?"

"No," he answered, with a rap of his rack tom and the ash fell from the cigarette, down his shirt front. He brushed it off. "It was just before Gabe left."

"I wonder if I should take a look at his guitar," I mused out loud. "He seems to be having some trouble with it."

"I wonder if she hasn't just fucked his brains out, is all," he muttered, stone-faced, adjusting the position of a cymbal stand and executing a series of noisy percussive fills.

KC came back and began tuning up an old Telecaster. A pre-CBS model, around '62 or '63, by the looks of the bridge and headstock decal. After it was tuned up, he started a drone, with the small E string ringing against thirds and fifths of the B and G. Every fourth measure he would throw in a flatted seventh, giving it just enough dissonance to make it sound mean. I picked up the bass, turned up the volume and felt my way into it. I started out pumping muted eighth notes on the root, then picked up on the flatted sevenths, noticing a nice effect when I played a ninth on top of KC's fifths, and threw that in every other bar. The guitarist gave no clue that he had noticed my contribution, but I knew he had. He expected it. I was his bass player.

I was still bent over watching my fingers work when Billy came in pounding a disco pattern with a hard rock accent to it.

A low moan I first thought was feedback started coming out of the monitor by my feet. It was Frankie, with a haunting baritone moan. Several minutes later, words started coming out. I couldn't tell what they were about, if anything.

The Telecaster attached to KC began to wail. A B.B. King-style stringbending exercise argued with the howls of feedback from the Marshall amplifier. His solo became a harmonic storm as the bent tremolo bar conjured the screams of a load of scrap steel sliding down a glass mountain. KC seemed to have a little bit of his tone back.

But no one acted excited about it.

4

The jagged melody still ran through my head as we sat around the patio picnic table on the healthy side of midnight. Pedro had gone out to County Line for barbecue ribs and brisket and all the trimmings. Now there wasn't much left except a pile of grease-soaked paper plates, bones, lots of spent napkins, and empty Heineken bottles. KC and the redhead sat across from me, and I tried not to let our feet touch under the table.

"Hey Martin, wake up," said Billy. "You OK? You look kinda pale."

"I'm fine," I answered. "Guess I have dirt road lag."

KC paid more attention to Diablo than anything else. Lorraine fidgeted, played with her hair, and scratched on the table top with a kitchen knife. Once in awhile she would purposefully touch KC with her elbow or put her face close to his, but he would ignore it, petting the dog or puffing on his cigarette instead.

"Christ," groaned Billy, rolling his eyes, turning around so he didn't have to face the couple.

Frankie sighed disgustedly and howled in the direction of the canyon, then tilted his head, waiting for an echo that never came. To no one in particular, he started whining about the heat, the dust, the fact that he'd much rather be inside the city limits.

The dog abruptly dipped his head, barked, and trotted off.

"You just wanna party with your friends at Club Slither tonight," said Billy, "with that limp-wristed artsy crowd and the frat rats. Jesus, what a combination. You dance with guys when you go there, Frankie?"

"No, Billy, I don't dance with guys," he answered. "And I don't do X, except once in a while."

"X?" said Billy.

"New designer drug, Ecstasy. Like a coke, speed, and Spanish fly cocktail. It's a new synthetic, so it's legal," he answered. "Makes you feel great, makes you wanna party all night long with people whose names you don't even know. Girls come up to you and complain that their clothes are making them so uncomfortable they just wanna take them off."

"Synthetic drugs make synthetic music sound better I guess," said Billy.

Frankie glared at him with a look of mock contempt. He grinned lop-sidedly and winked at me. "Martin, you're not saying much. You're getting, what, two thousand for this gig, or fifteen hundred? I forgot."

"Two thousand," I said. On the other side of the house, the dog was barking.

"We're each getting four," he said. "That's fair, you think?"

I shrugged. "It's your band. I'm just the hired gun."

Someone could have denied it, but no one did.

"Hey guys, I brought dessert," said a new voice.

Only Johnny could talk so loud. Only Johnny Craft, who'd been on the road with more bands than U-Haul—fixing amps, changing strings, harassing club owners, accidentally blowing up amps. I'd been in at least half those bands. Topped off by a big Borsalino hat, he was five and a half feet of thrift shop fashion. A bright yellow shirt underneath a light double-breasted jacket, smartly pleated baggy gray pants and English brothel creepers that the dog was sniffing. He had a broad flattened-out face, slightly slanted eyes under dark bushy brows, and a wide grin that could have belonged to a used car salesman.

KC wiped his mouth with the back of his hand and said, "Who told you where to find us?"

"Hey KC, what's happening?" Johnny said, ignoring the

question. "Martin, why didn't you call me? I didn't think they'd talked you into it . . . Lorraine, baby, you're looking good. Frankie . . ." shaking his hand, ". . . and Billy, still funny looking as ever . . ." and so forth, around the table he went, shaking hands and sniffing at the leftovers before he sat down between KC and me.

He had a blue Anvil briefcase covered with backstage passes that he placed underneath the table. He reached inside his jacket, pulled out a pack of cigarettes and a baggie containing what looked like a half ounce of blow. He lit a cigarette and gave me one. I could hear one nervous foot tapping the object under the table.

"The money you owe me in that case?" asked KC.

"So how's it going, fellas?" Johnny asked. "I been over at the 123 Club making sure they got the sound system wired up right. And the video. This is gonna be a grand opening that'll go down in history. And to celebrate, how would y'all like some blow? This is 99% pure Peruvian marching powder." Whipping a switchblade out from somewhere, he shoveled out some of the coke and gestured to KC. "I'll take care of you, Bub."

KC stiffened visibly, shaking his head.

"KC doesn't want any," said Lorraine, reaching around her boyfriend's back to tap Johnny's shoulder. "But I'll take a line."

Crickets were chirping, or maybe my ears were ringing. Everyone was quiet and Lorraine, Frankie, and Billy seemed to be trying to decide what to look at. The shiny knife blade with the pile of drug on it wanted their attention, and it was certainly easier to look at than KC and Johnny. KC was unyielding. Johnny was suddenly sweating and uneasy, the hand holding the knife and drug shaking.

"Got my money, Johnny?"

"Listen Bub . . . I wanted to talk to you about something," said Johnny. "I'm doing one last deal before I go full-time video jockey at Ward's new club. But it's a babysit job, with some . . . *amateurs*," he said, spitting out the word, "trying to get into the drug business all a sudden, all a sudden trying to make a quick buck." He put the knife down and tried putting a hand on KC's back. "I'll take care of you tonight. If you want to drive into town with me we can square up and then some."

KC didn't answer. We sat there like statues. But none of us looked as stony as the mask of dark stubble and smouldering cigarette.

"Look, I don't need this shit," said Johnny, shaking his head. He scooped a generous pile of flake out of the baggie and dumped it on a clean paper plate. Probably a gram and a half of someone else's money. "Here—whoever wants to take some without giving me a hard time can have it. I'm splitting. I got bidness to attend to." He got up, tugged on his hat and picked up the briefcase. "In case y'all didn't know it, all this equipment out here didn't get out here by itself. Ward hired me for this gig and I rented all this shit and hauled it out by myself. If y'all need strings changed or an amp fixed, why don't you just аᴀк Pedro. Martin—"

"I'll see you Saturday," I said.

"All right," he said, shaking his head. He turned and headed back through the house. And KC followed him.

The other three got busy with the coke. Billy started spreading it out with Lorraine's knife, chopping it finer, separating it into little piles. Frankie watched eagerly and Lorraine pushed KC's Gitancs pack aside and said, half under her breath, "He's *your* friend, Martin."

"Well, you're not going to take candy from a stranger, are you?" I said.

She snickered. So did Frankie. Billy shrugged and didn't even look up. I stood up and let them move in closer around the drug, which did not interest me. If I wanted a headache I could always hold my breath.

The people at the table were starting to remind me of hogs, bent over the quickly railed out lines, sniffing through a rolled up twenty. I went inside.

I looked down the long hall with the little depressing room at the end and hated the thought of it. I decided to go back into the practice room.

I pushed through the swinging door to the dining area, as the hired help had no doubt done nightly in years past, around the big table with its yellowing linen underneath the chandelier, found my way through the darkness to the couch in the living room, plopped down without spilling any of my beer and hauled the bass onto my lap.

I was tired, full of red meat and in a weird mood. I felt bad about Johnny, but as well as I knew him, I figured he'd brought it all on himself. He always did.

The house was quiet—a big, hard, lonesome thing intermittently pestered by Lorraine's laughter.

I let my hands run down the scarred metal flake finish of my instrument. That bass suited me like the dark suits the night. There are all kinds of guitars, but a Fender bass is special. It had nothing to do with my last name. A Fender is the archetype. You look up bass guitar in the dictionary, you'll find a picture of a Fender Precision. Its contours and the arch of its neck make themselves at home in your grasp, familiar as an old lover, as a cop's revolver. I popped the old G string hard—once, twice, till it broke. Suddenly there were voices outside the front of the house.

It really sounded like they were saying "rhubarb, rhubarb," over and over. Finally, "Get the fuck out of here," from KC's ragged voice, like that was the end of that, and the sound of something, maybe a foot, hitting the side of a car, probably the rental van, since Johnny didn't have a car.

The starter ground the engine over, gears found each other noisily, and caliche crunched in the drive. Soon the side door slammed and KC's boots stomped down the long hall to his room.

5

It was ten-thirty in the morning and I was trying to sweep the cobwebs from my brain with some black coffee and fresh air on the patio. Under the table, flies fussed over a bone that Diablo had given up on. I slung it out into the canyon. The sun got in my eyes whenever I tried to look up and there were a couple of bluejays making a lot of noise in a cypress tree next to the house.

She was inside, making bread. KC loved her bread, she said. It was the only thing she knew how to cook. I'd watched her rolling over the lumpy cylinders of dough while I'd poured my coffee and she asked how I slept. I told her it wasn't worth rating, as she sprinkled the dough with flour and shaped it in her hands. You should have brought a girlfriend along, she said. A good-looking guy like you shouldn't have any problem finding a girl to take out to the country for a week.

She was wearing the cut-offs again, and another T-shirt with the sleeves ripped out but no bra today. Sometimes as she bent over the table to get the flour sifter I could see her breasts.

"Wait till you smell it baking," she'd said, licking her lips. She sprinkled more flour and I saw them again. She had to know. Squeezing, pounding, twisting the dough, pinching it with fingers that ended in nails that were bitten short. I tested the coffee and tapped a pack of Camel non-filters on the table top. No matter how hard you pack them, some tobacco still gets in your mouth.

I gave the pack one last tap, unwrapped the cellophane,

pulled one out and lit up, pausing to dab a fleck from my lip. She smiled at that. I asked her if she wanted a cigarette.

"No," she said. "And you smoke too much."

"So?"

"I'm worried," she said.

"About my health?"

She shook her head. "He took off this morning," she said. "I guess he found the spare set of keys in my purse."

"When did he leave?"

"Before I woke up. There was a note on the typewriter saying he had to pick up some strings. I hope that's all he picks up, because if he gets drunk and blows it . . ."

"I hope so, too." I tried the coffee, wondering what was wrong with it. Country water, probably. I was wondering, too, if I should have gotten an advance from KC. "Why was he so upset with Johnny last night?"

"Johnny owes him money."

"So what else is new? He owes half the people in Austin money."

"He really needs it now, Martin. And Johnny can be so annoying."

"Even when he doesn't owe you money. I thought KC was still doing some studio gigs."

"I haven't seen any money from them," she sighed, tossing her head back so that her hair moved in a big wave and her breasts jiggled. She stopped kneading and rubbed her eyes and turned away from what she was doing. It looked like she was staring at my hands. I looked at them myself. They looked OK. Then I looked up at her, and she wasn't looking at my hands anymore, but at my face.

Outside the window, the sun went behind a cloud, and that seemed to break the spell. Lorraine went back to the dough, biting her lower lip till the color went out of it, and I tried to think of something to say, but couldn't.

So I'd walked outside and sat there, hating the coffee, staring at my hands, wondering where the dog was. Thinking how the baggy pleated pants I was wearing today would be a lot cooler than the jeans I'd worn yesterday. When I finished the cup I got up and walked back in, somewhat sun-blinded, to get more. And collided with the redhead in the doorway.

She looked so startled that for a moment I thought I'd hurt her. I said I was sorry.

She swallowed hard and said, "I just wanted to tell you, he's back."

How did she know? A noise was erupting inside, sounding like a buzz saw tuned up to high C, ready to rip the roof off. She brushed some flour off my black shirt. There was flour on the crotch of my pants from our collision, too, but she didn't touch that, she only looked at it and smiled. Things in the kitchen rattled as the guitar made wounded dinosaur sounds.

"Maybe he did just get strings," she said.

We rehearsed. No one talked much. KC made a lot of mistakes, but still no one appeared to notice. No one ever looked at anyone else, other than to bum a cigarette or ask about a certain piece of equipment, and even then the focus was on the cigarette and the match, or the instrument, like when Frankie suggested KC use his big, semi-hollow-body Chet Atkins model Gretsch on "August Snow." KC said his Stratocaster could make the same sound if he adjusted the intensity setting on his Space Echo, and he didn't have the big Gretsch anymore anyway.

"Bullshit," said Frankie. He kicked the mike stand over as Billy watched, frowning, but not at Frankie.

I looked at the two of them and shrugged. What was their problem? KC should know if he still had the guitar or not. And he was probably right about being able to get the same sound on his Strat. But all it did was make me feel like the odd man out.

The afternoon dragged on, and it seemed like the weekend was a long ways away.

Once in a while Billy would get up from his throne and pace around the room, whooping and clapping his hands—"checking the acoustics, man"—since he was going to tape his drum track that night after rehearsal.

Lorraine padded in on bare feet every couple of hours, bringing Heinekens and saying it sounded great, but did we have to play so loud? No one ever answered that question, and I was the only one who ever thanked her for bringing the beers. Pedro came in twice, bringing cheeseburgers, onion rings, and hot pups from Dan's Hamburgers, and chicken fried steaks and mashed potatoes with white cream gravy from Trudy's later on. But nothing overpowered the sweet smell of that bread in the oven.

It was after 2:00 A.M. by the time the last song ended. Nobody said "that's a wrap" or anything remotely like that. We just quit. Frankie and Billy went off to the kitchen. I got out a screwdriver and began making adjustments on the bridge of my bass.

KC bopped me on the arm. "You sound good, chief. You're a natural."

"Natural what?" I asked. The saddle on the D string was giving me some trouble. The individual bridge pieces can be adjusted to fine tune the intonation. The D string saddle had a tendency to slip after a few hours' hard playing, but didn't want to budge when I tried a screwdriver on it.

"Natural earthquake machine," he laughed. "Really keep that bottom end down." He leaned over, sitting on the couch, elbows on his knees. One hand held one of my cigarettes, the other absentmindedly pulled on his earlobe. I finally managed to get the screw to move a half turn. I gave the guitarist the once-over.

He looked hard. Four-day beard now, big wet eyes that caught the light, the flesh around them a rim of shadows. He blew out a cloud of smoke and grinned.

"You doing OK, Martin?"

"Yeah, I'm fine. How about you?"

"Oh, I'm all right, I guess. It ain't quite falling into place for me like I'd like it, but I'll get it. It's gotta be good."

"So it will be," I said. "Might take all week, but at least someone else is paying for the beer. Something you'd like to talk about?"

He shook his head. His cigarette hand was shaking.

"Well, don't worry, KC. We'll get it back together."

"Yeah, I guess so," he said hoarsely. "But not tonight."

"Where'd you go today, KC?" I asked, finally twisting the stubborn bridge piece into the position I wanted it, reconciling the harmonics with the fretted notes according to the tuner on the couch.

"Just taking care of business."

"I was a little worried," I said, "and Lorraine was, too. You know any time you want to talk . . ." I looked up from the guitar and tuner and realized I was talking to the air. He'd left the room.

Soon after that, I was in my room, wondering what the cracks in the ceiling reminded me of, listening to the rat-tat-tat of KC's old manual typewriter. It was a sound that I'd gone to sleep to many nights when we shared rooms on the road. KC had written a lot of blues lyrics on that typewriter. I wondered if a person could tell what the song was about by the rhythm of the tapping keys.

Tired as I was, it was hard to sleep. As far as I could tell, everyone was in bed but Billy. That was the problem. World War III, I hoped, wouldn't be as noisy. The living room was on the other side of the house, and he wasn't playing the tape at deafening volume, but the intensity and dynamics of the drum sounds were jarring and disconcerting. Elephant stampedes, Godzilla doing a tap dance, artillery practice, thunderclaps . . . all these things went through my head instead of sheep, and the comforting thoughts that sleep should bring.

The room was almost cool, though, and the noise gradually settled into a kind of hypnotic rhythm that blended in with the rattling screen on the box fan and the squeaking of the bed springs as I settled down. The lumpy bed felt good against my tired back, and I was the star in my own movie. It wasn't really a movie, just something I seemed to be remembering for the first time. I was riding a big white pony, galloping across the Hill Country, crossing the Pedernales where it was rough, perch and catfish jumping out of the water, the sun glistening on their backs. Riding hard, riding fast . . . rough and smooth at the same time, deeper and faster, and my crotch was warm down by the saddle. Mane brushing against my arms in the wind . . . I opened my eyes. Lorraine was sitting on top of me. I was the horse, she was the rider, and it was no dream.

She ground herself into me harder and harder, whispering things that don't look good in print, clawing my hips with the spurs of her fingertips. When it seemed that the whole world was going to explode in time with one of Billy's drum fills, she rolled off me suddenly, hunkering down by my side, her head under my armpit.

She convulsed and writhed there for a long minute, moaning and breathing and touching herself. I wanted to ask her if something was wrong but thought better of it. Finally she mewed a couple of times like a little puppy, then fell silent, her breathing gradually slowing down.

Bizarre. My heart and respiration were far from ready to go back to normal. The crazy drums kept up their house-shaking beat, blood kept pumping. And here, lying beside me, about to doze off, was the guitarist's girlfriend, wearing a man's denim work shirt with only a couple of snaps fastened, covering one plump breast, half a moonlit shoulder and not much else.

She raised herself up on one elbow, leaned over me, and licked me on the lips. "Didn't know I was a sleepwalker, did you."

"Don't give me that," I shot back in a whisper. "What the hell do you think you're doing?"

"I need you, Martin." Her eyes were wide and glistening. "I love KC, but I need a man who doesn't need me."

"I need a beer."

"OK, I'll get us a couple. Don't worry about KC. I'll be right back," she said, getting off the bed, snapping a couple more buttons.

"What do you mean, don't worry about him?"

"I need to explain some things, Martin. KC's out like a light, since he got up early. And I can't . . ." she stopped, pulling on her hair with both hands, "think with all that racket. You think I can get Billy to knock it off?"

I nodded. Then shook my head. She put one finger to her lips and said she'd be right back. Soon the drums stopped.

The door opened again and she came in with two lit cigarettes in her mouth and a Heineken in each hand, the hands that moments before had pulled my hips to hers like a cowboy bull-dogging a longhorn. She sat on the edge of the bed.

I tasted the beer. It was warm. Like the room. She stroked my hair.

"You've got such nice hair, Martin. You remind me of that guy in *Blade Runner*. I know the perfect hairdresser for you. He used to cut Joe Ely's hair."

"Is that what you wanted to talk about?" I asked. I was surprised I had a voice. I would wake up any minute now and realize it was all a dream. I'd go across the hall, say goodnight to KC, and go back to sleep.

"I love him, Martin. I take care of him. But he's so dependent on me, sometimes it's like I'm his mother, not his lover. I have to make sure he doesn't drink, I have to make sure he eats and gets his clothes cleaned once in a while. He's so dependent on me, I don't know what he'd do without me. So I could never leave him, of course."

That didn't do anything for me. I wanted her out of my room. But I also wanted . . . something. An explanation, an apology, anything to fix the situation. I drank some more beer and looked at her, then looked away.

"Why are you looking away now, Martin? When you came in my room that time you didn't look away. You just stood there. You just looked at me like I was a tree or something."

"Right now maybe I wish you were."

"So you could climb all over me?" She didn't give me time to answer, and didn't act like there could be but one answer. "You pissed me off that night and I never forgave you. Looking at me like that." Leaning her head forward so the long red hair brushed over me, sucking on her cigarette, as mine burned between my fingers. The hair around her temples was wet and I smelled sex. *Our* sex.

The pounding in my ears and throbbing of my unrelieved loins were feeling more like symptoms of guilt and sickness than the mindless call of nature. No, it wasn't a dream. And once my brain accepted that, it began to search for ways to rationalize the whole thing. Although we were in a house with three other people, we were miles from anyone else. No one had to know but us. Maybe . . .

No. No way. Guys have codes, I told myself. The musician across the hall was more than just another human being, more than just a friend. I could imagine my bass falling out of rhythm with the grooves he conducted, knowing I had done the business with his girl. The thing would stand between us forever, like the silence in the room that grew between me and the mostly naked, sweaty thing beside me, like the smoke from our cigarettes, now making crazy patterns up by the light fixture and cracked plaster.

"It's going to be hard," I said, "but I'm going to lie here and pretend to go to sleep. You're going to leave this room and you can do whatever you want, but hopefully as I pretend that this never happened, you can go back to your room, get back into bed with your boyfriend, and do the same, whether that's best for him or not. But it'll have to do for now."

She was mad all right. She pinched some of the sheet between her fingers and looked like she had something nasty to say to me.

But that's when we heard it. A lone popping sound. Her body jerked and she squeezed my leg. First I assumed, annoyed, that Billy had gotten into the stash of leftover Fourth of July firecrackers we'd found in the house. We decided that Billy had no sense of consideration. Then we decided that only one thing sounds more like a firecracker than you think it should.

A gun.

6

He was hunched over the typewriter, a dark red stripe of blood leaking out of a nasty exit wound, a tangled mass of hair and stuff by his left ear. Out of the corner of my vision I could see a mess on the wall. His arms hung limply, monkey-like, his fingertips almost touching the floor. Just below his right hand on the floor was a nickel-plated snub-nose .38. I didn't want to look at his eyes, but I did. One of them wasn't where it was supposed to be. I felt the big vein in his neck. No pulse. KC would never have a pulse again.

Lorraine touched him on the shoulder, then recoiled as if she'd put her hand in a fire. She began hyperventilating, shaking from head to toe. I made her sit on the bed, where she hunched, slack-jawed, hands between her knees, making little sounds.

Frankie and Billy were in the room now. I told them their eyes weren't playing tricks on them—KC had shot himself. Frankie said something about being sick. Pedro stood in the doorway, his big, tired face and kind eyes looked at me, and he shook his head. Call the police or the doctor? he wanted to know. I didn't think we needed a doctor, I said. Pedro patted me on the shoulder and escorted the girl out of the room.

I dialed 911 with shaky fingers.

We had time enough to put on pants and shirts, all of us, and time enough to watch the seconds blink away on the tacky digital timekeeper I hated, until I smashed it with one of the many empty green beer bottles.

"Your name?" A big black, sleepy-eyed cop with an East Texas accent and a couple of acres of razor burn on his neck wanted to write it on his clipboard.

"Martin Fender," I said, even though I was sure Lorraine, whom they had interviewed first, had already given all the names. But more police had arrived since then, and everybody was getting interviewed at once now in the living room. Except for KC, who would get a ride back to town before any of us. It seemed like a couple of years had passed since I'd gone back into that room and noticed a scrap of paper in the old beat-up typewriter's carriage, almost hidden by the dead guitarist's hair. I'd ripped the scrap of paper out of the machine and stuffed it in my pocket. I could feel it crinkle there as Lorraine's eyes, red and swollen but dry, shifted from the cold tile floor to me. We're guilty, they said.

"Fender . . ." he said slowly as he scratched it out, saying, "like the guitar . . ."

"Like the guitar." Guilty. What right did I have to the last words of the deceased?

"Occupation?" he asked.

"Musician," I answered. One who backs the guitarist up, picks up his cues, picks up on a leading note that signals they're going to the chorus even when it's too soon, all without being told.

"I need a home number where you can be reached, and a work number."

"I work out of my home most of the time, officer. If you want, I can give you a number at an office where I keep irregular hours."

The living room seemed small now, as other officers—some in uniform, some not—asked Billy and Frankie the same type of questions. There was a lot of shrugging of shoulders and hands running through hair, a lot of sighing and staring at the floor.

"Music office?" he asked, rubbing his chin with a big ugly thumb.

"Collection agency," I corrected. "I look for people, try to find out where they move, where they work."

"You're a skiptracer, then."

"Yes."

"Part-time musician," hyphenating the words "part-time" with a clicking sound behind his teeth.

"Part-time skiptracer," I said.

He nodded, unimpressed. Men were carrying cameras around with them, going back toward the bedrooms. Some EMS workers stood around looking at our equipment. KC had forgotten to turn off his amp, and the red power indicator sat there glowing, with no one willing to go over and extinguish it.

"You at this home number most of the time, then?"

"Most of the time," I answered. "When I'm at home."

He gave me a sort of irritated look and hitched up his pants, like maybe his utility belt was wearing a blister on his hips. "Well I think that should be enough. We need to talk to you, I'm sure we'll be able to find you. Let's take a walk."

I followed the uniform through the kitchen and den and down the hall. We stopped just short of the room. Men were coming out with their cameras and towels, talking in the matter-of-fact, gruesome manner of homicide investigators. They called it a "GSW" instead of a "gunshot wound," and talked of "powder tattooing" and the "scorch zone." Shop talk. Radios squawked and flashes went off, the last time they would go off for the guitarist.

The policeman leaned on the wall opposite the doorway. The stuffed deer head above the cop looked as if it was trying to read over his shoulder. There was a patch of whiskers about a half inch wide on the cop's neck he'd missed when he last shaved, and he worked at them now with the big thumb.

"Kind of music you play?"

"R & B, soul, and is there anything else?"

"Prefer jazz myself." He started using a soft, confidential tone reserved for man-to-man stuff: "That's a lotta woman there, you know."

"I guess so. Sir. She's . . . I mean . . . she *was*, his girl-friend."

"Was," he said, nodding. "You mean 'was' before he shot himself or 'was' before you and she started *talking*?"

"Before he shot himself," I said tersely.

"OK. I guess we'll be seeing you later, uh, Martin. As I told her, I imagine they'll be doing an autopsy." He brought the clipboard out from behind his back and tucked the pencil under the clamp. "And if it turns out you need to come visit us or be present at an inquest . . ."—pointing at my cheek—"I don't think you should wear that shade of lipstick. It's not very becoming."

"Sorry you had to go through that bullshit," said the bearded cop plucking my bass.

I shrugged, not knowing what he meant and not caring. I'd almost made it out of there. Lorraine had already driven back. Billy was wrapping up the cords for his tape recorder, and some of the younger cops were helping him. The late-arriving cop turned out to be a big R & B fan. He was Detective Sergeant Jim Lasko. I heard some of the other cops call him Alaska. He'd seen me play at Antone's ("Home of the Blues") hundreds of times and thought that the only guitarist better than KC was Stevie Ray Vaughan.

"I was photographing some blood spatters in a motel on the Bastrop highway when this came on the radio. You shouldn't have to explain who you are to some uniform, Martin. Wish I'd gotten here sooner."

"Yeah, I'd much rather get the third degree from some guy in jeans, cowboy boots, and a Hawaiian shirt. What are those?" I asked, pointing to the garish splashes of color on his front.

"Supposed to be hibiscus. And don't be making fun of my clothes just because I don't wear black all the time like all you night-crawlers. People don't wanna talk to a cop who looks like Lou Reed. So was he drunk?"

"No. I mean, I don't think so."

"Was he ready to do it?"

"What? Kill himself? How should I know?"

"The gig. Was he psyched up for it, or was he in some kinda funky state of mind?"

I got my bass and started packing it into the case. "Detective Lasko, I don't know what to tell you. I'm tired and . . . I'm more than tired. Can we talk about this later? KC was kind of rusty, but he was here, wasn't he?"

"Did y'all tape any of it?" he asked, hopefully.

I shook my head.

"That's a shame. Damn shame. I'd sure like to have heard some of those old True Love tunes one more time. Guess I better go to work."

"Yeah. Let me get out of your way. We can talk tomorrow?"

"Yeah. What's this collection agency number here?"

"Part-time job."

"You have to work part-time?"

"Sorry to disappoint you."

"I guess that's so you can be selective about your gigs. I imagine another one will turn up."

"Yeah. They know where I live."

But they didn't bother me there. I drove back that early Wednesday morning while there was still some dark. I wanted to get drunk, maybe go out and get in a fight with the first person that looked at me funny. I wanted to walk down to Town Lake and listen to the ducks squawk, sit on a park bench and watch the poor folks fishing. I didn't do those things, though. I just sat in my apartment until it was Thursday morning, doing nothing, with the TV on and the phone unplugged.

7

I plugged the phone back in just before "The Rockford Files." That meant it was 10:00 A.M. A news announcer came on before the prologue and talked about the heat wave. It was already 101°. By noon, the air out there would be palpable. It was a terminal weight, an airborne cancer. It would get in your face, under your skin . . . making the simplest outdoor task near impossible. But I was almost out of cigarettes and clean black shirts, so something would have to give. First, the phone rang.

"Where the hell have you been, man?" asked Ward. I could practically hear the gold chains rattling around his neck. "Been trying to get you since yesterday. I'm real sorry about KC. It's hard to believe, you know."

I said I was sorry too.

"Say, you know that Grandeville guy is pretty good."

"What?"

"Grandeville, the guy who plays in the Trainrobbers."

"Yeah, so?"

"So you guys have worked together, and . . . well, dammit Martin, have you thought about a replacement? It's Thursday, all right? I know you're probably in a state of shock . . ."

"You don't really think that we could do your gig with another guitar player."

"Well, hey. I've got a lot of money tied up in this deal and I guess you never know who's going to flake out on you like this when things aren't going exactly perfect. Just tell me straight, OK, do you still want to do it or not?"

"No." I downed the rest of the beer. Out of cigarettes. I had a stash of whiffs in the silverware drawer. They were Brazilian cigars, small but dense and powerful and they satisfied. I lit one.

"OK, OK, OK. I thought you might do this to me. Just bend over Ward, get used to it, right? Yeah, just forget it. After all these years I mean, that's business, right? Things are always happening out of the blue like this when you don't need them to happen to you. *Dammit*. OK? You could have kept this thing happening. You know? I mean, I don't know what was going on out there but . . ."

"Nothing was going on out there. Just a bunch of guys trying to drag something up that should have been left alone."

"Now you tell me."

"You never asked," I answered.

"Oh, never mind. That's how it goes. Listen, have you seen Johnny?"

"No."

"I need to talk to him."

"I don't know where he's staying these days. Have you tried Lorraine?"

"No. KC's girlfriend? I haven't talked to her. I mean, I'm not very good about that kind of thing. Don't you think she's probably being taken care of?"

"What I meant was, Johnny might have been in touch with her. You should ask her."

"Oh. Well, I'm sure she hasn't seen him. No one else has. How about the bug?"

"What bug?" I was really starting to regret plugging the phone back in.

"The Texterminators bug, for chrissakes. Have you seen it?"

"Not lately. I've been in my apartment for the last thirty hours."

"No, man. It's been *stolen*. Happened early Tuesday morning."

"So what?"

"Listen, Martin, you know how crazy the frats are for that

bug. Every year they put up a pot and if somebody steals it without getting caught they get the money. Well, I've got six hundred special free admission tickets out to the fraternities, and I want at least that many frats in my club Saturday night."

"What does that have to do with me?"

"Because this weekend is pretty damn important to me, man, even if you don't give a rat's ass. I'm working my butt off here and I'm not about to let something like this blow it for me, especially after my band cancels out on me. It'll screw things up if the fraternities' top dudes are in jail. You know what I'm saying? So listen, I'll give you a chance to make the money you were going to make on the reunion show. Plus I'll throw in a couple of Bruce Springsteen tickets. Just find the bug and let me know who has it so I can get it back to George over at Texterminators before it's too late. He's a very good friend of mine. Whaddya say?"

"Ward, I may have been born yesterday, but I was up late last night."

"Does that mean no?"

"I hate to rain on your parade, Ward, but you were right about me not giving a rat's ass. Not for the 123 Club, the Alphas, Betas, or Zetas."

"All right, all right. Martin, let's play a little game. I'll tell you the truth, then you tell me the truth."

I groaned into the receiver, but he took it as a green light.

"I got a little high the other night. I guess I was trying to think like a frat, trying to figure out how to get them into my club. And I'd rented that van for you guys, and Johnny was anxious to get on my payroll, so I guess I said something like hey, wouldn't it be cool to have the bug here for this weekend, spinning around over the dance floor instead of the old traditional mirrored ball?"

"So you told Johnny to go fetch, is that it?"

"Well—"

"And now you've come down and you can't find Johnny. You don't want any trouble for yourself at your party, and you didn't really mean for Johnny to actually steal it. Maybe you were just kidding around. Now you figure he's got it and he dropped it off at a frat house for a big fat reward since he's such an enterprising guy. Is that it?"

"That's right, Martin. I'm not very happy with Johnny, OK?"

"And you're sending *me* to go fetch now and you'll pay me two grand for either the bug or the roadie?"

"That's right, Martin." ·

"That's the stupidest thing I've ever heard of," I said. And before I could find out what he wanted me to tell the truth about I hung up on him.

I called Frankie and Billy. They were taking it pretty well. Frankie blamed Lorraine, saying he could tell she was a ball-buster the first time he met her. Billy blamed KC, saying it was a really selfish thing to do. He wished the guitar player had tried to talk about his problems with one of us, but then KC always was the quiet one—except when he had a guitar plugged in—and how do you know what's going on with someone like that? He thought maybe someone should look in on the widow. He would, he said, but he was too busy. It seemed like everybody was.

I opened another Labatt's and looked for the list of ingredients on the label. There was no list. I hoisted one for the guitar player. No more midnight jams at Steamboat on Monday nights doing Wilson Pickett medleys. No more giving him cigarettes. No more applause for the bourbon-soaked guitar hero who not only did impossible things with six strings, but did them without falling down. Some people who said they were his parents were having his body shipped back to some little town west of here. I'd never really thought of him having parents. His body. It wasn't KC anymore, it was his *body*.

Human bodies are made of enough chlorine to disinfect five swimming pools, about two ounces of salt, fifty quarts of water, three pounds of calcium, and enough fat for a bar of soap, iron for a six-penny nail, sulphur to kill a dog's fleas, glycerine for an artillery shell, and phosphorus for twenty thousand match heads. I could just see some guy in a white lab coat taking an inventory of KC's mortal coil, the things he left behind. There would be a blank somewhere, something not accounted for at check-out time, like the occasional pillow we nicked from motel rooms on the road.

I'd had it in my pocket since that night, taken it out and read it over and over, wondering what it meant. Was it a three word command? The beginning of a confession or a suicide note? Or just a last minute stutter, like a car engine dieseling after being turned off? I took the scrap out again, fingering the letters that had been written under a splatter of blood.

Do the do

they said.

If I was going to find out what they meant, I'd have to turn off the TV and leave the apartment. I looked outside and the squiggly rays of heat coming off the asphalt parking lot were either mocking me or warning me. The first step is always the hardest.

8

I stood by the balcony door, still staring at the heat rays on the blacktop, here and there colored green from the spilled coolant of ruptured radiators. It seemed that nothing moved out there except for cars. No birds, no wilted leaves on suffering oak and pecan trees by the dried up creek bed and the straw-colored bermuda grass of its banks. No one out there walking around who could tell me where to go to do the do.

A roach the size of a guitar pick made its way across the TV screen, onto the stereo cabinet and my record collection. There was a knock at the door. I answered it.

George Garrett, president of Texterminators Pest Control, walked into the apartment wearing a light tan suit, white button down, a tie too wide to be Mod and too narrow to be vintage '30s, slightly flared trousers, and brown shoes with tassels. His reddish hair was combed straight back in a way that showed off a lot of creased forehead. The hair, wet at the temples from sweat, was trimmed to about mid-ear. He had a broad mustache and walked with a long easy stride that said he was used to having a lot of elbow room. I let him sit on the couch by this week's still folded newspapers and Monday's black shirt and jeans.

"Sorry about your bug, Mr. Garrett," I said. "Would you like a beer?"

"No thanks, Mr. Fender," he said, resting an arm on the back of the couch. "Can't we cut out this mister stuff? I know who you are and I guess you know who I am."

"No problem." I watched as he unbuttoned his jacket and fanned himelf. "I saw you on TV about six months ago when you had the bug repainted. He's a real superstar."

"He sure is," Garrett answered with pride. "That's good and bad, you know. It's saved me and my dad at least twenty, thirty thousand a year on advertising. When you figure twenty years, that's a lot of money. But it's not just the money, you understand, it's not just the . . ." gesturing with his hands, like he was trying to conjure he bug out of thin air, "publicity. For us, it's our contribution to the community. You know what I mean?"

"Austin's Statue of Liberty," I suggested. "Better looking than an armadillo, and it'll never get run over, torn down, or voted out of office."

"But it does get stolen."

"Good and bad, like you said. Excuse me." I went into the kitchen and retrieved another of the whiffs from the silverware drawer. The apartment was already as fog-laden as an after-hours joint, but I thought maybe I could smoke out my guest. I wanted to be alone again, so I could mope about not doing anything.

Wrong strategy. His face lit up as I did. "Oh?" he said. "Mind if I?" He pulled a package of fat King Edwards out of the tan jacket. I walked over after he had it unwrapped and gave him a light. He took a big lusty draw and started to unwind on me.

"But that's the way it is. The way Dad feels, we've got a responsibility to the community. You know, people call us when he has an eye burned out, or when we take him down to be painted. We couldn't get rid of that bug if we wanted to."

Relieved that he'd clarified that he was talking about the bug and not his father, I drained the last ale.

He went on: "Hell, he weighs twenty-five hundred pounds, and one of these days somebody's gonna get hurt trying to steal him. That's what Dad and I are afraid of."

He looked around the room, at the collection of beer bottles by the sink, on the refrigerator, on the coffee table and the television. At the overflowing ashtrays, piles of dirty laundry, Rotosound Roundwound Long Scale Swing Bass Medium Gauge Bass String wrappers. Detective novels.

"You live here alone?"

I nodded.

"I'll give you a hundred dollars a day to find the bug."

"What makes you think I can find it?"

"You've been around, you need the money, and I know the guy who owns the collection agency you work at and he says you like this kind of stuff."

"Is that what he said?"

"Well, basically, that's what he said."

"Yeah," I said. The room was getting pretty smoky, sort of like a "Twilight Zone" set. "You have any leads on the *bugnap*, George?"

He scratched his forehead and leaned forward on the couch. "You know about the fraternities and sororities." I nodded. "Whoever did it used that yellow nylon rope to slide it into or onto whatever they drove off in, because they left some of it behind, with a hook and pulley. Nothing else. And other than that, I got nothing else to go on. One more thing, though . . ."

"What?"

"Like I said, we want him back. Dad and I want this to stop. Buggy is an Austin tradition, but that doesn't mean stealing him has to be one. We want to prosecute the people who did it. That set OK with you?"

"Oh, yeah. And after I find the bug maybe I should fly out to Disneyland. Maybe they'll need me to find Donald Duck's spare bill or Mickey Mouse's gloves or something."

"You're not taking me seriously, are you, Martin?"

"Well, it's just that I've got a lot on my mind right now, and I've got other things taking up my time."

"Doesn't look like it to me. And I know that you hang around with this fellow and he's been spotted in the campus area the last couple of days driving a silver Ford rental van."

"What's the pot on the bug up to this year?"

"Five thousand, I believe. I guess I could match it."

I told him I would see what I could do. He gave me a two hundred dollar retainer and I told him we'd be in touch. Just as they were rolling the last credits on "Perry Mason."

9

Under twelve or thirteen socks without mates, under a tangle of black T-shirts and underwear, mangled neck ties and one of the cat's chew toys, at the very bottom of my closet, I found it. It was pretty wrinkled, but it had the traditional polo player on his polo horse over the heart, his mallet raised high, ready to swat me on the nipple. Pants would be more of a problem. I went through the closet, shaking my head. Frat boys didn't wear thrift shop baggies. Tight black jeans pegged at the bottom? No. The gray WilliWear slacks would have to do. For my feet, wing tips were definitely out, along with the black leather lace-up high tops and pointy toe alligators. That left only the lipstick red loafers. They might give me away, if nothing else did, but with the right buzz words, a blonde girlfriend, a Trans-Am and a pet iguana, I could be in line for the vice presidency of Texas Commerce Bank in a couple of years. Or all set to look after Dad's Texas Instruments and IBM stock.

I didn't have any of those things, and five thousand dollars wouldn't get them for me, but it was enough to get me out of the apartment. Somewhere out there was the meaning of KC's last words, somewhere out there was Johnny, who had had some kind of problem with KC the night before the night he shot himself, and somewhere out there was a place I could rub out the memory of what had happened with the redhead. I hung the wrinkled shirt in the bathroom, took a hot, steamy shower, and gave my face a close shave. I moussed my hair down a bit and used the blow dryer on it. Most of the wrinkles came out of the polo shirt during the steam bath. I was still a little too old to pass for a student, but the Ray Bans helped.

I packed my Walkman, grabbed a Tina Turner cassette and one with a combination of the Fabulous Thunderbirds, Rufus Taylor, Rita Lee, Sade, Aretha Franklin, the Bar-Kays, and Ann Peebles, set the answering machine, and hit the road, hoping I had enough camouflage to blend in on fraternity row.

It was a good time to curse the people who'd passed on the opportunity to synchronize the city's traffic lights. I could have left the top up but the breeze and scenery were worth the grilling every time I hit a red light. It was almost a shock to see that Town Lake hadn't dried up. A few hardy joggers braved the noonday blast, running red-faced around the hike and bike trail. The redbuds were still red, but the willows and cypress trees hung limp and faded.

I drove north, toward the University of Texas, hoping I'd find Johnny, anxious to be doing something other than wondering what those three words meant, making excuses to myself for my petty theft. I never let myself think that I'd snatched KC's last lyric because I'd wondered whether he had known just where Lorraine was and what she was doing when he put the gun to his head and had used his last few seconds to tell everyone else about it. Some people might have thought that, but not me. I was his bass player, the guy who was supposed to be able to read guitar players' minds for a living, and if he'd left a note for his girlfriend, he would have put her name on it. Wouldn't he?

I took 12th Street west and turned up Lamar, to avoid the congested campus drag. The route took me right past the Tavern and Texterminators Pest Control where no twenty-five hundred pound, termite-toothed, glass-winged bug with blinking red eyes and steel stinger rotated on top of a sixteen-foot perch.

The Sigma Chi house was an uneven marriage of Greek Revival and "Leave it to Beaver." I'd played for parties there a number of times, so I knew the general layout and I knew that they were wild enough to get involved in the kind of prank I was supposed to be investigating. Also, since Johnny had roadied there for me, he'd be familiar with the group, too. Johnny was good at getting to know people, though he did have trouble with long-term relationships. From my parking place on the side street I could watch people going in through the front entrance on Nueces, as well as the traffic in the breezeway between the main house and entertainment room and the dorms in back.

The breezeway opened into a back yard with patio furniture and a swimming pool. No one was out. I turned off the Walkman halfway into Ann Peebles' "I Didn't Take Your Man (You Gave Him To Me)" when I saw a late model compact pickup with a camper cover back up to the front door.

Some of the senior Greeks barked orders and six or seven younger ones came out of the house and quickly fell into line around the back of the truck. The tailgate dropped open, and the junior leaguers tugged something covered with army surplus camo net out of the bed, up the steps, and into the house. It was a little smaller than a Volkswagen. Had Johnny already made a deal?

I lit a whiff and pondered my next move. When I'd last seen the U.T. Tower clock it had read one o'clock. Barely two hours after taking on the bugnapping job I could rush into the frat house and yell "Freeze," or I could go call the police. I could collect the reward money, take the rest of the week off, and go back to work at the agency on Monday. Maybe a couple of days at the lake, try to write some songs, then drift into work next Wednesday. I could even call Ward and see if I could collect my two grand reward. But I wouldn't have Johnny.

Maybe it wasn't even the bug, maybe it was a dead pledge they were going to use for a poker table. I decided to go in and look around.

The place was wrecked. Half a dozen junked TV sets sat in the foyer. Old tires, junk car parts, and steel drums littered the dining area. The floor was knee-deep in shredded newspaper.

The main rooms were deserted except for more of the same. I checked the restrooms. Cutouts of naked girls, in all manner of sexual orientation and activity, were pasted on the walls. When I came out of the ladies' room, three guys were waiting for me.

"Find the right one?" asked the tall one. Both of his friends had acne and knee-length baggy shorts. They looked like they played a lot of racquetball or something.

"Yeah," I said. "No problem."

"What are you doing here?" asked the tall one, hands tense at his hips like a gunfighter ready to draw.

"Oh, I was looking for Buff. I've got his Australian Psychology notes."

"Buff who?"

"Buff A. Lowe," I answered.

They had never heard of him.

"Say, I think I got the wrong frat house, and I'll be going. What's going on here, anyway? Looks like you guys are all majoring in interior decorating."

"*End-of-the-World* party this weekend. Have one every semester. Johnny Reno and the Sax Maniacs are playing in this room, and in the dining hall that guy from *The Blues Brothers* movie—what's his name, Boyd?"

"James Brown."

"Yeah," said the tall one. "James Brown. Playing in that room, the dining hall. That way we don't have to hook up a tape deck for music during the breaks. Non-stop party music, dude."

"Very practical," I said. "That last thing you guys carried in—what was that?"

"Laser video game—World War IV—one of those where you sit in the cockpit. Gotta have lots of video for the party. Video's the future, man. See?"

Boyd pointed to the adjoining ballroom, where the camo net was being pulled off the machine by a couple of fresh-faced pledges. "Fucking A," he said.

"Fucking A," said the tall one.

"You fellows haven't run into a guy by the name of Johnny, have you? Wears a hat and pleated pants, looks like a gangster?"

"Was he in *The Blues Brothers*, too?"

I left.

Fucking A.

They were more concerned with the present on Leon Street where the Alpha house was located. It was a much busier neighborhood, with a couple of sorority houses practically next-door, and two or three co-op dorms around the corner. Everywhere people were carrying books, going to or coming from school.

The house was a rambling affair of red brick and white shuttered windows. A wrought iron fence with ornate scrolls and star-topped pickets surrounded the lush green yard. Sprinklers were going full force and a wet sidewalk led up to the front door where Greek letters were emblazoned on a brass plaque above the fan light. There were no Ford rental vans parked anywhere.

But as I set the hand brake on the Ghia, a green Monte Carlo pulled up behind me. The driver, a business-major type, hopped out of the car, leaving the motor running, and ran inside the house. His passenger, another button-down, waited in the car drinking a beer. The driver came out in a couple of minutes and they drove off.

I counted four more drive-ups in the next fifteen minutes. The fifth one was a Thunderbird full of kids who looked too young to be in college. This time, a boy and girl went in the house. When they returned, one of the girls in the back seat leaned forward, asked the driver a question, and squealed with delight at the answer. They roared off in a cloud of dust and rubber.

The next suspicious arrival definitely broke the mold. A '57 Ranchero, black, license plate #AAA 59, stopped at the curb. The driver, who looked to be a hard-lived fifty or so, with short curly hair, Ray Bans, and beer gut, glanced over his shoulder after getting out of the car, then walked splayfooted up the sidewalk.

When he came out of the Alpha house, just a couple of minutes later, he was carrying a red and white Igloo ice chest. I saw a big scar across his throat showing white underneath his whiskers, and splotchy patches on each arm that had to be tattoos.

Maybe the bug was inside the house, and people were dropping by to look at it, or to pick up their share of the pot that had been netted from its capture. It was hard to imagine him ending up in this house. Anyone and anything that came there would be seen—depending on the time of day or night—by at least dozens and maybe even hundreds of witnesses. It seemed ridiculous.

But so did the whole bugnapping event. And I told myself I knew it, and had just swapped watching daytime television for sitting in my car, dressed not really like a student but more like a boring prick, getting my kicks out of watching people who had nothing better to do than go to school.

Just like I had nothing better to do than to follow the '57 Ranchero. So I did for a few blocks, without getting too close or running over anyone. The four-way stops were a problem, though, and soon a pair of almost identical Trans-Ams got between me and my quarry. When one of them stopped in front of the Sigma Phi Epsilon house on Pearl Street to talk to someone in a blue MG coming the other way, the Ranchero turned down 26th Street. I honked my horn, but no one ran for cover.

I was hungry. The last thing I'd eaten was a chicken fried steak at the last reheasal. That was Tuesday. This was Thursday, and the clock on the U.T. Tower read two-forty. I was ready for the take-out cheeseburger, fries, and milk shake I ordered at Dirty's Cum Bak Burgers on the Drag. The big black man behind the grill stood there, talking about how hot it was, as he squeezed the ground meat into balls with his big black hands, how hot it goin' to be, as he smashed them on the grill. This one of the hottes' jobs in the world, he said.

I bought a six pack of Labatt's at Snaps Buy and Fly. The little white burger bag smelled good on the ride down the Drag, which eventually became just one-way Guadalupe again, then South 1st, and then I was back home. Being a detective wasn't too bad, I thought, even when you were just looking for a ridiculous steel insect. The day seemed to have a little more life in it since I'd turned off the TV. Everywhere I looked there were green leaves, summer clothes, construction cranes. Blue sky that wouldn't quit. People working, bums looking for shade in the parks. A couple of girls walked by me on their way to the pool, bronze-skinned, bikini-clad. One of them turned around and smiled. Being alive wasn't that bad a deal, no sir. I only wished KC would've given it more of a chance.

I checked my mail. Bills and circulars. I tossed it all in the plastic trash can conveniently located by the rows of mailboxes. I loaded my arms up with food and drink again and headed up the sidewalk to my building.

I saw the bare outstretched leg when I first entered the hall, like a log across a road but more attractive. Lorraine was sitting on the carpet in front of my door.

10

A shiny green miniskirt hugged her upper thighs and her breasts bounced heavily underneath an oversized paisley shirt with big ornamental buttons. She was barefoot again, a pair of green Springolators sticking out of a very large tapestry purse. I got the impression she wanted one of the beers in the six-pack. It wasn't till we got inside and I handed her an open one that she looked up, and then only briefly.

"Thanks," she said, giving the word a taste of the red lipstick that moistened the full lips on her emotionless face. After a perfunctory sip she set the bottle down on the cheek of Bryan Ferry, the singer who graced the cover of a British magazine on the coffee table. By the time she sat down on the couch, Ferry's cheek and lip were puffed out from a ring of water blisters.

"I really loved KC. It's still so damn hard to think of him as . . . you know . . . Well, that's what I came to talk to you about."

I nodded, but she could have been talking to Bryan Ferry, because she wasn't looking up at me. Her hands were working at freeing something from the inner depths of that purse. She pulled out a pillow and put it on the coffee table. She reached back in the purse, deliberately, and pulled out a pack of Kools. I tried to light one for her, but she lit it with a green Bic— green to match her skirt—while I fumbled with a matchbook. I started pacing the room.

She took a long drag on the cigarette, extending the silence as she inhaled. I took one of the Kools for myself, lit up, and grudgingly sucked the noxious menthol stuff down my own chest. I replaced the Bryan Ferry coaster with one of the unread daily newspapers. It was something to do besides sitting down beside her, or not sitting down beside her.

She leaned forward, cigarette in one hand, pack in the other. "KC was murdered," she said finally.

"Lorraine," I started, shaking my head.

She exhaled sharply. "Look." She tapped the cigarette pack on the coffee table. Out rolled a spent .38 cartridge.

"Well?" I asked.

"Well, I found that in a crack between the baseboard and the wall of our room at the ranch. I went back out there to look for KC's old Gretsch guitar but it wasn't there. I was pretty sure we took it out there. I looked around some more and found this," she said, indicating the pillow. "Look."

There was a hole in it. She reached inside the pillow case and pulled out a copy of some coffee table book on the Rolling Stones. Mick Jagger was on the cover, all lips and sweaty hair, one jewelled wrist limply dangling behind his head. There was a crater about the size of my ring finger in his nose. I opened the book to the middle, where there was a two-page photo of the riot at Altamont. And a slug, which dropped onto the floor. I didn't pick it up.

"KC's .38 never had more than four bullets in it," she said. "I know, because that was how many came with it when he bought it at the pawn shop. I thought it was odd when one of the cops said something about there only being two rounds in it, one of them spent. But I was so freaked out, I didn't think about it at the time."

I looked at the ceiling. "You mean somebody used this stuff to muffle the shot when they put the gun in KC's hand and fired it to get his prints on it and cordite on his hand for the cops' paraffin test?"

The ceiling didn't answer. Like any other ceiling in any other living room, it had been lit up often enough by the procedural details in TV cop shows to be way ahead of me.

Lorraine sipped her beer and wiped her nose with the back

of her hand. "I don't know what this means, Martin . . . how it fits together," with a shaky voice, "but you've gotta help me."

She started crying. Tears rolled down the face that had been so overly composed minutes before. A lot of her eye makeup came off with the tears. I said a few things, I don't remember what, but they weren't especially clever. I kept talking, hoping the monotony would help.

It didn't, so I gave in and sat down. The smell of her perfume got in my nostrils and when I touched her shoulder it reminded me of things and I decided I couldn't take any more crying.

I got my feet under me again. "We've got to go to the police," I said. "I'll take you."

Her eyes suddenly opened and glared at me, all red and wet, circled by melted eye makeup. "No," she said.

"Yes," I insisted, trying to take control of the situation.

"No no no no NO!" she screamed. She started hitting me.

Her balled up fists were hammering away at everything in their reach, and that meant me. At first it didn't hurt, or maybe my nerves were slow. There must have been some reason, because when I did begin to feel it I stepped back, forgetting the coffee table was there, and I tumbled backward over it. A nearly full bottle of Labatt's took the tumble too and foamed out on the rug.

I got up and went over to her, managing to grab one of her hands while the other fist smashed into my face once, twice, more before I could pin her onto the couch. I got on top of her as she bucked, kicked, and elbowed. She was crying again but I didn't feel too good, either. Teeth gritted, big red lips drawn back, she breathed violently and grunted unmelodiously.

We struggled like that for some time. Finally, while she was trying to bite me, her right wrist jerked free of my now sweaty grasp and found its way to my crotch, quickly darted under the elastic of my underwear and grabbed me. I let go of her other wrist, and thought about kissing her bared teeth as her free hand raked my back. I let myself fall on her as she tightened her grip and hissed at me.

"No," came her hoarse whisper.

We glared at each other, gasping, mute, and hot. The sweat that dripped down my face and soaked through my shirt mingled with her sweat, which plastered her hair to the sides of her face. I felt her hot breasts and stomach through our clothes. Legs that had kicked and kneed me were now wrapped around mine, locking me down. Her face was wild with fear and will. It was scary. My voice was as hoarse as hers when I said: "You're not kidding, no. Let go of me."

She pulled her hand out of my pants and wiped her face with it. I extricated myself and walked to the refrigerator.

I got out three more bottles of Labatt's. Bracing myself with one hand on the countertop, I twisted the top off one with my teeth. I chipped a tooth doing it, and relished the pain. I drained the first beer, opened the other two, and straightened my trousers with difficulty. I think I hated her a little then.

The pillow lay on the coffee table. It was doubtful KC had used it for target practice before putting the gun to his head. If the gun had had *two* spent shells, wouldn't we have heard about it by now? And why hadn't the police managed to stumble across the book and pillow, or weren't they Stones fans? These things were puzzling, but the biggest enigma of all now sat straight-backed on my couch, sniffling and regaining her poise. She pushed the big purse that still looked bulky enough to contain more secrets away from her feet, got up, and padded over to the sliding glass door of the patio. "You think he was a pretty cool guy, don't you," she said.

The soggy carpet, the indentations in the couch where we'd wrestled. The note in my pocket.

"You think he was pretty hip, right? A guitar hero, so cool he wore leather even in the summertime," she sneered. "Well, sometimes when he got drunk he'd talk about how cool he thought *you* were, too. What a tough guy, he'd say."

The TV sat there, blank, extinguished. But I could see her reflection in it. She went on.

"Oh yeah, he talked a lot sometimes. I know you think he was the strong silent type, and in a way, he was. Strong, when he got too drunk—that's when he'd hit me. And silent the next day, when he'd remember what all had happened. First he got drunk, then he'd throw me around. Next would come the 'sorry' part. When he realized he'd hurt me. So whiny and sorry, and that was when he'd say things. He needed me so bad, but didn't deserve me. And he'd say, Martin Fender, that's the kind of guy you want. You spent all your dad's money trying to make me into something, and all I do is beat you up for it. I'm not making this up, and I don't mean little love taps, either. I mean the black eye kind of stuff."

She tapped the glass with her fingernails and sniffled. "Martin Fender, that's the kind of guy you want. That's what he'd say."

"What's all that got to do with it?"

"It's why I know I can trust you to help me. We can find the kilo of cocaine he had stashed under the bed. Whoever shot him stole it from us. I know you can do it." She turned around and looked at me for an answer.

"I'm gonna make some coffee." I went into the kitchen, got the cheeseburger out of its bag and put it in the cat's bowl. He came running out from wherever he'd been hiding during the excitement. I freshened up his water bowl with an ice cube and made a pot of Guatemalan coffee. Strong.

Johnny had brought the kilo of cocaine out to KC Monday night, she said, after Johnny had stolen it from some Mexicans. The Mexicans had burned Johnny and KC on a deal before, she said, and Johnny was just trying to even things up. A large shipment had come into town the week before, but it was being handled by some college students who had more enthusiasm than expertise in such matters and Johnny had merely taken advantage of the confusion when he went along with the Mexicans to make a purchase from the students.

Right away she started running Johnny down. "He's such a fuckup. It's his fault KC is dead."

"Now just hold on a minute," I said. "Whose idea was it to rip off the Mexicans?"

"Johnny's, of course. I guess he thought he was doing a favor by bringing the stuff out to the ranch so KC could make his money back. But that's not the kind of thing KC would want to get involved in. That's about all I know about it."

"Did Ward call you?"

"No. Why would he?"

"No reason," I said. No need to go into the bug episode. "Just how much money did Johnny owe him?"

"I don't know," she sniffed. Slightly indignant: "KC didn't deal that often anymore, you know."

"What do you mean 'anymore'?"

"He and Dan Gabriel used to when Dan was still in the band. But that's been years."

"Well, the important thing is that this time it blew up on him. There's no need to put the whole blame on Johnny."

"Why do you take up for him? KC said you wouldn't have agreed to doing the reunion unless he was on the wagon, but you still hang around with someone like Johnny. What a hypocritical bastard you are."

"If Johnny happens to lose track of three or four grams out of an ounce of coke he's supposed to sell for someone else, it doesn't affect me, because I don't give a damn about the stuff. If a guitarist shows up at a gig so drunk he gets the band I'm playing in a bad rep, I do give a damn."

I didn't say anything about not wanting to stand back by the drummer, trying to help keep time, all the while watching somebody with a lot of talent flush himself down the toilet. And I didn't say anything about Johnny taking me out for burgers every day for five weeks when I didn't have a gig or the part-time job.

I tried a few numbers I had for Johnny, all with the same results. The parties who answered my queries did so with such bluntness that I knew I wasn't the first, nor the second, person to ask. He had a beeper but it didn't seem to be working.

I ducked into the bedroom and exchanged the pseudo-student disguise for my black suit. When I came back out, she'd fixed her face up again. Her hair was dry, her lips re-moistened with the vivid red lipstick. I sat at the bar, she stayed on the couch, and that was the way I wanted it. But I knew from the way her foot started rocking after she crossed her legs that she was about to come up with a zinger.

"Do you give a damn that KC's dead and your friend Johnny's nowhere to be found and I was in your bed when it happened?"

"I'm sure that Monday night when you came to bed all wired and KC told you he had a kilo under the bed and where it came from, you told him to go give it back. I'm sure you didn't even look at it. I bet you didn't even dip your finger in it and give it a lick."

That shut her up.

The last sip of coffee tasted as black and bitter as it looked.

I told her I'd help her. Or at least I'd try. I told her to stay at my apartment with the door locked and not to answer the door unless she knew it was me. Maybe they were still looking for the coke. Maybe KC had made a deal or stashed it somewhere that Tuesday he was gone all morning, and when they'd come out there looking for it, they'd killed him. They could have done it. Billy had made enough noise to let anything else go unnoticed, and she and I had given them enough time to get away, sitting there in the dark, thinking about firecrackers and other things. Now they might think she had the kilo, or the proceeds from it.

I told her I'd go out to the ranch, take a look around, look for Johnny, get some questions answered, either by him or by some other people I knew. If the killers were dumb enough to try to pull the fake suicide stunt, maybe they were dumb enough to drop a name tag or monogrammed coke spoon at the scene. Or overlook the kilo. Especially the kilo.

Who was I kidding? Cops are supposed to look for killers, and at least two people had already checked under the bed for the drug. But it wouldn't hurt to get away from her for awhile, and if the coke *was* lying around, the widow could have it, as far as I was concerned. Guitar players don't usually carry life insurance.

11

Angel Funeral Home is on South Congress just next door to Dye Automotive. I wasn't really in the mood for morbid puns, but I had to notice the irony along with the time on the funeral home clock as I passed by on my way to the Shamrock station. It was four o'clock.

As I filled the car with regular, the heat rays danced like little question marks on the hot pavement. Whose couch was Johnny sleeping on this week? Had it really been necessary to tell Lorraine where to find my gun? I hadn't brought it and wasn't sure why except that just knowing one was in your dresser drawer seemed like protection enough. At least, that was what I'd told her before I'd left. She actually seemed worried about me, and I'd actually promised her I'd be careful, and that I'd call her from the ranch. I showed her around, where the cat food was, how to operate the stereo without scratching any of my records, and how to keep the dead bolt and patio door locked. We agreed that it was a pretty safe place for her to hang out, with neighbors up and down the hall, across and above, and a twenty foot drop off the patio. She'd given me her house keys and a list of things to pick up for her there later. There had been a few more awkward moments, but I gave up on trying to light her cigarettes.

As I paid for the gas, a blind man was raising hell inside the station. He stumbled around, lead-footed, arms outstretched, feeling around with a white cane. He wanted to know where the cigarettes were. After he bought a pack, he wanted to know where the trash can was, so he could throw the wrapper away.

He kept stumbling around, careful but obnoxious, all the while loudly announcing, "I'm blind, I'm blind," as if it had just occurred to him and no one else could tell. Every time the clerk tried to count out my change, the blind guy would yell, and the clerk would start counting all over again. I wanted to push the guy out into the street and tell him to play in the traffic. I had to wonder who felt the same about me—stumbling around in the dark, not knowing what he was looking for, not knowing who killed his guitar player and made it look like suicide. At least the blind man's eyes just didn't work, period. Mine played tricks on me. Or people did things to make them play tricks on me. I was about to stumble off into the burnt orange sunset myself. Who would be waiting when I fell?

"He's blind, too!" yelled the blind customer, pointing his finger in the air as a Prince—not Stevie Wonder—song moaned and percolated into a fade on a loud radio. At the end of the song, the DJ announced that the new Prince concert date added for Austin had sold out early yesterday in record time, just like the first one had. The announcer noted that the Bruce Springsteen date that had been added had sold out again, also, and there was talk of a third date in Austin. More details were promised for later.

I finally got my change and used some of it to call the homicide detective, Jim "Alaska" Lasko, at work. He sounded concerned when he answered the phone. "Martin," he said. "Been trying to call you. You feeling any better than the last time I saw you?"

"Not really," I said, letting a little silence build up on the wires before I said I'd been wondering if he or any of his pals had any doubts about KC's death being a suicide.

"Just wondering, huh. Calling from a pay phone. You at sound check somewhere?"

"No, but it's just as unpleasant. Could you just tell me? I'd feel better if I knew. Any doubt . . ."

"Not really," he rasped. "Cordite tests show he fired the weapon. Thirty-eight caliber registered in his name. Died from GSW, self-inflicted, one round fired, just behind the ear, several exit wounds from exploded bone fragments . . ."

"Spare me the details, please."

"Sorry, Martin. Guess we talk a little different up here. Why you askin'? Know something to make us think different?"

"Just wondering. You know. You talked to Johnny yet?"

Hell no, he said. And he said something else, too, but I wasn't listening. I was watching the blind guy again. What was that he'd bumped into? A red Igloo cooler. What was interesting about that? They were handy items in the summer. They were handy items for a lot of things. Lasko was asking me something. I cut him off.

"Do me a favor. Run this license through DMV. It's a Texas plate, AAA 59."

"Why?"

"It'd be a personal favor, Jim."

"No shit, I thought I was your mother. Did some guy run into you or something?"

"Sort of."

"Well . . . aw, I'll be right back."

"MY GUARD DOG DIED," the blind guy brayed as I waited on Alaska. "WHERE'S THE RESTROOM?" The clerk went over and straightened out the stack of coolers. Johnny used to use them to carry drugs around. The character I'd tried to tail after coming out of the frat house had been carrying one, too. Johnny didn't normally hang around campus, and what if the stupid bug didn't have anything to do with . . .

"OK. It belongs to Bud Salvador," he said. "Know him?"

"No."

"Guy's a real sweetheart. Ex-something-or-other. Burn-out. I'm sure you seen him around, especially at the clubs you play at. Still talks about 'Nam like it was yesterday he was over there. Real low life. He's been in some pretty bad traffic, but don't know what he'd be up to right now."

There was a pause on the other end of the line. I didn't know how to fill it in so I thanked him and hung up.

The road to the hacienda was still dusty, still bumpy. The big house was still there, too. But no dog barked when I pulled up. And why hadn't he barked when KC's killers had come to visit? A blue Volkswagen sedan with a broken left taillight lens was parked out front.

Two men were coming out of the front door, Pedro trailing behind, shrugging his shoulders and shaking his head. One of the men was tall with a heavy build and thick neck, cherubic red face and disappearing hairline. He walked with a bow-legged swagger. The other was shorter and smaller, with a hurried, worried look on his bearded face that seemed to affect his whole body. Both of them wore baggy blue jeans and T-shirts with ads on the front and I knew them both. The big one was Cole Slaughter and his companion was Neil Popkin. Rock critics.

"What are you doing out here, Fender? The Mafia garage sale is two miles down the road," said Cole Slaughter with his usual too-loud Fort Worth twang.

"Yeah," said the sidekick, bubbling with conspiratorial giggles. Then, with a shaking head and solemn tone—"We're sorry about KC, Martin. Seriously, it's a real tragedy for us all."

"Yeah, yeah, I know," I said. "So what are you guys doing out here?"

Cole stared out towards the barn as he said: "*Texas Monthly* wants a feature on KC." Elbowing his partner, "We're collaboratin' on it." He adjusted his wire rims and looked down at my car as if it were a record he was about to rate.

Neil came around and put a soft hand on my shoulder. "Martin, we know you probably aren't ready to talk about it. We just came out here to get a feel for the place where it happened." He wiped a band of sweat from his forehead with the heel of his hand, then wiped that on the back of his Levis. "We tried to talk to Pedro but he doesn't seem to understand English or my Spanish, so you know . . . actually what I was thinking—well, and Cole, too—was we could talk to you, over lunch maybe early next week. I just discovered the best ribs in the world over at this little dive on the east side. You'd love them, I just know it."

"Got another gig lined up, Fender?" twanged Cole.

I stared at the critic's threatening gut and shook my head. Why did I have to run into these hyperactive losers?

"But who we really need to talk to first is Johnny," piped in Neil. He looked at his companion when he said it, but I knew it was intended for me.

"Really," I said.

"Where is he?" asked Neil.

"I don't know."

"Didn't think you would," deadpanned Cole, hooking his thumbs in his belt loops.

Neil leaned closer and said softly: "It's very important that we speak with the son of a bitch."

"Did he run away with your thesaurus or something?"

"Such a wit," spat Neil.

"Shit-wit," drawled Cole.

The hand that had been on my shoulder now jabbed at my chest. "I know," Neil said, wide-eyed, "that Johnny came out here Monday night. He kept us waiting like a couple of assholes. But if you want to help a couple of old buddies out, they could help you out, too. Know what I mean?"

"Old buddies. Hmmm. That wouldn't be two gentle souls from the fourth estate, would it?"

"Hey, this fella's been takin' smart pills," beamed Cole.

"Two gentlemen who never pay to get in anywhere, get all their records for free, sell the ones they don't like to the record stores, then take it on themselves to decide what's cool for the public and what isn't? Two smug, self-inflated stooges?"

No answer. Just silence. No eye contact. Diablo came running up and started sniffing at Cole's shoes. "Love that dog," I said. "He knows where you're coming from."

"Let's go, Cole. This farm grows nothing but sour grapes."

"And bullshit," added Cole. "I need to get back. The rates are down now and I gotta make some calls for that Robert Cray piece I'm doing for *Rolling Stone*."

Neil said he had calls to make, too. Cole said Neil would have to make them on his own phone since he hadn't paid him back for the last batch of calls. They were cackling and clucking at each other like a couple of brooding hens by the time they weighted down the VW, slammed its doors, and left me in a cloud of dust.

"They come here, try front door, then go 'round, don't say nothing to me," said Pedro. "Just go look round in room, act real important. I been working other house for Mr. Ward, don't have time to clean up much since you stay here. They left in such hurry," wiping his brow with an old bandana, "I never get to say maybe this what you look for." Out of a cloak closet by the side entrance, the old man pulled out a blue Anvil briefcase, covered with backstage passes. "I don't know," he said, pushing out his lower lip, "found it under KC's bed."

I tripped the latches. It was empty.

I asked him about the dog. It was a little difficult, but with a little effort on both our parts, he realized what I was asking.

"He's no good for wash dog." He smiled and scratched behind the animal's ears. "He like to run around, down there, in arroyo, shase things at night. Mebbe he look for romance."

There wasn't much to see in KC's room. The wall had been cleaned but the place was a mess. The mattress and box springs had been flipped over, the sheets pulled off. The only pillow on the bed had been ripped open. The carpet had been pulled up in one corner, and a wicker wastebasket in the corner had been overturned.

There were three empty Gitanes boxes, some used Kleenex, a matchbook from the Roadrunner Motel with no phone numbers inside, five wadded-up sheets of typing paper, and the most recent issue of the local music rag.

The sheets of paper from the basket had one sentence written on them over and over, double-spaced:

The quick brown fox jumped over the lazy dog.

The magazine had the usual club listings, the usual reactionary record reviews, an anti-CIA piece, and a lengthy dismissal of a recently released bootleg live recording of True Love.

While it praised the "dependable relentless rhythm section of Billy Ludwig and Martin Fender," it attacked the "inadequate nasal exhortations of singer Frankie Day, who is as frequently off-pitch as he is off-center, missing both the melody and the message of the song entirely." But that was nothing compared to the barbs that lashed out at the "cliché-ridden excesses of guitarist KC Williamson, whose overamped angst derails any sensitive moments the music might potentially aspire to." Unbelievably, it went on to deride the guitar player's hair style, smoking habits, and slouchy posture.

The headline read:

> TRUE LOVE
> SHOWS TRUE SLEAZE
> IN ONE NIGHT
> STAND.

The byline read: by Cole Slaughter.

I sat on the window sill and lit a whiff. Outside the house an armadillo was rooting around for grubs and bugs, turning over small rocks and sticks with his snout. Almost deaf, slower than an old man on crutches, with his beady eyes and less-than-keen nose, the armored anachronism rooted along, sure of what he was after, sure where to find it.

I wadded up the damn paper and threw it at him. It landed a couple of feet behind him, unnoticed. There wasn't a screen on the window, and I'd been thinking about crawling out and looking around, but what would I find out there? Footprints of the coke-killers? Was I supposed to be Daniel Boone now? I had a dead guitarist with writer's block, a shot-up pillow, a dust jacket showing Mick Jagger with an extra nostril, an empty briefcase, a big redhead. And no idea how they all fit together.

I slid off the window ledge and crushed the cigar butt on the floor. Now I had something new: a white and powdery blotch on the leg of my trousers. I tried brushing it off. It was stubborn. Must have happened when I sat down, I decided.

The source was a brown-black burn spot on the outer sill of the window where I'd rested my leg. I sniffed the sample on my hand. Toothpaste. A cigarette burn disguised by toothpaste. It didn't seem like something Pedro would do. My shoe crunched on a dried crust of homemade bread as I left the room.

I used the phone in the kitchen to call Lorraine. She was glad to hear from me. I told her about seeing the critics, and about the big story they were supposedly going to do on KC for *Texas Monthly.* As I talked, I looked up their addresses in the phone book.

She didn't say anything for a moment. Then, "Those guys hated KC," she hissed. "They're not about to write a kind word about him. They never have. Did you see that review of—"

"That's what I thought," I said. "I just saw it. They're after the coke, not a story."

"Those bastards," she snapped. "Do you think maybe they . . ."

"I'm afraid to think. I'm going over to Cole's house first. The tables are turned now; this bass player is gonna interview some rock critics. Takes about an hour to get back to town with the traffic, I guess, so give me a couple of hours and I'll be back with your stuff from the house. We'll order a pizza."

"Be careful," was all she said.

Diablo loped over to the car and dropped something in my lap as I was starting to pull out. I tried to give it back to him but he let it fall there in the dirt. I gave him a pat and started rolling, trying not to run over the chewed-up blue Frisbee as the sad-eyed dog barked at me and my dust.

I chainsmoked all the way back to civilization. Every other time I pulled a cigarette out of my shirt pocket, I re-read KC's last words. Do the do.

12

Cole Slaughter had a small clapboard A-frame on the corner of Nile Street and Pleasant Valley Road on the east side. It had taken over an hour to get there. The sun was going down fast.

Just around the corner was Boggy Creek, and as I walked up the cracked sidewalk the air smelled of wet grass and moss. There was a broken rocking chair on the porch, and the screen on the front door was pushed out at the bottom from a cat or dog. Thirty years ago, the little bungalow wouldn't have been a bad place for a pair of newlyweds to start out. Now it was broken down and seedy, perfect for a bachelor who leaned more toward barbecue, books, and records than dinner parties, PTA, and a new Chevrolet every couple of years.

I knocked several times. No response. A long-bodied yellow cat disappeared into the overgrown hedge that had taken over the right side of the house. Through the screen I could hear an electric fan running. The VW was in the drive.

The door wasn't latched, so I went in. I called out hello. No answer. It was a small house for such a big man. The hardwood floors creaked underfoot. A couple of steps into the living room I stopped and surveyed the wreckage: cinderblock and plank shelves, piles of magazines, books, records, and posters, along with a component stereo system, an old acoustic guitar—everything tossed and scattered. What had probably been a housekeeper's bad dream to begin with had been turned upside down by someone looking for something. Violently.

The kitchen was the same. Dirty dishes were broken on the

linoleum. Cereal and flour containers had been opened, their contents spilled out.

Cole was in the bathroom. His eyes were open. He lay fully clothed at the bottom of the tub, the water spilling over the edge, colored red from the blood that had pumped out of deep gashes on his wrists. I lifted the toilet lid and threw up.

A rusty butcher knife lay on the soap dish next to a bottle of creme rinse which promised to "beat the frizzies." I touched the body tentatively several times before I got the courage to turn it over. More water splashed on the floor, and my feet got wet. No other visible wounds, nothing at the bottom of the tub. On the back of the head, a lump, big and hard as an avocado pit.

Maybe he slipped in the tub, lost his marbles and decided to end it all. After he decided to take a bath with his clothes on. Yeah.

The phone rang. It rang six times before I answered. It was Neil Popkin.

"Martin, is that you?" even more rushed than usual . . . "Lemme speak to Cole." More pushy, "Lemme speak to Cole, please."

"Cole can't come to the phone. I just found him."

"What do you mean, you just found him? Lemme talk to him."

"I'm sorry, Neil. I don't know how to tell you—"

"Tell me what? Lemme . . ."

"He's dead. I'm sorry. It looks like murder."

Long pause. Strange whimpering sound. Voice quavering, he said: "My god, we just wanted . . . you know . . . one easy thing. It's not fair . . ." voice rising in pitch, deteriorating in tone, "I mean, goddam, we just wanted to do this one time, after working so hard and having nothing . . ."

"We need to talk, Neil," I said firmly.

He muttered something.

"Was it the Mexicans?"

"What?" He didn't know what I was talking about.

"I'll be right over," I said.

Cold shivers were working their way up my backbone, like someone had just dumped a glass of ice tea down my shirt. I waded through the wreckage in the living room, poking at some of the papers and magazines piled around the typewriter on an old rolltop desk. It was a waste of time.

My thoughts wandered back to Cole. There was nothing I could do for him. Back there in that tub was his dead body. Never one for beauty contests in life, his corpse wasn't going to win him any prizes either.

I wiped off the door knobs and frames and telephone with my shirttail and split.

I drove down Nile looking for a short cut to Holly, but found myself back at the intersection with Pleasant Valley where I'd started, the victim of a cul de sac. My errors were compounded as I took Pleasant Valley north instead of south. I pulled over and took some deep breaths. Concentrate. Yelling the names of the streets helped drown out the noises in my head. Right on Cantebury. The bright white lights of the Holly Street power plant pierced through the tops of the trees, illuminating the neighborhood. The sound of churning turbines and rushing water, the sound of power being made, grew louder and louder as I neared Holly. I went a block past Neil's street, turning in at a lit-up baseball diamond adjacent to Town Lake. There was a game going on. I parked next to a truckload of sand where a jogging trail cut through the weeds.

Neil's house was on the corner. The noise was a giant thing, like being inside a sea shell. How the hell did people sleep? The houses in this neighborhood were small and spare as bird houses, huddled together under the trees on close lots, many of them painted colors that you only find in neighborhoods like that. Pink, turquoise, peach.

Neil's was white with black trim, a small porch with a rotting balustrade, a dirt yard, and an old Cutlass on cinder blocks poking out from the back. The tar paper roof was weighted down by bricks and tires.

Once again, no one answered my knock. I went in. It was

so loud here, people probably didn't knock anyway. A thread-bare carpet of no distinguishable color covered the living room floor. Old movie posters hung on imitation maple wall panelling throughout the room. All in all, it wasn't as ravaged as Cole's house had been, despite the upturned record boxes, scattered papers and magazines, disemboweled sofa, and overturned ash-trays. The whole scene could have passed for the aftermath of a wild party except for one thing: Neil was hanging from the overhead ceiling fan by a length of yellow nylon rope.

If this kept up, people were going to quit inviting me over. I lit a Camel, sucking the smoke down to my shoes. It couldn't have been more than fifteen minutes since I'd talked to him. Maybe twenty. Twenty-five on the outside, counting getting sidetracked going the wrong way. I wondered what time it really was. Lorraine was probably expecting me back by now. Neil still had a plain Texas Instruments digital watch strapped to his wrist. I approached it.

The phone rang. A nerve-jangling, inappropriate thing to happen. As I walked over to it, a red light lit up on a cheap answering machine that clicked into gear. "Hi, this is Neil and I can't come to the phone right now but if you'll leave a message at the sound of the tone . . ."

The speaker beeped and a voice said: "Neil . . . are you there? Is this thing working? Listen, uh, Neil, this is James, and we definitely want 1969. I'm leaving the office now, but why don't you touch base with me in the morning. OK. Ciao."

1969? I glanced at Neil. Better get someone else for your psychedelic '60s retrospective, pal. I wondered if someone had been listening when I'd talked to him on the phone. Then stepped out from the closet and hanged him. For chrissakes . . .

Someone knocked at the door. I peeked through the ragged curtain on the front window and saw a freckle-faced kid with a flat, square box balanced on one hand and a money changer on his belt. Pizza.

I stood there, quiet. He was persistent, about to open the door and yell "Anybody home?" I could tell. He was that type.

I did the only thing I could think of to get rid of him, fast. I opened the door a crack.

"How much?"

"Six ninety five—large pepperoni and anchovy, extra cheese."

My wallet was empty except for the two hundred dollar bills George Garret had given me. "How about it?" I asked.

"Gimme a break. You think I carry that kind of change around in this neighborhood?"

I told him to wait and shut the door. Neil's wallet was on the desk. There was twenty inside. I paid the kid and gave him a dollar tip. The pizza and wallets came into the kitchen and ended up on the table. As I was putting the change from a twenty in Neil's wallet, a pink slip of paper fell out and drifted to the dirty tile floor.

I was no stranger to pink slips of that particular sort. I recognized it instantly. It was an overdraft notice from his bank. He was overdrawn from a $10,000 check.

I pulled up a chair and sat down at the chrome dinette. I hadn't eaten in almost two days, and the pizza smelled pretty good, and I was worried that my mind might be playing tricks on me because of starvation. A lot of barefoot guys had seen God after they'd gone out and sat under a fig tree and fasted for a week or so. Then they wrote books about it. I wanted no part of it.

The pizza was still hot. Neil was still rotating a bit on the rope. People don't order pizza and then hang themselves. I sprinkled some red pepper on a slice. You can't find New York pizza anywhere but New York. Something about the spices, the consistency of the sauce, and the greasiness of the cheese. Texans' idea of good pizza is a big doughy slab of cheese with Thanksgiving dinner piled on top of it.

I doubted a small-time writer like Neil made ten thousand dollars in a year. Why would he write a hot check for that amount? The notice didn't say who the check was made out to, only the amount and the number. I took a big bite out of the slice to fortify myself on the search for the checkbook, but never got to swallow.

Something came down on my head. I saw colors and heard myself hit the floor, only it felt like the bottom of the world. I took a break.

I came to on the dirty linoleum, face to face with a couple of cockroaches. Cockroaches can live six weeks after you cut their heads off. By the way mine felt, it seemed like a good trade— no head, no pain. I got up slowly, doing a little soft shoe as I tried to get my balance. The world was my teeterboard.

It was dark. Still hot, though. The floor was wet from my sweat where I'd been lying, and some of the dirt had turned to mud on my face. I peeked into the living room. Neil was still there. In fact, Neil's twin brother was there, too, hanging from an identical overhead fan. There were two of almost everything. I lit a couple of Camels with a couple of matches, went over to the sinks and splashed some water on my face. At least I only felt one face.

I noticed the power plant noise again. It had been there the whole time, I just hadn't been thinking about it. Maybe I was starting to like it.

I'd been out. How long? I made my way into the living room with the dead man in it, intent on looking at his watch and not his face. His wrist felt more alive than it should have, and that gave me the creeps. Gravel crunched in the drive out front and I let the wrist fall before I saw what time it was. Maybe my blind date had sent for reinforcements, more sledgehammers. I hit the back door, stumbled down the steps and over a short fence into the neighbor's garden. I squatted there, between rows of sun-scorched tomato plants. Two blue and white APD cars had pulled up to the house. Radios squawked and black institutional rubber soles clomped up the steps to the front door.

The big noise seemed normal now, like the sound of blood rushing in my ears. Over it, I could hear the crickets chirp, and another patrol car pulling up on Riverview, in front of the garden owner's house. I was sandwiched in. I didn't think I could hack my way through back yards all the way to the other end of the block. Someone was bound to have a nervous Doberman with a taste for skinny white boys. The Karmann Ghia was a dangerous thirty yards away, equidistant between me and home plate on the baseball field. The jogging trail was much closer, just the other side of the fence, between me and the power plant. I needed to get out of the house. Then get my car. But I couldn't do both in one smooth motion. No way.

I ripped off my clothes. From a distance, my boxers could pass for gym shorts. Luckily I'd worn my Converse All-Stars for the trip out to the ranch. They weren't jogging shoes, but . . . I twisted my clothes into a tight cylinder and tucked it all under my arm.

Sweat was no problem. I had enough of it for ten joggers. I made my way across the garden, keeping an eye on the house. Sounded like a home run from the ball game—cheers and honking horns—so I hopped over the fence and hit the track with my eyes open and my fingers crossed.

I ran west on the track, passing just a few yards from the blue and white on Riverview. One of the uniformed cops was watching the ball game while I passed, the other was on the radio. I jogged down the trail to the banks of the lake. The colored lights of the Ramada Inn over on the opposite shore reflected on the murky water's surface.

OK. I'd had my little break, and now it was time to get back to my car. I put my clothes back on and walked back in the direction of the baseball game. My vision was getting back to normal, and by the time I rounded the back of the bleachers, my heart seemed ready to slow down to the speed limit. The cops were still parked on Riverview, more of them now, as I walked just a few car-lengths away from them to retrieve my ride.

It started the first time, and I rolled out of the ball park pinching myself for never having bought a pair of fuzzy dice for the rearview mirror.

At the pay phone outside the 7th Street Pay-N-Take-It I dialed a number I had for Johnny one last time. No answer. When I hung up, my quarter didn't come back. I didn't have any more, so I reached for my wallet, planning to go inside, buy a six pack and more cigarettes and get some change. No dice. No wallet. I'd left it next to the box of pizza at the scene of the most recent murder I'd come across.

I had to warn Lorraine. I didn't know what I'd say, since I wanted to tell her about Neil and Cole in person—maybe together we could calmly figure some of this out—but I wanted her to be prepared when the police came looking for me. I used my credit card number to call my apartment. The phone rang twenty nine times before I gave it up.

13

I needed a place to hang out for awhile, think things out. I couldn't go home. I needed someone who wasn't involved in this mess yet. I turned the car around and headed for Travis Heights, South Austin.

Ladonna DiMascio answered the door on my second knock. She'd been getting ready for bed. She was wearing the big white cotton shirt that she wore instead of a robe in the summer. That shirt had once belonged to me. Her face was still a little wet from taking off her makeup and her platinum blonde hair was pulled back with a white head band. But those silver hoop earrings she always wore were still dangling, and that shirt looked a lot different on her than it did on me.

"Better come in, Martin, before we let any more of those June bugs in here," she said. "The cat just loves to eat them. It's so gross."

Her condominium was a cool, tidy, white-carpeted nest. A lot of Sundays had been spent at flea markets accumulating the art deco and '50s furnishings—the black lacquered bookcases and the pink boomerang coffee table in the living room, the round chrome '50s toaster and martini shaker and other Machine Age artifacts alongside the platinum white high tech food processor and matte black German espresso maker in the brightly lit spotless kitchen. I sank down on the pink couch under a black velvet Elvis painting. The '50s clock radio on top of the TV said it was a little after nine.

"Well hello, stranger," she said, bringing out a tray with some glasses and a crystal decanter and setting it down on the coffee table. Though her face could have belonged to one of the exotic models pictured in the stack of *Vogue* magazines on the coffee table, she was a young single mother of Italian descent tempered with Texas frontier practicality. Her cat was rubbing her small black and white body against my pants leg. The cat's name was Betty, after Lauren Bacall. "You look terrible," Ladonna said.

"Thanks. Cigarette?"

She nodded.

"Sorry it's wrinkled." I lit them. We inhaled as she waited for an explanation. "How's Michael?" I asked instead of giving her one.

"He's just fine." Her voice was tentative. She was either going to give me a little time to work up to it, or she didn't care if I did. It was hard to tell and I didn't trust my senses just then. "You know he's going to be seven years old pretty soon? I just can't believe it. Remember you gave him that Walkman for his last birthday? I can't believe a whole year's gone by."

"He's some kid. He's in bed already?" I said, noticing that both the bedroom doors were shut. She nodded as she poured us a couple of drinks. The kid was lucky to have such a pretty mother. But where did I fit in, especially now? I felt pretty damn awkward. I didn't feel like a part of her world at all. Her calm, matter-of-fact beauty, her art deco, books, bright kitchen, and humming refrigerator was too much too soon, after what I'd seen. She sat cross-legged on the white carpet, the boomerang table between us.

"Martin," she said softly, touching my hand, "you're in trouble."

"No. Just trying to help some people out, fell down in the mud by the lake."

"Sure."

I nodded.

She touched my hand again. "I'm so sorry about KC. I was planning on taking Michael to the gig. I heard about the reunion on the radio, and I was so glad for you. I've been trying to call you . . . I guess you've got a right to get drunk and fall down."

Since I only nodded, more at my own distraction than her

statement, she changed the subject, saying, "So I guess instead of your gig I'll take him to Bruce Springsteen. I got tickets today. Paid $100 each for floor seats. I've never seen him, and Michael really wants to go."

I was still nodding, thinking about just how I wanted to approach my situation. I was a little relieved that she'd veered off the subject, but Springsteen was a little too far. There'd been no escaping him on the radio for the past week.

"Were you and KC very close? True Love was before I knew you."

"Well, you play in a band with a guy, you share rooms, you spend a lot of time in a van or on a stage, to where maybe you don't even know how to spell his last name or where he came from, but you know things about him without even talking." But what *did* I really know about the guy? I didn't know much about his drug deals, and I certainly hadn't suspected him of *the black eye kind of stuff*. I wasn't the one to eulogize him. All I knew, I told Ladonna, was that "He sure could play guitar."

"You're feeling the loss even though you didn't know him as well as you might have. That's normal, Martin. And very human."

"I still feel like I'm his bass player."

"Oh, Martin," she sighed. "I wonder how Big Red is taking it."

"You know her?"

"I know who she is. I don't *know* her. One of the realtors at work is handling the sale of the house around the corner from them. She's a trust fund brat. Her dad was a wildcatter before becoming a drunk, but he managed to set up her trust fund before the oil business went bust. Now he just spends a lot of time using the free phones at the Forum Club, pretending to make deals, but there's nobody on the other end."

"When you guys sell a property, you really investigate the neighborhood."

"It's all on the grapevine, Martin. The guys I work for are just regular guys who happened to get rich off a crazy deal a couple of years ago and they like to gossip more than any girls I know."

"Well, I'm worried about her. She's staying over at my place, and something weird happened with KC, and like I said about the band thing . . ."

"Go ahead, fuck her, I don't give a damn."

"That's not it, dammit. KC was murdered."

"What? I'm sorry, Martin . . . for saying that, but. . . . Are you *sure?*"

"No, not really. Yes, I am. So were a couple of other guys. Tonight. Cole Slaughter and Neil Popkin, the critics." There, I'd gotten it out.

"No," she said, trembling. "Do the police . . . ? They don't, do they? You, and your friends, Martin . . ." She shook her head. "Why? How?"

"It's bad," I said. I tried to do better. "It's stupid, it's a trap, but I don't know. I don't want to worry you. Maybe it's not that bad."

She didn't believe the last part any more than she liked the first. "What are you going to do?" She grabbed my hand and gently tugged.

I started to tell my reflections in her eyes I wasn't in that much trouble. Her eyes were too big to say that to. But I counted on the strength of her aristocratic nose and high cheekbones, the resolve of the strong bony shoulders and proud chest when I said I had to get at something, to plow through just a little longer because . . . "It just wouldn't be right not to."

"But why can't the police handle it?"

"Because it's a little complicated." I was thinking of the kilo. "And because evidently KC thought of me as some sort of extra cool guy, according to Lorraine."

"It doesn't mean you have to get yourself . . ." she hesitated.

"I won't. But Johnny's mixed up in this somehow."

"Just call the police, Martin. The last time . . ."

"But the last time is how you and I got together."

Her lips quivered a bit, and her gaze took in my hands, my wrinkled clothes and jitters. I could see a melancholic smile start to take the frown away, if not the worry. I was just about to tell her I needed a place to stay the night when I heard a loud belch come from the bedroom. It didn't sound like the kid.

"What have you got in there, a grizzly bear?"

"Martin, I haven't heard from you in three weeks." She blushed.

"Two and a half. I haven't had a band to bring you to see and because of that I've been broke and couldn't take you out. I've been in a bad mood and I didn't want to . . ."

"You don't have to make excuses. But you've got no right to come over here in your new wave Humphrey Bogart suit, smelling like the Swamp Thing, and make me feel guilty." She stood up, hands on her hips. It wasn't fair that her perfect skin glowed with a just-scrubbed purity, now accentuated by the faint blush. She was right, she was perfect, and I was either wrong or confused. Maybe both.

"Hey, I know I've got no rights." I finished the drink. "I was just leaving anyway. I just wanted to look in on you and apologize for not calling. I guess this means it's off."

"What's off?"

"My timing, I suppose." I excused myself and went to the bathroom, splashed clean cold water on my face, and combed my hair back. My suit, after a little touching up with a wet cloth, had that roguish, ruffled look that was so popular that year.

When I came back out, Ladonna was wearing a robe. She asked where I was going.

"Oh, I don't know. Don't worry about it."

"You can't just walk in here, drink my Scotch and use my hair spray and make me all worried, then brush me off." She wasn't going to whine or scream, she wasn't going to lock the door and keep me from leaving. And she wasn't going to say anything about the trail of muddy footprints I'd left on the white carpet, either. "And you didn't come here to say you were sorry."

"I am, really. About the carpet, too."

"To hell with the carpet. Please be careful. Please go to the police. Please . . . come back."

"I'll call you tomorrow, when your company is gone," I said, reaching for the door.

She came up and stood on her toes to kiss me hard. "How do you know he'll be gone tomorrow?"

"I'll call you," I said, walking out under the yellow bug light into the hot August night.

14

It was Thursday, and I could think of only one place for a hip fugitive to go. It was a place for people who sold drugs and people who bought them, as well as people who dropped by to strut their stuff, touch base, get lucky, and maybe just to dance. I had no hopes or inclinations for any of those things, but I figured I could borrow some money there so I could get something to eat, and maybe, just maybe—Johnny would be tucked into a dark corner there.

Club Slither was the place. And it wasn't even a place.

It was a floating club. Most of the venues that hosted it were gay discos, though it occasionally touched down in empty warehouses and other surreptitious locales that had the requisite quantity of space and darkness. Thursday nights the scene was at the Sindrome, a post-modern glass tile box near the railroad tracks, and from fifteen hundred to two thousand trendy insomniacs would be there.

I cut to the front of the line. The proprietress, Queen Bee, stood to the side of the box office, smiling a little Mona Lisa smile at all the money prancing in. She was a tall, thin thing with a lightly teased chocolate brown wedge cut and mannequin cool, and she'd found her niche. She'd never have to wait tables again. Before she started her club, people rarely remembered her name when they were introduced to her. But I did. I could see then that she had something, and I told her so. I told her she was a real princess. But I was wrong. She was a queen bee. She knew it, and now everybody else did, too, because that was what they called her.

Once I got her attention, she nodded me in through the out door. I pried my way through the throng, kissed her on the cheek, and said that I needed to talk to her. We went upstairs through the club and out a door that opened onto a catwalk outside above the club's patio.

"I need to borrow some money," I said.

She smiled and said, "Sure, Martin," and a roll of bills appeared from somewhere, two of which she peeled off and put in my hand.

I looked down. Two Ben Franklin notes. "I . . ."

"You don't have to tell me what it's for, Martin. I know you wouldn't ask unless it was . . ."

"Important," I said, nodding. She gave me a matronly peck on the cheek and patted my shoulder.

"Frankie was here earlier, and I thought about you. That was so terrible about KC."

"Yeah. I don't suppose he hung out at your club?"

"No. But his girlfriend, Lorraine, would come when he was out of town."

"She's kinda wild," I offered.

"She looks wild. But all she'd talk about was KC this and KC that. He was her pet project. He didn't have anything to worry about. I mean, I understand how it is," she added with a sly smile. "I paid the rent on a relationship like that for a year and a half."

Below us it was all boom crash thunder, digital echo, and urban chants. Hi-rise hairdos were bopping and swaying on the dance floor like tribal headdresses. "Have you seen Johnny?"

"Oh, it's funny you'd ask. Those guys were in a bunch of times last week. It was odd."

"What guys? What's odd?"

"Well, you know, Martin. Those critics are always turning up their noses at anything trendy like this. They don't wear the clothes, the girls wouldn't look at them twice . . ."

"Johnny is not a critic."

"Yeah, but Monday night he was with Neil Popkin and Cole Slaughter. That's what I'm saying. There's nothing unusual about

Johnny hanging out at my club, but we don't get many rock critics. I haven't seen the three of them since Monday night, when Johnny was going out to drop in on your rehearsal. Wasn't he your manager or something?"

"Just the roadie," I corrected. "And, you know, an old pal."

"Well, you know Johnny, then. One of those guys who carries his ego around in an Anvil briefcase. Would you like a drink?"

"No. I don't really have time." Boy didn't I. This might be my last night out for awhile.

"You look like you could use one. You look stressed out."

I shook my head again. "So what were the critics doing, besides looking down their noses at all the high fashion and low bass frequencies?"

"They had some kind of drug deal going. They were pretty excited about it."

The dirty graverobbers, I thought. I asked her if she knew anything about the deal.

"She shook her head. "You know I don't do the stuff. Everybody around here is on Ecstasy, in case you can't tell. I think it's kinda cute—they're all having so much fun. They say it gives you a nasty hangover, though."

"Queen, didn't you at least see the writers talking to anybody in particular? I kind of need to know who they were expecting to sell to. Or who they were buying from. Were the guys Mexican?"

"No. Like I said, Monday night they were talking to Johnny. I mean, so I assumed their deal was with him. That's who they talked to, you know, like—*Hey, Johnny*—when they'd see him. And you know they wouldn't have been glad to see him otherwise. He's not the kind of guy they hang out with."

I must have looked confused.

"I don't know, Martin. You know I don't keep up with that stuff, either. I just watch. But people are pretty damn obvious. Neil and Cole were smirking all over the place, they held their wallets different when they pulled them out to pay for drinks, you know, that kind of thing . . ."

Below us the disco beat pounded away. A tuxedo came and

whispered something in the party magnate's ear. "I gotta go, Martin," she said. "Later?"

"Thanks, Queen," I said, then added, "for the loan, too."

She smiled as she turned to leave. It was nothing, the smile said.

My mind was racing. I needed to get out of there.

I had a puzzle on my hands. A widow staying at my apartment whose boyfriend was supposed to have been killed over a kilo of coke supposed to have been stolen by Johnny from some mysterious Mexicans in the middle of a transaction with some amateur dealers. I had some dead critics—the amateurs Johnny had mentioned Monday night at the ranch—who'd had some deal going with Johnny. I had a missing steel insect which Johnny had been hired to steal. Johnny had been awfully busy. No wonder everyone was looking for him.

Maybe I was just lazy, but I wanted to pare things down, so I started throwing out things that didn't fit. The stupid bug didn't at all. If Johnny was supposed to be stealing it, why didn't he have the van Monday night? The sound of gears shifting in front of the ranch house was clear in my memory as a bell. Rental vans are all automatics. Sure, he could have borrowed someone's truck that had standard transmission, but like I said, I was getting lazy, and wanted to keep things simple. Just like Johnny would.

Then there was the matter of the critics. I couldn't imagine them being involved in ripping off the mysterious Mexicans, too. And simplifying things was getting to be so much fun, I threw the Mexicans out, too. I just couldn't get a mental picture of them.

Murder must be like that, I thought. You decide who stands in the way of your life being easier, and then you eliminate them. Not with malice, just a yearning for order in your life. Some bright person would probably build a cult around that kind of thinking. Someone probably already had. That was the 1980s for you.

So what did that leave? Two dead critics, one dead guitarist, and three little words: Do the do. Suspects? I never once suspected anyone in the band. They weren't the nicest guys in the world, but . . .

I found a reasonably quiet pay phone and called them anyway. Maybe they could help. Billy's roommate said he was in the studio. That could mean all night. Frankie's answering machine was on. His recording started off with the usual thing about how he was sorry he missed you, but it had a jarring postscript: "and if this is Ward or Lorraine, I'm ready to get paid now. Billy said that one of you guys would have my cut. So let me know where I can pick it up, OK? Later—"

I didn't leave a message. I was too busy thinking. Maybe I had some consolation money coming from the cancelled gig. Evidently Ward had cut some kind of deal with Lorraine and the surviving members of the band. Maybe Ward had a conscience after all. I wondered why Lorraine hadn't said anything about it. Well, she was upset and anxious to get the coke. But why hadn't anyone else told me about the money? Maybe I didn't have any coming, after all. But that wasn't what bothered me. What bothered me was that Ward had said he hadn't talked to Lorraine.

And Lorraine had said she hadn't talked to Ward.

I called back again to make sure I'd heard the message right. It said what I thought it had said, so I hung up again. What did I give a damn if Lorraine and Ward talked to each other? I had two quarters left. I used one on True Love's original bass player, Dan Gabriel, who Lorraine had said KC used to deal drugs with. He wasn't asleep, but he hadn't been expecting any calls, either.

"You must be drunk, Martin," he growled.

"Not hardly. Meet me in front of the capitol in half an hour."

"Not hardly, yourself."

"Dan, you spent a lot of time with KC and you used to sell drugs with him. He was murdered and I've got some questions for you."

"You're drunk, all right."

"Then call the cops and tell them that in forty-five minutes a drunk bass player is going to be over at your condo breaking out all the windows."

He didn't want to call the cops.

Everybody was go-going to an electro-funk version of a James Brown song as I made my way through the throng, through the cigarette smoke, late night party talk and poppers, and on out through the Colorado Street door.

As I stepped off the curb I could hear car doors slam in the alley. I half turned in time to see a couple of men in inexpensive suits undiplomatically cut to the front of the line. I turned up my collar and kept walking. They weren't musicians, I decided, and not just because the bulges in their jackets were too big to be made by guitar picks.

They were cops. I'd left just in time.

15

Dan Gabriel was sitting at the base of a statue on the capitol lawn. The statue was a life-sized cowboy trying to rein in his mount as it reared back on its hind legs. The horse had good reason to be spooked. Under his belly, only an inch or two away from his horse-sized genitals, was the top of a large colony of Texas prickly pear. It seemed humorous in a surreal way, the cold bronze memorial to the rugged cowboy with the soft outline of a retired rocker in a jogging suit sitting at the foot of it. But the capitol grounds are always eerie at night.

Gabriel felt bad about not returning KC's phone calls, and it showed in his face. Now every time the phone rang, he heard a Stratocaster moan from the grave. But he wasn't too surprised when I told him that Lorraine was heir to a kilo of cocaine, and that the two critics had apparently been killed over it.

"Why shouldn't KC have been trying to make some easy money?" he said. "I'm not saying I get the part about it being ripped off, but when you get to be KC's age and you don't have anything, no security I mean, no car or health insurance . . . Know what I mean?"

"I guess he should have bought a three-piece and gone into real estate like you did."

"Now Martin, you're getting me all wrong. I've turned a few keys in my time, yes sir. Me and KC made the run across the border more than once. More than twice. Hell yeah we did. I'm plenty familiar with the lure of easy money."

"It's not the lure that has caused all the trouble. I just don't understand . . ."

"Shit. You seem bright enough. I could get you set up in my outfit where you'd make the same kind of money you'd make off delivering a kilo of blow—what, about fifty, sixty thou these days? It'd take a few months. It'd be legit, though. You could pay income tax on it and everything."

"Uh huh."

"However, you wouldn't get the same kick from it. That's why you're hanging around with the redhead, trying to do a good deed, I bet. Yeah," he growled, low and hoarse, lusty. "The thrill, man. The chance to make a big score. That cocaine is shiny stuff, you know, especially compared to a couple of wrinkled twenties from a one-nighter or a paycheck from a local rag that pays a buck or two per column inch. You can't fault Neil and Cole."

He laughed. I shot him a look.

"It's just the thought of those two shitbirds trying to play "Miami Vice," Martin. It's funny, you know?"

"No, it's not. Especially not from where I've been standing."

"Sorry. You gotta excuse me, I need some sleep." He got to his feet and leaned back on the statue, rubbing his hands on his warm-up suit. "Hell, Martin. I wish I could tell you something that'd be a help. I'm hip to where you're coming from. But maybe you should just leave it alone. It ain't like KC left instructions for you in his will. Damn that moody bastard. Notice how everybody always had to come to him? When was the last time he gave you a phone call, or dropped in to see you? I don't hear from the drunk bastard in five years and then he calls me. What am I supposed to think, huh? He coulda dropped by the office, but it always had to be on his turf. And she'll be OK, Martin. She can take care of herself."

"Probably so. I just felt like . . ."

"You aren't fooling around with her, are you?"

"I'm just trying to help her out."

"What's wrong, she strain her back pushing thirty?"

"KC must've seen something in her."

"She's part of the reason I gave up playing," he said. "Girlfriends break up more bands than any other damn thing. Why didn't you *call me* from Baton Rouge, they say. Why do you have to *rehearse so much*. That *bass player* hogs the spotlight during your *guitar solos*. Or they find a pack of rubbers in your road laundry. She had KC by the balls, man. Course she co-signed for one of the vans and paid for studio time, too, but we couldn't get through a rehearsal without her calling and reminding him to bring some groceries home from the store. And she'd call our rooms on the road, leaving messages like 'don't forget I love you' for KC, and it'd be kind of embarrassing for him in front of the girls, lemme tell you."

"But he didn't let that stop him."

"Hell no. He liked to get his wick wet after a show no matter what town we were in. She had to know. How can you respect a girl like that?"

I didn't answer. "Respect" didn't quite cover the situation. "It wasn't quite like that when I was in the band," I said. "Maybe he'd settled down a little bit by then."

"Gave up, more likely. Found himself a new friend."

"We weren't all that close."

"No, Martin," he said, shaking his head. "One named Jack Daniels."

I didn't say anything. It seemed true enough to leave alone.

"I will tell you this, Martin, with these guys' places being ransacked like you say, right after you found them at the ranch snooping around, it looks to me like somebody is looking for that key all right. And killing whoever's laying on the bed they wanna look under. So as far as that goes, you're getting there. Maybe you'll beat them to it and see that they pay the cover charge one way or other. But you gotta ask yourself: Is it worth it?"

"It's worth it. If it's worth it to them, it's worth it to me. But who are *they*?"

"I don't know. But there's all kinds of amateurs out there. Just trying to be cool. I heard they got assholes that prance around at Club Slither with an X button on their shirt, fucking advertising the fact they've got the shit for sale. No self-respecting drug dealer would do something like that—those guys just wanna get laid. Think about it."

"What's the point?"

"Amateurs. Only amateurs would go around killing people, trying to make it look like suicide."

"So I'll be in good company. Looks to me like I'm just a couple of steps behind some killers who don't know what they're doing, either."

"OK, all right. I don't know. I don't know what it's all about, suicide or no. And I hate to stand here and play devil's advocate. But good luck to you, and if any police come up to my office asking me questions about this stuff I've been out of for years now, I don't know nothing."

"Seems like you've got a Ph.D. in nothing."

"Always a smartass, Martin. That's OK. You're all right. I'll see you around. In fact, why don't you drop by my office, maybe I can get you a job as a courier or something," he winked.

"No thanks."

"OK. Just remember. Is it worth it?"

He sucked in his gut as he offered his hand. I shook it, let it drop, and watched him amble off to his BMW.

I strained my eyes trying to see down Congress as far as the Joe Koen and Son Jewelry Store clock at Sixth and Congress. I guessed it would say about 12:45.

As I got in the Ghia and lit a Camel, I wasn't sure if I should be relieved about Gabriel's amateur killer theory or not. Amateur drug dealer killers can kill you just as dead as the professionals. I popped the boot and got the tire iron out of it, resolving to keep it close at hand for the time being. The bump on the back of my head was solid evidence that I had reasons to be paranoid, or at least, careful.

I drove across downtown. The streets were almost empty, and what traffic there was consisted of people shuttling between bars and the automated teller machines, so they could buy more Coronas and cocaine, more Ecstasy and etcetera. I cut across

Lamar at 12th to get to Lorraine's house. I made sure I had the list she'd given me before I got out of the car.

There was a barbecue smoker on the stoop, no abandoned cars on cinderblocks out back, and no dead bodies inside the front door. Not in the living room, kitchen, or bedroom. No dead rock critics in the ringed bathtub. There wasn't even a ceiling fan for one to hang from.

The fearless house-wrecker had been there, though. Albums had been pulled off shelves, curtains ripped down. Mattress and pillows had been slashed in the bedroom, pots and pans scattered in the kitchen. An old tweed Fender Pro Reverb had been knocked over, the tubes knocked out and broken on the floor.

KC's belongings stuck out in the wreckage—milk crates full of guitar cords and gadgets, a ragged canvas overnight bag full of cassettes, and in the living room, a half dozen wooden crates full of records, most of them dog-eared and belonging to other decades. Something caught my eye—an album propped up against the wall behind the couch. I retrieved it and it turned out to be the Howlin' Wolf album I'd loaned KC back when I'd come over to this house and seen the big redhead for the first time. I decided to take it with me.

It was a little disturbing and awkward, but I gathered up the things Lorraine wanted. A couple of pairs of jeans and some T-shirts from the bedroom where KC's guitar cases lay open like caskets, her makeup remover and toothbrush from the bathroom. Some vitamins from the kitchen, and a grocery bag to put it all in. I took it out to the car, then went back in and called my apartment. She answered. "I'm at your house," I said. "I got your things."

"Martin, I was so worried about you. Thank goodness you're all right." Her voice trembled with fear. "Somebody has been calling here all night then hanging up when I answer."

"I called earlier but you weren't there."

"I just quit answering the phone for a bit after all the hang ups. Don't be mad. Did you have any luck? Is everything OK?"

"No. Have you got your car?"

"Of course. That's how I got here."

"All right. Now listen . . ." I told her to wait fifteen minutes, then drive down South 1st to the laundry room by the Circle K store, and her things would be in one of the dryers. "Then go back to the apartment and keep the door locked and keep the answering machine on to monitor the phone calls. And keep the door locked."

"You already said that, Martin. What's going on?"

"Cole Slaughter and Neil Popkin are dead. It looks like murder, and the police are probably looking for me, because I'm stupid and have lousy timing. They're probably waiting for me to come home, but I don't have the time to talk with them right now."

"That one named Lasko has already been here. I didn't answer the door."

"Oh." I looked around the house, and didn't have a good reason to ask, but wanted to just the same. "What happened to the cedar outside your bedroom?"

"I chopped it down."

"Why?"

"I hated it. I always did. It rubbed against the house and I couldn't sleep."

It was just a tree.

"Martin, please be careful. I'm sorry I got you into all this."

"Don't worry about it. Just do as I say. I'll find a better place for you to stay tomorrow, and we can talk then." I thought I heard her sniffle as I hung up the phone.

I dropped Lorraine's things off at the laundry room and kept heading south.

16

4700 South Congress, Hill's Cafe. Next door is the Goodnight Motel. If you lived much further down the street, your neighbors would be dead automobiles and live armadillos and rattlesnakes. The junkyards stretch southward until Congress Avenue joins up with Interstate 35, which you could follow to San Antonio or all the way to Laredo where it dead ends. If I had any sense, I'd be on it, I told myself. I could sell my car and use the money to bet on the dog races across the border. Or I could park the car and hide out in the junkyards. But I didn't.

I pulled my lapels up around my face and curled up in a corner booth. A waitress who ground her teeth a lot brought coffee and a menu with pictures of the food by the descriptions. I pointed at a picture of an omelet and waved her on. I knew I was taking a chance being there but I was taking a chance driving around all night without any coffee in my bloodstream, too. I nabbed yesterday's newspaper from the cigarette machine to hold in front of my face so I could think.

The smell of hot grease and coffee, the Tex-Mex and frontier motif, the too-bright lights, the busboy with the bad complexion, and the waitress with varicose veins and itchy gums all seemed too normal for two o'clock in the morning after being wanted by the cops, beat up by a woman, and finding two fresh corpses all in one day.

The newspaper was full of facts. A gangland style shootout had occurred in another part of town between Vietnamese roommates. It seemed that three of them had been kicked out for not paying their share of the rent, so they came back, tied up the other six, shot and stabbed one to death, one nearly to death, while the rest escaped. There goes your deposit. A prominent ecology group had evidently taken a $10,000 bribe from land developers. More people are killed per year by barnyard hogs than by sharks. Cows hate spinach.

My omelet arrived on a big white plate with a sprig of parsley and a greasy brick of hash browns. I lowered my newspaper shield—I was safe. The only way a cop would get a full view of my face was by sitting in the same booth, across from me.

Lorraine was probably asleep in my bed. Probably naked. The cat would be curled up on top of her, and in a few hours would start licking her hair and hitting on her with his paws, letting her know he was ready for breakfast. She'd wake up, sleepy-eyed, reach out to pet him, and he'd gallop off to the kitchen and wait for her nervously by the food closet. After he ate, he'd probably roll over and play dead, lying on his back in front of the fan. She'd feel sorry for him, call him "poor kitty" and feed him some more.

She'd fall for that, just like she'd fallen for KC's overly complex tale about the drug deal, with Johnny ripping off Mexicans and neophyte dealers. KC had lied to her before. Maybe it was all a game to him, with her trust fund and all that manic energy expended to get him somewhere, somewhere he never got. So she was dumb. Or naive. Or maybe she didn't really know where the coke came from and just improvised some story about it to make it more exciting for me. Or maybe she was a liar. She'd lied to me about talking to Ward—that I knew.

Maybe she'd feed the cat out of respect for a fellow con artist.

"Come in to get a grease fix?" said a familiar voice whose owner had his hand on my shoulder. A cattle prod wouldn't have made me spill any more of my coffee.

Billy Ludwig slid into the booth across from me, a newspaper under his arm. "Kinda jumpy, aren't you?" he said. "Pulling these all-nighters will do it to you. How was it?"—pointing to the empty plate.

"It cured my appetite. Maybe permanently. I hoped I'd run into you here. Been recording?"

"Yep. Got a cig?" I loaned him one and he lit up off the one I had going in the ashtray. The waitress, showing off her familiarity with his needs, brought him coffee and extra artificial sweeteners without being asked. "Well, it's good you ate. I was wondering what this would do to you on an empty stomach."

He held up the newspaper. It was the early morning edition, and its headline read: "LOCAL WRITERS FOUND DEAD IN HOMES"

"Says they committed suicide, looks like," he said.

"Give me that." I snatched the paper away. The details were sketchy. From a lead sentence that also mentioned KC's death, the copy went on to describe the crime scenes, quoting a police spokesman about the paucity of details "at this time." It didn't even mention the word "murder." Nor did it mention my wallet. It didn't say that KC had been a helluva guitarist, that Cole Slaughter had been fat, or that Neil Popkin had giggled too much for a man his age. It was just three lives reduced to a few column inches between ads for auto parts and hair restorer.

"You're pale, Martin," he said. "You seem to be taking this pretty bad."

I told him what I knew. It took a while, and when I was finished, he said: "So for all we know, KC's murder could have been suicide, but somebody made it look like murder just to throw you off track while they got rid of the critics, which they made look like suicides to buy them more time and throw the cops off the track."

"That *might* be a possibility."

"Uh-huh," he said mechanically, staring at me. After a cautious sip of coffee, he said, "Martin, I think you're paranoid. You've got yourself all worked up into a nervous state over something you should just leave alone. KC got into trouble without you, why not leave it that way?"

"I can't. Know where I could find Johnny?"

He shook his head.

"Do you know who he got his drugs from?"

"Hell no. And you know I never pay money for that shit, unless somebody wants to go in on a gram during an all-night session. Even then, we send the assistant engineer out for it."

"Frankie?"

"Ha. Damn gigolo. You know it's an insult to Frankie to have to pay for anything. Girls are always slipping things to him. He even asked me one time what was more, a pound or a kilo. That's how smart he is. One thing on that boy's mind, and it's between every girl's legs. KC always kept to himself, anyway, except when Gabe was in the band."

"Gabriel made it sound like Lorraine made KC feel trapped. Maybe . . ."

"Martin—you trying to prove KC was pussy-whipped, or murdered?"

He wasn't going to be any more help than Gabriel. I told him he was getting on my nerves.

"I'm sorry. Look, just do whatever you think is right. But be careful, OK. I'd like you to come by the studio and play bass on that drum track I recorded out at the ranch. It's a killer, Martin. I could use you."

"I'd like to get paid for the last deal first."

"Oh," he said, scratching his chin. "I don't know. What'd you get worked out with Ward?"

"My deal was with KC. Do I have some money coming or not?"

He shrugged. "I'm sorry, Martin. I'm just a drummer. It's my understanding Lorraine went ahead and deposited the check and Ward made a settlement with her. He said I'd get a grand, but she has the money. I figure I'll wait till she's feeling better. I got other jobs."

"I see. Well, it might be this weekend before I make it to the studio. Might be never."

He nodded understandingly and got up, then reached inside his jacket and pulled out a shiny hip flask. "Brandy," he said. "Have some on me. Bring the flask back when you come by the studio. My mother gave it to me."

I nodded.

"Be careful, Martin." He smiled grimly. I watched him walk out the door after pausing at the cigarette machine to buy a pack of Kools.

Soon I got the urge to move. A lady with one too many chins stuffed my money in the cash register on my way out. She told me to have a nice day. It was almost 5:00 A.M.

17

I drove. I smoked. I found myself sitting on the top of Mt. Bonnell. Below me, the lights of the city sparkled like broken glass on a roadhouse parking lot. I suppose I hoped that as the night gave way to day it would give up some of its secrets.

Some things make sense. You drink brandy, and it burns your throat going down. Cigars taste good, but smell bad to people not smoking them. Of all the people down there, who could make sense out of the mess I was in?

I wasn't even sure if I was confused about the mess or about the way I felt about it. I'd run out looking for a kilo of cocaine that a falling guitar hero had evidently found to be a fatal stumbling block, then I'd blundered in after the killing of two rock critics who'd been trying to use it to scramble their own way to the top. And did I really care more about the fact that the guitar player's widow who sent me on such a cynical errand had lied to me about the setup, or the fact that she'd been talking to the clubowner, even though she'd denied it?

What did I care that they'd been talking? What did I care if she hopped into somebody's bed in the middle of the night? Every night.

I took another belt from the flask. I was glad the brandy wasn't V.S.O.P. What good was it if it didn't peel a layer of skin off the back of your throat?

She'd lied about the setup, all right. KC was too cool to have made up the story about ripping off the Mexicans.

I sat there motionless until the sun started peeking its head above the hills, pulling back the covers on East Austin. It was a helluva view at seven in the morning.

My city. What did it have to do with me? I didn't even have a home to go to because an apartment with cops waiting for you there is not a home. I did have bar tabs at a couple of clubs, a few friends, my bass, hamburgers at Dirty's, tacos at Tamale House, blues at Antone's. A big striped cat. A girlfriend I hadn't been paying enough attention to. Not much to live for, but better than hanging around on a windy mountaintop feeling sorry for myself.

Johnny had to be down there somewhere. For as many detractors as he had, as many people as he owed money and favors to, he belonged as much as I did. There was nowhere else to go. The music, the food, the places we got our clothes at a discount, the damn smell of the place, was in our blood. We were hooked. I'd find him.

18

Crouching in a cluster of bamboo, I surveyed the parking lot in back of my building. No cops. They would be on the other side, watching the entrances—one in front and one on the other side, by the pool.

My balcony was about twenty feet off the ground.

An old knotted live oak sidled up next to it. In his younger days, the cat used to jump from the balcony to the tree's main fork, then scamper down its trunk to the ground. I was no cat, and there was no guarantee that there weren't cops watching from inside the apartment building across the way, but I needed my gun and a change of clothes. I'd rather go to jail than look like a bum.

The first few feet were the hardest, as there were no branches or knots to hang on for eight to ten feet up. The bark was rough, and some kind of vine had taken over the west side of the trunk. Finally I made it to the main fork and was able to grab the balcony railing and swing over. The door was unlocked. The cat was hungry and alone.

I fed him and read the note Lorraine had left me. It said:

Dear Martin: I hope your ok. The phone calls never stopped and it worrys me. It's too hot to sleep. I went out for a while don't worry I'll be careful. Love, Lorraine.

I didn't know what bothered me more—her disappearance or her spelling. I went to the closet, picked out another jacket, black cotton shirt, baggy black pants, and the two-tone Stacy Adams wingtips. Fresh underwear, a couple of cassettes, and a pair of socks were tossed in a grocery bag. I tied a long extension cord to the handle of my bass guitar case and lowered it off the side of the balcony, letting the cord fall after it.

At the bottom of my desk, under the Chilton's Karmann Ghia manual, where my 9mm Beretta should have been, was only a dead cockroach.

By nine o'clock, I was in my fresh clothes and sitting in my car just downwind of the Alpha house. Well-scrubbed but bleary-eyed, they came out carrying books. Sometimes they took off down the street on foot and some went to their cars in the gravel parking lot on my side of the house. There was a freshly topped-off hedge that gave me some cover. I lit another cigarette and waited for signs of Johnny, the sound of the Ranchero driving up, or a mesage from Elvis.

A girl with a pink mohawk, fringed leather skirt, and man's undershirt flew up on the back of a Lambretta. She propped the scooter up next to a fire hydrant, trotted up the sidewalk and into the house. Moments later I saw her appear out back where one of the fresh-faced ones relaxed on a deck chair under a Cinzano umbrella. His back was turned towards me, but it looked like there was a briefcase open in front of him. They spoke for a moment and transacted some business. He handed her an envelope, she handed him some money, and that was that.

The sound of the scooter whizzing away was almost drowned out by a suddenly loud radio coming from the house. A DJ was making an announcement: advance tickets for Springsteen's recently expanded stand at the Frank Erwin Center were *all sold out.* For some reason, the announcement elicited a loud whoop from the students on the patio.

Someone wearing a rugby shirt and Bermuda shorts joined the businessman in the back yard. He was drinking a Budweiser, and he raised the can in a toast. Another car pulled up. It was the black Ranchero. Bud Salvador was back, walking up the sidewalk carrying an Igloo cooler, same as yesterday, except today I knew his name.

Soon he was out on the patio with the two younger men. He wasted no time accepting a Budweiser from the rugby shirt and wasted no time draining it. A minute later I was tailing him down 24th Street.

Bud Salvador was in a hurry. I had to punch the Ghia hard several times to keep up, but I managed. As we headed south on the Mopac expressway, he swerved sporadically, driving with one hairy, tattooed arm hung out the window.

It was getting hotter by the minute. I hoped the Howlin' Wolf album wouldn't melt.

As far as I could tell, Bud Salvador never used turn signals. Just past Barton Creek Mall, we took Loop 360 south for less than a minute, then pulled onto a narrow two-lane, followed that for a few minutes and took a right on Noon Street.

Noon Street turned out to be a one lane bumpy ride through the middle of acres of gently rolling grassland, dry and undisturbed. A map would show that Barton Creek was nearby, and that the area was called Barton Bend. The land was just sitting there, undeveloped. Going to waste, some would think.

I kept my eyes on the cloud of dust made by the pickup on Noon Street. Suddenly it went off the road, bumping across the grassy field to the left. I stopped where he pulled off the road and squinted out over the grassland and saw his destination: A black Cadillac limousine about fifty yards away.

Things happened fast. Salvador got out of the car, spit, and walked over to the limo. The back door was held open by a boyish figure in a chauffeur's uniform. A Hispanic man in a white suit, shades, and hat got out. The hat was white, with a low crown and wide, flat brim. Not a local variety. Salvador held out his hand, but the hat didn't shake it. They didn't appear to care if they were being observed or not, though the tall grass gave me a bit of anonymity. I heard a plane overhead. They must have, too, because all three looked skyward. A small twin engine plane made a pass over the area. They waved, shielding their eyes from the sun. The plane circled around, came back. The second time it was overhead, it tipped its wings and flew on.

The meeting was over. The hat got back in the limo and Salvador got back in the Ranchero. I turned the Ghia around. I wanted to be in the lead this time. As I looked in the mirror after making the hundred and eighty degrees, I could read the sign jabbed into the dirt where the cars had left the road. Evidently Jefferson Stubbs was the realtor selling the land, and evidently the address was 1969 Noon Street. It gave a phone number in case I was interested. Maybe I was. I wondered if Jefferson Stubbs could tell me why someone named James had left a message on Neil Popkin's answering machine saying that they wanted 1969.

19

Anxious to add to the tangled coil of clues, lies, and odd scenarios, I headed for the collection agency, suddenly very curious about Neil's bounced $10,000 check and a few other things I might be able to find out from my office there. The agency was just a couple of miles away, down Bee Cave Road, and though excited, I was careful, using my turn signals, not running any lights, not littering. I found a spot under a big cedar tree in the back parking lot of the building, the one you couldn't see from the street, and I covered my bass and the album with my jacket, put the top up and locked the doors. So careful, so cautious.

I was even proud of myself when I didn't bump into the cop who greeted me when I reached the top of the back stairs, which he led me straight back down and then around to the front of the building, where a blue and white was waiting. He held the door open for me and said to watch my head.

But I felt like looking at my feet.

Lasko, looking tired and troubled, was glad to see me. Billy and Frankie did not appear to be, though I only saw them for a moment. They were in an outer office, which I was escorted through on my way to Lasko's office. The door was shut and we were alone.

"Serves me right to be tired," he rasped, "waiting all god-damn night for you to get home. I ain't gotten close to a bed in three days."

"You've been wanting to talk to me."

"Goddamn mind-reader you are." Scratching his beard, he picked up a styrofoam cup, sniffed it, and tossed it in the trash. "You've been scarce. Call me yesterday afternoon and hang up on me. Wanting to know about Bud Salvador. Best stay away for him, Martin. He's not nice. But I've been wanting to talk to you about KC. Wednesday morning when I ran out there, you said you hadn't suspected KC of being extra depressed or anything."

"So what?"

"Didn't want to talk about it. Said you was tired."

"So what?"

"So why wasn't there a guitar in his room?"

"What?"

"So why wasn't there a guitar in the guy's bedroom? This guy was the consummate R & B guitarist. Don't tell me he wouldn't normally sit on the bed and pick. That's normal. If a guy is feeling normal."

"I've got important things to do, detective. My bass is in the back of my car. One of my favorite records, too. They could get stolen or warped while you're holding me up here asking me about a guitar player's personal habits. I'm not in the mood to talk about normal."

"Whoa, Martin. I'm not holding you, I just wanted to talk. This ain't TV, ya know, where the cops are always the dumb guys. Maybe I know what I'm doing."

"If you did you'd stop trying to solve a suicide," I said. "KC was murdered."

"As in killed by another party?"

"Or parties unknown. And the critics. Even though you guys for some reason don't think so."

"You *must* be a mind reader, Martin. But whose mind have you been reading? I'd like to talk to him."

"It's a long story."

"I guess we need to do lots of talking."

"Some other time, Lasko, " I said, getting up. "And since all you're interested in is suicides, you might as well give me back my wallet."

"What wallet?"

I sat down.

"Talk to me," he said.

And I talked. About the extra .38 casing, the gunshot Stones book and pillow . . . Everything except the cocaine.

"Where are these items now, Martin?"

That put the brakes on. I replayed the sight of my living room when I'd last seen it this morning. Her note said she'd just stepped out. But why would she take the gunshot book and pillow?

"I don't know."

It didn't go over. He sat there and stared, then blinked, hard, squeezing his eyes into fleshy cracks of tanned skin.

"One of us needs to get some rest, Martin."

"Sleep is the last thing on my mind right now."

"But look here, Martin. You say KC was murdered and your proof is a missing pillow and book. You say the critics were murdered and your proof is that you were there but you split when we got on the scene."

"Just what prompted your men to go there?"

"Anonymous call. Said there was a guy dressed all in black, driving a yellow Karmann Ghia, in the process of B & E. Two doors down someone reported a hit and run fender-bending by a silver Ford van. Know anything about that?"

Johnny. I shook my head. "I drove right by one of your cars."

He looked embarrassed. "There was a little mix up. One of those officers had a kid playing in that softball game. And I didn't know till later what kinda fucking car you drive. But there was no sign of forcible entry. In fact, all the signs pointed to the mess on the scenes having occurred after the deaths."

"Oh, I guess that cleared things right up."

"Martin, do you know how many burglaries are committed on that side of town per hour? We got scumbags over there who read the obituaries so they can go clean out the bereaved's house during the services. Maybe this time they got a jump on the papers. Do you know . . . ."

He interrupted himself, thinking out loud. "Aw, just hold on. What am I doing here? I never had any idea what a smartass you are. Look here, I have, believe it or not, an investigation going on. And I can't sit here and explain the facts of life to you. I suggest you leave the police work to the guys who get paid for it, and if you have any helpful information to lay on us you give me a call. In the meantime, don't take any out of town gigs, and go home and get some sleep. I gotta tell you though, if I had me a crystal ball, it'd most likely show you getting charged with accessory after the fact in the real near future. But before we get around to any of that nastiness I wanted to run these items by you. You know it still bugs me that KC never even deposited or cashed that fourteen thousand dollar check for the gig. His girlfriend did Wednesday morning, but wouldn't you think KC would've stuck that sucker in the bank already if he was really gonna do the gig?"

"Look," I said, realizing that maybe I had underestimated the detective. "Why don't I help you out, and you help me out?"

"Go on."

"Give me a break. I haven't killed anybody. You *know* that. And if you've got an intuition about this case . . ."

"I've got a lieutenant who can't spell that word, Martin."

"Just a little time, Lasko. That's all I'm asking. I know you need to interview Johnny, in any case. When I find him I'll make him come down. He might know something. I'm a lot more likely to find him than you are."

"Don't be an asshole."

"I'm sorry. But I'm close to this. I'm . . ."

"Yeah." He opened his desk drawer and removed a short, fat, maduro cigar, bit into the cellophane, unwrapped it, sniffed it, and stuck it between his teeth, all without looking at anything but me. I knew what he saw, too. I was a musician, he was a cop.

"No one gives a shit around here," he said, the cigar shifting from one side of his mouth to the other, "if you're a cool guy or just some dickhead off the street. They probably think you're somebody trying to sell crack to their kids in school. They don't know from Adam all those old black guys from Chicago and New Orleans that you know, that you've played with. And don't give a shit."

He got up and walked over to the window, but barely looked out. From where I sat, all you could see was a blue sky and construction cranes. "They're tearing everything down out there," he said.

He wrote his beeper number on a card and gave it to me. "They'll give you a ride back." He looked around the small closed room, but he was thinking about things just on the other side of its walls. He reached back and clamped his big hand on the back of his neck, squeezing it, saying, "I don't have to tell you . . ."

I nodded. We shook hands.

20

"Well if it ain't Dick Tracy, skiptracer, back from the dead. Before noon, too."

I looked up, but just barely. This time I'd made it all the way into the collection agency office, with a warm but hopefully not warped Howlin' Wolf album in hand. The drawl had come from Gary something-or-other, the only other employee who was in at the moment. One of the other male collection agents was out on a repo, he told me, and the females—"ran down to the print shop, but I suspect they mighta run over to the mall. They been squealing about some sale over there all morning." Gary lived in a mobile home in deep South Austin, drove a pickup truck—his wife usually had the station wagon—with a rifle rack in the window and a "Jesus is the Way" bumper sticker on the back.

"This stack of files for me?"

He nodded.

"I'll be in next week to sort them out."

"I'm still working on the last batch of skips you smoked out. Glad you're not in here full-time or I'd never get a break. Have a flat tire?"

He'd noticed the tire iron on the desk.

"Paper weight," I said.

After he pointed out the stack of pink phone message slips on my desk, he left me alone in my small corner cubicle with its work table big enough to command a microfiche viewer, computer terminal, and telephone. A metal bookcase in the corner held dozens of area phone books and assorted directory volumes, including two reverse phone directories. The computer was hooked into the downtown retail merchants' credit bureau. For the microfiche viewer, I had files from the phone company and city utilities, with similarly cross-referenced information, and they were updated every month. These were the tools of my part-time trade.

One of the biggest tools the agency had was in another room down the hall. It was a computer programmed to spew out late notices. The color-coded generic bills went out on a regular schedule, using language that got harsher with each mailing. The first one might say: "You probably just forgot, but your account with _____ is now two months overdue." They would get nastier and nastier, eventually threatening the debtor with a lawsuit.

Collection agencies operate on percentages. Most of the late notices go unheeded and many never find their way to the right address. But a good enough percentage of them find their way to the type of person who would be motivated to pay his bill when threatened with a tainted credit record. Others would be motivated to pay when Gary got them on the phone, and found they'd rather part with money than have to listen to his spiel about how they could work something out.

Some people moved and thought that would be enough to get away from their creditors. But they didn't realize that before forwarding the agency's late notices, the post office photocopied the yellow change-of-address stickers and sent them back to us. That was what the "address correction requested" notice in the left corner of the envelopes was for. The collection agency paid a small fee for each one. And even if the debtor had moved again since their mail was forwarded, it still put us one step closer to being able to breathe down their necks. Those stickers found more people than a hundred skiptracers working overtime.

They gave me the hard cases, the ones that fell through the cracks. It was like I was peeping in people's windows. But I didn't lose any sleep over the right or wrong of it. After all, there was no way the collectors could force anyone to pay up.

If they were too poor, or just determined not to, they just didn't.

My biggest tool wasn't the computer, the directories full of names, or the mail. It was the telephone. It put those windows I needed to peek in at my fingertips as I checked out credit references, banks, former employers, neighbors, and those names you find in the blanks of forms that say "person to notify in case of emergency." Skiptracers probably use those numbers more often than anybody else. Now I picked up my number one tool and called my connection at Neil Popkin's bank. Like a lot of people I talked to from that cubicle, I only knew her by her first name and she knew nothing of my bass playing. I was just a guy she talked to at least once a week and we had a good thing going. She said she'd be able to visit customer service and look up the $10,000 check when she took a break, and she'd call me back. While I was still on the phone I typed out *Craft, John* on the terminal.

I didn't expect much, and that was a good thing. Craft, John, a.k.a. Johnny, had made a career out of slipping through the cracks. Sure, his credit file looked ordinary enough. Name, social security number, an address and several former addresses, some credit accounts with unpaid balances. Under occupation it said: "Roadie." The word looked funny in the squiggly computer font. But the file was 99% useless. There was nothing under spouse, a not surprising fact since I knew that Candyse Miller probably had credit of her own and didn't want anything to do with Johnny's paper history. She'd stayed Candyse Miller when things were going good with the two of them, and when they turned bad, well, at least she was still Candyse Miller.

The addresses were the really useless part. Though I recognized a couple of the oldest ones as places he used to live a long time ago, the one listed as current gave the best chuckle: 1315 South Congress, the address of the Continental Club. We'd worked together in the joint hundreds of times and spent way too many after-hours there, but as far as I knew, no one—not even Johnny—ever slept there past closing time.

I had better luck with Bud Salvador. First off, I found out his first name was Henry and his real last name was Maxell.

The file was under Henry "Bud" Salvador, a.k.a. Henry Salvador, a.k.a. Henry Maxell, a.k.a. Bud Maxell. Occupation: "Unemployed." His credit was not good. There were fifteen "charged to P & L (profit and loss)" accounts and one small balance account with Western Auto.

I called Western Auto, who had a current address as of two weeks ago. I looked up the address in the city directory. It said that Bud Maxell lived there. No phone number was listed. Directory assistance had no numbers listed under any of the names. The city utilities directories were of no help, either, since the apartment complex was all bills paid. I went out to the break room, got some bad coffee, and came back to my desk in time to answer my phone. It was my bank connection. Neil Popkin's check had been made out to Jefferson Stubbs. I asked if she knew who, or what, Jefferson Stubbs was.

"Oh, you know, Martin. He was just another bankrupt rancher a couple of years back. He's been selling off the family's land piece by piece. He had some over near Barton Bend and . . ."

"Yeah, I know. Thanks a lot." I had my finger on a listing in the white pages. "Does he have an office on Bee Cave?" She said yes.

I grabbed the tire iron. It was only a couple of blocks away.

"Howdy." A rusty cowbell on the door had already announced my entrance into the storefront office in the strip center next door to the Tom Thumb Supermarket. The tire iron was stuck in the back of my pants, hidden by my jacket. I hoped.

A woman, somewhere past middle age, with blue tinted contacts and a frosted perm, was smiling at me. She was wearing a smart turquoise suit and a lot of gold jewelry. She had the biggest desk in the office.

"I'm Martin Fender," I said. "I was supposed to meet a couple of guys here but I'm late." The air conditioner kicked in noisily, and the woman looked over her shoulder and frowned. Another woman, a little younger, entered the room carrying a big coffee mug with a Dallas Cowboys insignia on it.

"Turn that thing down, *Thel*ma," the woman in turquoise

said. "It's *freezin'* in here." Then she turned back to me and smiled again. "Now who was it you were supposed to be meeting here, young man?"

"Well, that's the funny part," I said. "You see, I work just down the street at the collection agency, and a couple of fellows came in and were going to hire me to drive down to the San Antonio court house to do some title searches. They drive a black limo and the main guy had one of those names that just goes in one ear and comes out the other." I scratched my head in my best "aw shucks" manner and added, "They said something about meeting here and then running out to 1969 Noon Street."

"Oh," she cackled. "That'd be Mr. Gonzales, from Mexico City. But you must have gotten your wires crossed, hon. Today's the only day this week they *haven't* come by. They just called, though." That smile again. Her teeth were too big for her thin lips.

"They ask if I was here?"

"Nope. Just called to verify the option. And they won't be sending you to San Antone for that one. That title would be right here in Travis County."

"The option?"

"The option taken out on the land. We haven't actually sold the property just yet, and no telling who'll end up with it by this afternoon, or tomorrow. People are flipping land like crazy around here. All we have to do is sit here and answer the phone."

"What do you mean, 'flipping'?"

She gave me a curious look.

"I'm new to all this, ma'am. I'm just a skiptracer who runs errands for people once in awhile to catch up on the rent. I don't really know what you mean by option either."

"Well, let me tell you, hon. If you see some land that you think might bring a pretty fair price but you don't exactly want to buy it or can't, you can option it for a fee. It can be a small deposit, even. Then you find a buyer, or he finds you, and you get a percentage on the sale price of the land. Or maybe someone else just wants to buy your option. Then that fella finds someone to buy the option from him, for a higher price, *or* the land. And so forth. It can go on and on. That's what folks call flipping."

"So I could come to you and say I wanted to option some piece of property you own, and we'd work out a deal."

"Uh huh. We have a standard contract, but people these days are scribbling out deals on napkins in restaurants and lord knows what all. Like I said . . ."

"Would you take a check on a deal like that?"

"Well, yes, but . . ."

"A hot check?"

"A hot check? Well it has been done. Some people will hold a check, especially if it's from someone they know. We don't do business that way, though." The smile was gone. Thelma was at her desk, eyeing a sandwich wrapped in cellophane, sipping from her mug, but the check business woke her up.

"Marge—" Thelma was staring at me. I'd been made. Her husband must have trotted her out to Antone's one weekend. "Hot checks, you say? Did you know those writers?"

"I did."

"They were such nice guys, too," said Thelma, unwrapping the sandwich.

"Mr. Stubbs still gave them a fair chance," piped in Marge. "Gave them till Monday to make good on that check. They probably could have sold their option by then. Wasn't no reason to kill yourself. No, sir. Mr. Stubbs was more than fair. Said they could put down the $10,000 deposit on the option and they'd pay him $100,000 once the land was sold, but they'd get a percentage of the sale price, or they could sell their option to someone else. Lotsa ways they could have made money. When they come in here last week I figured they didn't exactly have the money in the bank, but it sure wasn't no reason to kill yourself. Coulda been other reasons, though. . . ."

I started nodding my head, casually looking around the office. Trying to seem a part of it all, wondering if I could get the rest of the picture in just one more bite.

I said: "So after the writers turned up dead you turned around and let Gonzales buy the option."

"I didn't say that." The big teeth were coming back. "*Thel*ma, who were those old boys?"

"The Futura Corporation." She was still unwrapping the cellophane from a sandwich, taking her time, almost as if she was defusing a bomb.

Though I didn't ask, my puzzled expression did the work for me. Marge said: "I don't think I ever heard of them. They picked up the option yesterday morning, sold it to Gonzales today. You want to talk to him, he's over at the Driskill Hotel. Course he doesn't really speak English."

"Or you could ask Bud," said Thelma.

"Bud Salvador?" The tire iron was cold where it touched my back.

Bud Salvador, said their nods.

". . . is the Futura Corporation?"

They both laughed quietly. "I seriously doubt *that,*" said Thelma. "He just brought the ten thousand cash by for the deposit, what, Marge, about eight this morning?"

Marge said yes, not long after they'd opened up.

"Ol' Bud does a lot of running. No telling about him."

Marge laughed. "Yep, no telling about ol' Bud."

They evidently thought this character was pretty amusing. I thanked them and said to have a nice day. I tried not to ring the cowbell on my way out.

I was not going to get sidetracked, I told myself back at the agency. It was a little after noon and I'd learned a lot. The critics had had two deals go bad on them in one week. Then they got dead. While it had seemed out of character for them to suddenly go into the drug business, doing it as a way to join the real estate sweepstakes might make sense. A little, anyway.

The way I saw it was this: People don't go around writing hot checks unless they expect things to get better soon. When it's a ten thousand dollar hot check, they must expect things to get a whole lot better. So they expected to turn the kilo for a quick profit, use it to cover their option deposit, and make who knows how much from that. Still, there was the small question of how two writers, living off twenty, thirty cents, even a dollar a word, could come up with the cash to get 2.2 pounds of cocaine delivered to them.

Or how the deal had gotten them killed. And KC before that.

I was not going to get sidetracked on some damn paper trail trying to figure out who and where the Futura Corporation was. But I had to notice, as I thumbed through the phone book looking for numbers that might lead somewhere, that the Futura Corporation had no listing. I'd already tried out my Spanish on Mr. Gonzales, who was back at his suite in the Driskill, and I'd been fluent enough to tell that he wasn't too interested in my problems. I threw a couple of names at him—Cole Slaughter, Neil Popkin. He hung up on me. But that didn't mean anything, other than he didn't have the time or inclination to put up with my broken Spanish.

I imagined myself calling Bud Salvador. He'd answer the phone in a gruff voice and I'd ask him if I'd reached the office of the Futura Corporation. He'd say hell no, of course. You got the wrong number, he'd growl. But I'd be persistent. Just as he started to hang up on me, I'd say I supposed that meant he'd never heard of them, just like he'd never heard of Cole Slaughter and Neil Popkin. No, it wouldn't work that way. I'd call, and he'd have an answering machine. I could leave a phony name, but that wouldn't play, either.

No. I was beginning to have way too much respect for Bud Salvador to try something as junior league as trying to put him on the spot that way. I was even starting to like the guy, mostly because he was essential to the only scenario that made sense. The critics had picked up the option on 1969 Noon Street with a hot check. They were murdered before they were able to make good on it, either by coming up with the cash or by selling the option. Thursday morning Bud Salvador obtains the option and Friday morning sells it, probably for a tidy little profit. His motivation for killing the critics was pretty easy to comprehend.

Then my mood started to cloud. I started feeling irritated at the smugness of it all. It was all too messy, too casual, and convenient somehow. I was ambivalent about it. If the events of the last twenty-four hours hadn't been so hectic and confusing, I could have cared more about the Bud Salvador connection. I still didn't have quite enough to take to the cops, and I still had Lorraine to figure out.

I phoned my apartment. "You've got to stay put," I told her.

"I'm careful, Martin. Has something else . . . ?"

"Yes, it has. Believe me . . . just believe me, OK, Lorraine? What did you do with the pillow and the Stones book?"

"Don't get excited. I threw them away because they were bumming me out and I was afraid you'd take them to the police. And from what that cop Lasko said, it sounds like you were ready to."

"He picked you up?"

"No. He was waiting for me at noon when I got back here. Don't worry, I fixed it. I don't think he believes you. I think maybe he thinks you're a little bit crazy. I don't think the cops will be getting in the way."

"I'm not sure that's the right tack to take on this, Lorraine. We could be in serious danger. In fact—"

"Look Martin, I am scared. But somebody killed KC and I still want that coke. The pillow and book weren't doing us any good."

"They were about the only things we had going for us that might put the cops on our side," I said. "It's more important to find out who's doing all the killing than it is to get the coke."

She groaned. "The cops are no good. They find out about the coke and all it'll do is ruin what's left of KC's reputation. You go to the cops again and it'll ruin everything. I guess KC was wrong about you being such a tough guy. I don't know what to do now."

"You're doing all right," I said. The panic in her voice was real. I hoped the ambivalence in mine wasn't broadcasting as clearly. I had some questions for her and I didn't want her to get spooked till I had her in a corner she couldn't back out of. This phone business was getting us nowhere. "Just sit tight for once. You've got to quit leaving the apartment. I'm going to find us a motel. When it's all set, I'll send a friend of mine over. His name is Ray and he drives a cab. If someone is following you he can lose them, and you'll be safe. Don't worry. And bring my gun."

"What gun?" she said.

Damn. Things were worse than I thought.

I was ready to get out of there. My extension was ringing but I was ignoring it. Then it stopped. Gary came on the intercom and said it was for me. I picked it up and Ladonna's smoky low voice greeted me.

"I took the afternoon off," she said.

"I'm glad," I said. "And I'm glad you called. It's good to hear your voice."

"Why?"

"It's nice. Makes me want to invite myself over."

"You don't have to do that," she said.

"Why not?"

"Because I'm inviting you myself. I'd like to see you. And there's someone here who wants to talk to you, too."

"Michael?"

"No, Michael's at Mom and Dad's. Someone else. Someone you've been wanting to talk to."

I was probably out of there before she heard the dial tone.

21

Johnny was drinking a cuba libre, sitting in front of the TV. "Martin!" he boomed. "How ya been?" His hair was wet and slicked back. He wore a burgundy silk shirt and a vintage white suit, the jacket of which was draped on the back of the chair. Big feet wearing Stacy Adams two-tones and pink thick-and-thins swung off the ottoman as he stood up to greet me.

I put down my bass so Ladonna could kiss me and look me over while I did the same to her. She frowned when she felt the tire iron and looked puzzled when she saw the Howlin' Wolf album. I put them both on the stereo cabinet.

"The fugitive," I said.

Johnny gave me a lop-sided grin. "Martin—"

"Shut up, turn off the TV, and tell me everything," I said, shaking his hand.

He let go of my hand and plopped back into the big chair like it was an act of rebellion, then punched the remote control hard enough to break it.

Ladonna let go of me. "You need anything, Martin?"

"I'll take some iced coffee if you've got any coffee left." I pulled an Al Green record out of a stack and slapped it on the turntable. "Get started," I said.

Johnny was still clearing his throat when Ladonna brought me a tall glass of iced coffee, squeezed my hand, and sat down on the floor on the other side of the boomerang table. She wasn't going to miss a word.

"All right, all right." He lit up one of my Camels, took a big

drag, and began. "Ward is such a dickhead, Martin. I was over
at the club last weekend trying to straighten out the crew in-
stalling all the video monitors and sound system because they
were wiring it all wrong. But it ain't making me any money—
Ward says he can't pay me for that 'cause I'm not in the elec-
tricians union and there ain't an electrician consultants union.
And I wouldn't get paid for the work I was doing for you guys
until the gig. Well, Ward ate a couple of disco biscuits and
started running his mouth. Right during the thick of it the critics
come to him asking could they borrow ten grand. Instead of
telling them to fuck off like you'd expect, he says no problem.
He says they could work out a little deal for Monday night.
Guess what it was?"

"Just tell me."

"The dickhead wouldn't actually loan them the cash, he'd
arrange for a kilo of cocaine to be fronted them. I'd be the
go-between—pick it up and deliver it to the critics. But they
have to do him a favor first to get the credit—steal the Texterminators bug. Then I'm supposed to swap the coke for
the bug."

"Oh, for crying out loud."

"Well how do you think I felt about it?" he moaned. "That's
what I mean, the guy is, what's the word, egregious? As a kilo,
this stuff is worth around $60,000 easy, which is all Ward wanted
to collect on it. The profit could go anywhere from a couple
grand to twenty, thirty grand, depending on how you break it
up. If you sell it in eight-balls, ounces, or grams, you're talking
a lot of money. Sometimes police call the street value of a kilo
a million bucks—and it is, if you sell it by the gram. Just depends
on how much of a hurry you're in to get rid of it."

"They were in a hurry."

"I guess they were, the way they acted. Because I thought
the whole thing was just a joke, but it wasn't. Ward wanted
the bug, they needed ten grand. And they said OK, we'll do
it. I needed the money, of course, so I said OK. They needed
me 'cause Bud Salvador—you know him?"

"I know who he is."

"OK. Well, Bud won't have nothing to do with guys he don't know, and he don't know Neil and Cole. And Ward wouldn't *even* ask him to pick up no one-ton termite. But Neil fucked me up, man. I picked the shit up early Monday afternoon in his old Buick 'cause they were gonna use the rental van to steal the bug. The throw-out bearing on the Buick's clutch is going zing every time you shift gears. That makes me uncomfortable, 'cause they can't steal the bug till late at night and I'm gonna be driving to make the swap at 4:00 A.M. or something and the clutch goes out and I'm broke down with a felony there under the seat and a cop stops to see what's wrong and there you go."

"So why in hell did you risk driving all the way out to the ranch with a bad clutch and a kilo of coke?"

"What can I tell you, Martin? I fucked up, OK? I tried, man. I met Neil and Cole at Club Slither Monday night to trade Neil's car for Cole's, but when we got outside, that damn Volkswagen wouldn't start. I was starting to realize I didn't wanna make that damn swap at all. I almost let those guys have the coke right then before they got the bug. It would've pissed off Ward, but goddammit I wish I would have now. So instead, I drove out to the ranch. I had five or six hours at least to kill, and that'd be plenty of time to get more nervous." He shook his head and gave me a helplessly sincere look. "Hell, I was hoping to hear you guys rehearse. And I owed KC a favor . . ."

"How much?"

"About twelve hundred, all right? So I was gonna make it up to him, let him skim some off the top if he'd just do the swap himself."

"He didn't even have a car."

"Lorraine's car, then. Whatever. Anyway, he was a absolute pain in the ass about the money I owe him but finally he said he'd keep the shit and deliver it the next day. That would have been Tuesday, right? A little late but I figured what the fuck, these guys loan me a decent car and they'll get good service."

"All right. Go on."

"OK. So Tuesday afternoon I'm holed up over at the Imperial 500 Motel and I get a beep and it's the critics. They're mighty steamed. They were sitting on the bug and KC hadn't come by. I told them to cool it and I tried the ranch all that day. I guess you guys couldn't hear the phone ring because you were practicing and a couple of times Lorraine answered but wouldn't go get KC. I don't think she likes me. Finally that night, Ward's on my ass, too, so I start to drive out there and what do you know, that clutch goes out when I get out to the end of Ben White Boulevard, right where it starts getting spooky. I get the Buick towed over to an AAMCO and had to hoof it back to the motel. It was three-thirty in the morning by the time I get back to the room and turn on the radio. That's when I heard the news about KC."

"Then what?"

"Well, maybe that's where I fucked up again. Bear in mind, I'd been up for a couple of days, first with Ward and then I was just sweating this stupid deal."

"And snorting what you took off the top of the kilo for your trouble."

He just shrugged and curled a lip at me. "Like I said, maybe I panicked, but I knew there wasn't any sense going out to the ranch at that point 'cause Neil told me they'd seen KC in town. That way I *knew* he did something with the shit, and what he did wasn't what he was supposed to do with it. I hopped a cab over to Cole's and took the van with the bug in it, stashed it over at Candyse's mother's house. I don't know what I was thinking, maybe that it'd give me some leverage or something . . ."

"Or you could tell Ward you went through with the deal and the critics were lying about never getting the stuff."

"Would I be hiding out here right now if I did that?"

"I guess not."

"I called Lorraine and she said she didn't know anything

about it, hadn't seen any briefcase full of coke. Called you and you don't answer and your machine's not on. Called Donna here and she said I was really fucking up. Made me feel bad about the critics. So I go over to Cole's last night to try to explain what had happened. He's dead, he's in the fucking bathtub. I go over to Neil's, he's hanging from the ceiling fan and you're in the damn kitchen, laying on the floor with a slice of pizza. I thought you were both dead. I went and stashed the van and came over here and told Donna I was in a world of shit, not to let *anybody* know I was here. I was just working up the nerve to tell her about you when there was a knock at the door."

"Then that sound you made, the belch, was your expression of relief that the world wasn't really Martin Fender-less?"

His eyes glazed a bit as he looked at me. "Martin. I'm sorry, man. I really am. I fucked up. I thought you were dead. I've seen dead people before, but . . ."

"Guess you were more worried about getting that bug stashed away than you were about seeing if I was still breathing."

"You wanna go round and round or you wanna try to figure this out?"

"All right. You didn't happen to see my wallet when you were there, did you?"

"What? No, why?"

"Somebody's got it. I guess whoever knocked me out, because the cops say they don't have it."

"Damn. That's a helluva note."

"You like that, here's a whole symphony."

I spilled it. Most of everything I knew. It wasn't much, just why I knew KC was murdered and why the critics needed the money. About Bud Salvador and the Futura Corporation.

Ladonna knew all about flipping land. "People are going crazy all over this town," she said. "I see it every day at work. There's a mad scramble going on for any patch of ground out there, like it's the Gold Rush or something. So it wouldn't be an unusual thing for someone to snap up an option the day after the option-holders are killed. It isn't a good reason to accuse them of murder."

"But put the cocaine in there, and you have a whole new game," said Johnny.

"Well, I just find it hard to believe that somebody would kill all these people over some bag of drugs worth $60,000 when people are dealing tons of it every day," she said.

"Baby, I got people that want to see my guts on the floor for the fifty bucks I owe them," said Johnny.

The record had ended and it was quiet in the room, except for the soft hum of the air conditioner. "I've got some cold cuts in the fridge," Ladonna said. "Anyone feel like eating?"

"I have to make a phone call first," I said. "I'm going to get someone to pick up Lorraine, then come over and get me. We'll stay at a motel till we can straighten this thing out."

Ladonna wrinkled her nose like she'd just encountered a bad smell.

"I know how you feel about her, Ladonna, but I don't know if it's safe to stay here. I don't think anyone followed me, but . . ."

"Most people who know you don't even know who I am, Martin," she said, a little too matter-of-factly. "You can all stay here. If you want."

I called and left a message for the cab driver, then settled down with the others in the making of sandwiches and small talk. Making sandwiches was easy.

Ladonna was quartering an apple with a sharp knife. I watched her, taking in her porcelain complexion, the platinum hair swept up with a scarf, loose strands falling down over her delicately arched eyebrows. I watched her deftly use the knife with her small hands and it was a wholesome thing, not at all like the redhead digging her knife into the picnic table back at the ranch while flies buzzed over greasy bones that had had cigarettes put out on them. They were so different—Ladonna with her smart, angular features made Lorraine seem like a big, voluptuous mess.

Johnny was piling meat and cheese on a couple of slices of rye, a lit cigarette hanging off his lip.

"Why don't you put that cigarette out, Johnny?" Ladonna asked. She wrinkled her nose and patted his arm after he mashed it out.

"I don't like this guy Bud," I said. "What do you know about his little candy store operation at the Alpha house?"

"What operation? I saw him in the neighborhood once or twice this week, but I didn't stop to say howdy. Like I said, I been trying to keep a low profile. He gets his shit from Jake most of the time."

"What were you doing over there?" I asked.

He glared at me, a little defiance showing in his eyes. "Trying to get rid of that ounce I skimmed off the kilo."

"Who's Jake?" asked Ladonna.

"Big shot low-rider coke dealer," said Johnny.

"Jake Ramirez," I said. "You might have seen him once or twice when we had afternoon breakfast at Cisco's Bakery. He probably had a football player or newscaster or somebody like that sitting at the table with him."

"Hmmm," she mused. "Curly hair, pinky ring, greasy little mustache?"

"Pencil-thin," corrected Johnny. "That's him. He's a heavyweight, all right. Since the critics were supposed to get the coke Monday night and by Thursday evening it's not only missing but a lot of people are squawking about it, Jake might have gotten irritated. Irritated enough to clean house."

"But that doesn't explain KC."

"Nope," answered Johnny. "Unless KC definitely made a deal on Tuesday and word got out. Jake would have to do something about it then. It would be a matter of pride . . ."

"And *just business* . . ."

"Or," mused Johnny, rolling up a slice of corned beef, "maybe Bud just decided that snatching the coke from a tired guitarist and/or two rock critics would be like taking candy from a baby . . ."

"Except the babies didn't have it," I said. Ladonna's eyes were wide. She didn't like this kind of talk. "If Bud's the killer, he's got to be working for Jake."

Johnny agreed, reducing the tube of corned beef to a mere stub in one bite, then saying, "Ward is such a dickhead."

"What does that have to do with it?"

"Because, you know, he's a sleaze. Ward has lost $60,000 of other people's money plenty of times, and he's still in business. He should have been responsible for the loss, but nobody's put him on a slab. Greasy bastard." He licked his fingers.

Ladonna spoke up. "I still don't get all the hysteria over the coke. Maybe this guy Salvador killed the critics for the Noon Street option. Maybe he's the Futura Corporation. You did say the ladies at Jeff Stubbs' office said he brought the deposit by."

Johnny said, "I thought you were the one said it was no big deal that somebody showed up wanting the option the day after the critics get dead?"

"I definitely get the impression that Bud is not the corporate type," I said. "Maybe I got some bad info at Jefferson Stubbs' office."

"Maybe," she said, "but I'm going to look into it. The boys at work have had some deals with secret corporations before, and I can check with the comptroller's office and secretary of state. Who knows?"

No one said anything.

She tapped the glass table top with her fingernail to make a point: "You guys—listen to me. You're having trouble making the drug deal make sense. Maybe it's more about land than about cocaine. Maybe this Mr. Gonzales is a big Mexican drug lord who came over here to launder some money in a land deal. It happens."

"What would that prove?" I asked. "What would that have to do with KC getting shot in the head?"

"But maybe she's got something there, Martin," said Johnny. "What's this about secret corporations?"

"Just what it sounds like," she said. "People get together and use the corporation as a smokescreen when they don't want their identities known. The names of the people involved are very difficult to find out. Unless you know how," she added.

"So some corporation finds out that the critics still hold the option to a hot piece of property and kills them to clear the way," I said. "Nah, it's too simple."

"Simple," she said, calmly, taking a small bite of one of the apple quarters. "Simpler than chasing a kilo of coke around town for a crazy bitch?"

We looked at each other. I had the feeling that anything I said would be wrong. I started intensely wishing that we could get the whole thing past us. But that was silly. The dilemma was a monster, too big to move. We would have to do the moving. I wondered if that was what she was thinking, too. Probably not, I decided.

The phone rang. It was Ray. After I told him what was up, he said he'd have her over in fifteen, twenty minutes.

I put on a record, *Wilson Pickett's Greatest Hits*. Johnny and I sat in the living room and we didn't speak for a bit. After Ladonna put the dishes in the dishwasher, she came in and sat on the floor across from me again. She'd been thinking.

"Martin, did you happen to get the number off that plane that flew over the Noon Street property?" she asked.

"No. It happened too quickly and there was too much sun in my eyes."

"Damn," snorted Johnny. "You know, none of this would have happened if not for that creep Ward."

"Let's not be playing the 'what-if' game. I think we're looking at this all wrong."

"What do you mean?" said Johnny.

"Well, there are things we know, and there are things that we don't. Of the things we know, some of them aren't relevant, but we don't know enough to know which ones. And some things we think we know and some we've been told are lies.

Lies that were told to throw us off-track. Even some of the things that have happened might be lies."

"Uh huh," grunted Johnny. But Ladonna listened intently.

"Just look at it this way," I said, "the lies might be the most important things we have here, because once we figure out why they were told, we'll know everything."

They just looked at me for a minute, then Ladonna spoke up. "Martin, I'm just trying to get this straight in my mind, so help me out. Like, what lies in particular?"

I mumbled something.

"Do you think Johnny lied to you?"

"Well, at first he fudged a little about the deal with KC, about how they were each going to skim some off the kilo for themselves,"—Johnny started to protest but I squelched it— "but basically I think he's been truthful."

"And Ward, you know he's been looking for Johnny because of the coke, not the bug . . ."

I nodded.

"And the critics were looking for Johnny and the coke, not researching a story on KC . . ."

Right.

"All three suicides were lies, but we don't know who set them up and therefore we don't know who that liar or group of liars is . . ."

Right again.

"Martin—"

"What?"

"Who else has been lying to you and why are you still running around after her like a lonesome puppy?"

I started to say something but stuttered. Ladonna was right. Lorraine was a liar. Everything I could remember about her had a murky, confusing quality about it, from the time I saw her naked and she didn't seem to mind to that night she'd crawled into my bed minutes before KC shot himself. She'd lied to me about the coke deal—and it was a stupid lie, too. She'd lied about talking to Ward, and there didn't seem to be much reason for that, except maybe she was supposed to pay me some of the gig money but she'd kind of wanted to hang on to it.

Ladonna was sitting there, so pretty, so right. She didn't have to say a word. She didn't even have to look at me. Johnny was sprawled in the chair, a semi-elegant wreck. Lots of personality and presence, no luck. Suddenly I had an urgent need to explain myself to both of them somehow, to put it all in perspective, to—

The damn phone rang again.

Ladonna did the talking.

"Is something wrong?" I yelled into the kitchen.

"It's Ray. He says Lorraine has been in the bathroom for the last fifteen minutes. She says she has a cold. He wants to know if he can borrow your tape of *Beggars' Banquet*."

"Sure. Tell him to make her hurry it up."

When Ladonna came back into the room she sat down beside me on the couch. "Nothing worse than a summer cold," she said, stroking my hair, trying to smooth out some of the wrinkles in my pants.

"Summer cold," I said. But I knew that wasn't it. I looked over at Johnny, and I could tell that he knew, too. It looked like everybody who'd tasted that kilo was coming down with something.

"Martin," she said softly, "there's something else."

I looked at her and waited.

"He said the afternoon edition of the paper has a big headline. It says 'ROCK CRITIC MURDERS,' and says the cops are looking for 'associates of the dead writers.' He said when Lorraine saw the headline she snatched the paper away from him and threw it in the trash. Also, there's a message on your machine from some cop named Lasko."

"What did it say?"

"He said he's got orders to bring you in. Right away."

I just sat there and looked at my feet for awhile. Because whenever I looked at the ceiling I got dizzy. Why was everyone getting smarter at the same time?

"Martin," said Ladonna. "If you're not going to go to the

police now, you've got to get some rest. You talk about all these drug conspiracies and stuff, but you're so tired and stoked up on caffeine and cigarettes and shock that you can't see straight. You can't risk going out until after dark anyway."

No, this couldn't wait, I thought. But Johnny was agreeing with her, he and his white dinner jacket, the one with pulsating purple spots. I blinked, but they refused to turn themselves off. The cat was asleep on the other end of the couch. No spots on her fur. That meant she wasn't part of the conspiracy to make me go to bed.

"And Martin," she said—sounding so reasonable in her smoky Betty Bacall voice—"you're so smart and everything, but you've parked your bright yellow convertible in front of my condo like a big neon sign advertising that you're hiding out here. We're going to have to park it somewhere else, maybe at Candyse's mother's house, where Johnny's got the van hidden."

"I'll go cover it with the rain cover," I said, getting up on shaky legs.

"You want some help?"

"No." I put on my Ray Bans, peeked through a crack I made in the curtains, and went outside, taking the tire iron with me.

Boy, it was hot. Every step down the stairs was an effort. How were people supposed to live in heat like that? The air hurt my lungs when I sucked it through instantly parched lips. I was drenched in sweat before I even got the car cover halfway pulled out of the boot.

Boy oh boy. No clouds, no breeze. The Ray Bans kept slipping off my nose. I was in the mood to tell someone off. I wished Lasko was here now. I'd give him a piece of my mind. Orders to bring me in, hell. Why, so they could talk to someone with an IQ over 85?

I'd tell him, what would I tell him? I'd tell him, boy, it sure is hot. Look at those cracks in the pavement, too hot even for lizards like you. People from up north, they think of Texas as a desert, don't they? But most of the time it's not, not what they think. It's high tech, green prairies, it's all kinds of things.

But if they were out here today, out here in this parking lot wrestling this goddamn tarp with the purple spots dancing around on it like fleas, they'd say, yep, I knew it. The place is like hell, so I'm gonna be good the rest of my life, and you won't catch me down there.

Ever.

22

And that's the last thing I remember before waking up face to face with the Boss. The room was darkened, but rays of afternoon sun leaked out around the edges of the drawn shades. I was lying on my back on a twin bed. The poster of the guy who had sold out three arena concerts in one week was almost life-sized, and he was wearing his trademark bandana on his trademark sweaty brow, the sincere boy next door who just happened to be a multi-millionaire. It was Michael's room.

It was full of the usual kid stuff: skateboard, footballs, small boy-sized clothes sticking out of a dresser, lots of tennis shoes, a poster of a modern haircut band they were making a lot of on MTV, and a short-scale bass guitar I'd rescued from a pawn shop and given him last Christmas.

There was just one thing in Michael's room that looked out of place—the big redhead sitting on the side of the bed, painting her nails, humming softly. There was a record playing in the living room, but with the door closed I couldn't tell what it was.

"What time is it?" I asked.

"Oh, you're awake," she said, examining the nails, holding the fingers apart, blowing on them. "Thank goodness you're all right. They found you passed out in the parking lot. You could have gotten heat stroke. It's three-forty."

"What are you doing?"

"Painting my nails so I won't keep biting them. Do you like the color?"

"That's red, isn't it?"

"Um-hmm," she hummed, starting on the nails of her right hand. "Have you found out anything?"

I wiped some sleep from my eyes and backed up a little against the headboard, got a cigarette and put some fire on it as I looked over the room again. Things were still a little fuzzy. Sleeping in a kid's room with the shades drawn, hung over from death and danger, the most real thing in that room was the redhead. I sucked on the cigarette, comparing the glow from the lit end to her hair. It wasn't the same. Her hair was the color of copper wire, like the coils you find wound up inside an electric motor. It tumbled down around her shoulders, down around the ample breasts that moved with her breathing.

"That depends."

"On what?"

"Do you know what 'do the do' would mean?"

She didn't know. I told her why I asked. She stopped painting her nails and glared.

"You had no right to take that."

"Maybe not. But I did. And it means something, and I think it was meant for me."

She went back to her nails. "I think we need to find the coke."

"That's all you care about, isn't it?" I said.

"I'm not surprised you'd say that, since your weasel friend, Johnny, is staying here with you. I thought I could depend on you. I thought I could make you understand."

"I understand a lot of things."

"Then try to understand this: Maybe I exaggerated on the drug thing. Maybe I was afraid you wouldn't help me if I just told you that KC swiped the coke from Johnny. But I don't have any money. I spent all my trust fund on my lousy boyfriend. I don't even have the money to pay my rent next month. I need that coke and it's mine. I need the money. I'm almost thirty years old and I don't have a husband or the money to pay my rent. What am I supposed to do, *get a job?*" She smiled grimly, ridiculing the idea.

"You'll never have to work, Lorraine. Don't worry about that." I got off the bed and started looking for my shoes. She lay back on the pillow, digging her bare heels into the bedspread as she stretched out.

I puffed on my cigarette more and said: "I can get the coke."

That got her attention. She was done with her nails. Now the fingertips rested lightly, still outspread, on each of the bare thighs that went into the tight leather miniskirt. She was listening intently. Staring up at me with those big blue eyes, sniffling sometimes, but not making a big deal out of it and not looking sad.

"You're not the brightest girl I ever met," I said, "but I guess you've had some bad breaks, too. You deserve to have things go your way. If the deal were done right, you could make enough money off the coke to pay for a good part of a condo. Or you could invest it. Or just have fun."

"Oh, Martin . . ."

"Maybe the coke isn't yours, but why shouldn't you have it and to hell with everybody. Who deserves it more than you? Ward? Bud Salvador? You deserve it, baby."

Her eyes were half shut for a moment, then wide open. Wide with life, with—"Oh, Martin . . ."

I went over to her and started stroking her thigh. First just with the tips of my fingers, then with the whole hand. "You like that?"

"I'm wet, Martin. You're making my pussy all wet."

"I thought you'd like it."

She hiked up her skirt. She had no underwear on.

"Why don't you just fuck me right now?" she said.

"No."

"Why not, Martin? Fuck me. I know you want to. I'm so *lonely*."

"I doubt that," I said. I kept stroking, and her legs twitched underneath my touch. She didn't move her hands, but the tips of her fingers, shiny with the wet polish, dug in just a bit. She was breathing heavier, moaning a little, starting to arch her back.

Those things didn't make all that big an impression on me. I was thinking of other things. Lies, for example.

"You haven't been seeing anyone else?" I asked.

"No, Martin. Oohh . . ."

"Not anyone, not even all those times I called and you didn't answer—"

"Nooo—" Her lips quivered, even as her tongue darted over them. But it was my heart that got hard. Lies. She was just as much a liar as Ward, who'd denied talking to her, who'd made up at least two phony stories about the stupid insect scam.

"What about Ward?"

"What about him?"

"I'm sure you've talked to him, seen him."

"Why?"

"Why I know is easy. The check for the gig, the check you deposited. But why it's important is another thing entirely. And it's real important. Maybe because you denied it, maybe because you both denied it. He even made it sound like he wasn't sure he knew who you were. But everybody knows who you are."

"Big deal."

"At first it bothered me that you both lied about it. I even thought maybe that meant I was jealous. I know you didn't want me to know you had the money. But there had to be a better reason to pretend that you guys haven't been talking to each other."

"I didn't think it was important."

"Did you think it was important when he told you about the coke? That you two could work out a deal with the coke, as well as the check for the gig?"

"You're a sneaky bastard," she hissed. "You don't have the balls to fuck me, and you don't have the guts to deal with any of this shit."

"You're that horny, why don't you just use my gun."

"I told you I don't have it, Martin. You probably don't even have one."

I lit another cigarette and looked at her. Her skirt was still up, the dark mound of glistening red pubic hair still visible. I didn't think of it as the embrangled undergrowth of a forbidden fruit, I didn't think of it as the enticing bedding at the entrance of a damp and dark mysterious vortex of guilt and trouble. It was just pubic hair. It was just part of the body of a girl I almost felt sorry for.

But that wasn't scoring any points with her.

"You're just like KC," she said in a clipped manner. "Another loser musician. You don't know what you're doing. You don't deal with anything. You have a problem, all you do is plunk-plunk-plunk on your guitar so people will leave you alone and think you're cool. You wear those stupid retro clothes like a uniform and you think that makes you something, too. Well, you're something. Know what? You're stupid. Your fuck-up friend has been staying here with your Suzy-homemaker girlfriend in her trendy little condo, and I bet he doesn't have any qualms about fucking her. What do you think they've been doing behind your back?"

I didn't say anything. But I was starting to not feel sorry for her.

"I bet her cunt's as big as a house."

"Lorraine, listen—"

"Listen to this, Martin," she said, swinging her legs off the bed, straightening the skirt, picking up the nail polish and throwing it against the wall, where it smashed, and the red-red liquid ran down the white surface. "Fuck you."

She opened the door, swinging it hard so it hit the wall, too. "Fuck you, and the horse you rode in on."

And she stomped out. The front door opened and slammed shut, and the building shook.

23

The digital numbers on one of the food processors in the kitchen said it was 4:01. The Howlin' Wolf record was on the turntable, the record going around and around with the stylus stuck in the last groove. I put it back at the beginning, went in the kitchen, and splashed water on my face. There was no one else home. By the phone, a notepad was covered with doodles and phone numbers—the comptroller's office, franchise tax board, secretary of state's office—and words and phrases—S corporation . . . Futura Corporation . . . Bud Salvador . . . 1969 Noon Street . . . option agreement. Well, that was nice to know—Ladonna and Johnny were out doing some research.

Then something made my ears perk up. It was the stereo. I sprinted into the living room and listened, dumbstruck. A bottleneck slide guitar buzzed around an octave, hopping from the fourth to the root to the fifth, then back to the root again, like a fly buzzing around a window screen—

Doodle-loodle-loodle, do do-do-*do*.
Doodle-loodle-loodle, do do-do-*do*.

In a voice that sounded like whisky chased with broken glass and Chesterfields, Howlin' Wolf howled the words to that old Willie Dixon song:

Well I know, I gotta babe
What I know, her love is truc

But you ain't seen nothin 'til you seen her
Do the do.

The scrap of typing paper was still in my pocket, with KC's last words.

Thirty-four bust, twenty in the waist
Ever'thing, in the right place
Cool disposition, you love her too
When you see her
Do the do
Do the do, do the do
Do do do
Do the do.

The record sleeve was on one of the speakers. I picked it up and looked inside. Taped inside was a pink pawn ticket from Snoopers Paradise on Red River. The date was last Tuesday, the last time KC saw daylight.

I grabbed the tire iron and blurred out of there.

"Fifty bucks, Martin," said the skinny guy standing behind the counter at Snoopers, fingering the pawn ticket. "You say it's pretty important?"

"I've got a feeling," I said. "In a few days I should be able to bring you an extra fifty for your trouble."

"Nope, fifty's all that was borrowed on it, and fifty is all you're going to give me. If it was anybody else but you—" He left it hanging as he went back in the back room behind the counter. I could hear the five o'clock traffic backed up outside, piling up to get on the interstate, piled up getting off to try to crawl across downtown. I looked down the rows of television sets, stereos, power tools, and guns, wondering if I really wanted what I was paying for. People pawned things to pay bills, to get through the next day or the next night. Why would KC pawn something for fifty bucks right before a four-thousand dollar weekend gig?

It was a big guitar case. He gently laid it on the counter. He worked his jaw around on a piece of bubble gum. "Here it is," he said, blowing a bubble, letting it pop. "Chet Atkins Gretsch."

The guitar was still in the case. There was a cigarette burn where the dead guitarist had parked his butts one-night after one-night. Bigsby tailpiece, frets milled down almost to the fretboard on the upper quarter of the neck for those fingers-are-quicker-than-the-eye solos. I lifted the white guitar out of the case. A fat, semi-hollow body.

It was the kind of guitar you saw on "Hee-Haw," not the kind your average rock and roll musician played. It had a mellow, one-of-a-kind sound, though, and KC had found ways to use it that Chet had probably never dreamed of. The strings looked new as I plucked one of the few six-string riffs I knew, but they sounded dead and old. The guitar seemed a little heavier than it should, too.

"I didn't know you played six-string, Martin," he said between bubbles.

"Eric Clapton has nothing to worry about," I said. I put the instrument back in the case and shut the lid, thanked him, and asked if I could use his phone.

Ladonna and Johnny were back at the condo. Her voice was warm but her message was chilling.

"We've been busy," she said. "Johnny made a lot of phone calls and talked to some of his contacts while I ran down to the office and around town talking to mine."

"And?"

"Martin—that piece of land, Noon Street? The city council voted today to rezone it. The old zoning limited any construction there to low density, single-family residences, one per acre, on account of it being in the Edwards Aquifer area. I don't know why they changed their mind, but evidently the critics had some kind of advance word on how they were going to vote. The rich Mexican you saw out there waving to the plane?"

"Gonzales?"

"Yeah. He paid *five million dollars* for the option."

"You're kidding."

"No. The land is worth no telling how much now. The new zoning allows something like fifty units on each section of land you could only put one unit on before. It's going to be condo city." She went on: "The Futura Corporation made the big deal and it's definitely what we call an 'S corporation.' *Secret*. The chamber of commerce doesn't have them listed, but they do have a franchise tax number with the comptroller's office. I can't get in line to use their computer until Monday, and if it's set up like I suspect, all I'd be able to find out there is the address of the corporation, and that would probably be a post office box or a mail drop anyway. It appears that Bud did deliver the cash to Stubbs' office, but—and Johnny can back this up— it also does appear that Bud does stuff like that all the time. People hire him for security, errands, all kinds of things, and it might mean the deals are shady and it might not. The only other name I could get out of Stubbs' office was this lawyer, George Walters, who may have handled the paperwork, but he's out of town for the weekend, and even if he wasn't he probably wouldn't help us if he represents the secret corporation."

"When I was over at Neil's, someone left a message on his machine, saying they wanted 1969. I didn't know what 1969 was then, though. His name was James."

"Come on, Martin. You're not expecting miracles, are you?"

"No. I just thought maybe . . ."

"Well, there is one small hope. A friend of mine works for the secretary of state's office, and he was going to try to find something there. He'll meet you at the Continental Club later tonight. He's a big fan of Johnny Reno and the Sax Maniacs and they're playing."

"OK, I'll keep my fingers crossed. Is Johnny available? I'd better talk to him."

"Yes he is, but just a minute. Martin, I know how you must feel about all this, but I feel like we've found out enough that we can let the police look into the rest of it. Even if—oh, I hate to even say it—even if the police wanted to hold you over the weekend—and I don't know why they would, I hope they just want to question you—on Monday we can do this right, sort the land deal paperwork out and hopefully prove what really happened."

"But one way or the other three people have been murdered," I said, "I know that. The cops know that, too. I really appreciate everything you've done. But with the police, we'd have to bring this drug deal out into the open. It'd be bad for Johnny, and it'd be bad for KC."

"KC's dead, Martin," she said. "What can hurt him now? I'm sorry. But . . ."

"I'm not being sentimental. Something just isn't right. This mess is either just a little bit simpler or just a little bit more complicated than we suspect, and if we just try to dump it in the lap of the police, it'd be bad."

She sighed and said to hang on for a moment. I could hear her talking to Johnny with her hand over the mouthpiece. Then he came on.

"Martin, you got me off the needle," he said. "You got me off speed—"

"I tied you to a bed in a cheap motel for a week, Johnny. You were in bad shape and—"

"I don't wanna relive the details, Martin. I owe you, that's all I wanted to say. I owe you and I trust you. I know you're not a killer, and I know you're not going to blow the whistle on me unless it's the thing to do."

"Well, the three of us have been through a few things, haven't we?" I said.

"I guess we have. However it happened, Martin, I ain't complaining about it. You're sticking your neck out, and besides, maybe some of this is my fault. Whatever you want to do, go to the police, do a body slam on Bud, harass Jake Ramirez, just say the word."

"Just don't be surprised when or if I say it, Johnny."

"You got it. I'm sorry I haven't been much help. I wish I could get to Bud, but I don't think it'd be too smart at this point."

"Yeah. I'd be willing to confront him, I guess. Maybe he could be talked into making some kind of deal with the cops—"

"Don't be a dope, Martin. If you're looking for him, he'll be at the Cedar Door," he said.

"How do you know?"

"He's there every afternoon. He likes their margaritas. I woulda told you, but—."

"You're cool, Johnny," I said, "but stay paranoid, too. Get Michael's baseball bat and keep it by your side."

"I can handle that kind of cool."

"I knew you could. Don't go anywhere till you hear from me. Give Ladonna a hug and tell her not to worry," I said.

24

The timing couldn't have been better. When I pulled into the shaded parking lot behind the Cedar Door, Bud was getting into the black '57 Ranchero. He pulled out and I followed. We dropped over to 2nd Street and across downtown, down South Lamar. He still didn't use turn signals. Abruptly, at the corner of Lamar and West Mary, Bud whipped into the drive of a self-storage warehouse complex. I cut into the Casey's Coffee Shop parking lot just shy of it.

I sat in the car and smoked a couple of cigarettes. Nothing happened, so I locked the Ghia and walked across the street to the rows of storage rooms. There was a small office up front but it looked vacant. A couple of kids were unloading Igloo coolers from Bud's car about three-quarters of the way down row number three. A late '70s model Chevy blocked the front end of the alley. I backtracked a row and walked down, came out the other end and peered around the corner to watch the action in unit number 59G.

There were four kids, about college-age, sitting in folding chairs around a card table counting and baling mounds of greenbacks. From where I stood I could see several bulging canvas bags, and even if the bills on the table were only singles, there were at least enough there to buy me a couple more Karmann Ghias.

Bud gave one of them a sheet of paper, and I watched as the kid nodded and counted out bundles of cash and put them in separate manila envelopes. When I overheard multiples of tens of thousands used more than once, I decided I'd seen enough.

I walked back to the car, taking it slow, lighting up another cigarette, thinking. When I put the key in the ignition and looked up, I saw the Ranchero's ugly chrome grill grinning at me, blocking my exit. Salvador got out and walked over, put his face up against the glass and knocked, then stepped back and waited. His nose had left a greasy print on the glass. I rolled it down a crack.

"Yer that Fenner guy, right," he said.

"Close enough."

"Whacha lookin fer?"

"Just looking for a place my band can practice. But no one seems to be in charge over there."

"Aw c'mon. Yew can do better than that."

I just shrugged.

"C'mon outta there, faggot. Wanna talk to ya."

"Fuck off."

He rubbed the whiskers on his neck by the scar and said: "Ya shouldn't talk that way, faggot. I'll tear off yer head an' shit in yer neck."

I rolled up the window, put the car in reverse and backed into a Mercedes. Damn. I was boxed in, with trees to my right, the Mercedes in back, the Ranchero in front, and a rusty Eldorado and a Bud Salvador on my port side.

He came over to the door again and leaned over the car. There was a ripping sound and a shiny blade cut a slot in the rag top over my head. I yelled and leaned on the horn but he soon had a fist full of my hair and his other hand around my throat. The tire iron was in my hand but there wasn't much I could do besides beat up the interior of my car. I almost quit struggling, wondering what it felt like to have your head torn off, when he loosened his grip on my throat and unlocked the door.

A more patronizing but still guttural voice said, "Just wanna have a talk with ya, faggot. Don't be fraid. I won't hurtcha."

He opened the door and took hold of my right hand with a hairy vise grip before he let go of my hair. He motioned for me to move over into the passenger seat.

"Why don't ya drop that steel in the back seat, too."

I did.

"Nice little car ya got here," he said. "Now ya got a sun roof. What'd ya pay?"

"Fifteen hundred. I was going to get a new top anyway. Last owner's German shepherd tried to eat his way through one hot July afternoon when he got left in the car in a Safeway parking lot. See?" I pointed to the large rip in the back.

"Don't blame him," he said. "See he chomped on this seat too. Radio work?"

I nodded. My scalp was part numb, part on fire.

"How 'bout the cigarette lighter."

"Yeah."

He punched it in, looked over at me and grinned. He said: "You should learn to mind yer manners, Fenner. Ya could wake up one mornin with a tag on yer toe." He winked, crow's feet shooting out from the eye like cracks in the ground. He held my hand up in the sunlight, turning it over to look at the fingers. "Bass player, I hear."

I nodded.

"Right-handed."

I nodded again.

"Callouses. Play with yer fingers, not a pick." The lighter popped out. Bud Salvador pulled it out of the dash and mashed it onto the tip of my middle finger.

It hurt. My lip, too, hurt where I bit it to keep from screaming, and the hairs in my nose tingled too when the odor of melting skin filled the car interior and mingled with the sadistic asshole's boozy odor.

After a while he took the lighter off, dropped it in my shirt pocket and patted me on the cheek. "Don' fuck wimme, Fenner, 'cause Ah'm bad. M'all kinda bad. Nex tahm it'll be yer dick."

I nodded. There was a chirping sound. He glanced at his car, said, "Be right back. Don' go 'way now, hear?" He took my keys and got out, walked over to the Ranchero, and pulled a phone out.

He said a few things and then nodded and looked at me with a new expression. If it wasn't exactly respect, it was closer to recognition. Or something. I was just about to make a run for it, but I didn't want to leave my car and KC's guitar. Or miss out on what was next.

He motioned for me to get out, smiling again. "Boss wants to see ya."

I didn't think he meant Springsteen. He gave me my keys, I got my jacket, locked the Ghia, and got in the Ranchero, desperately wanting to suck my finger.

25

"How do you like it, Martin?"

The clubowner's amplified nasal voice seemed to come from nowhere and everywhere. When I looked up from the drink that had been shoved in front of me at the bar, there was an image to go with it. The ten-foot video screen overhead had flickered to life, and Ward was on it. Sandy blonde hair combed over to the side, gaunt, pock-marked face, big Adam's apple, light-colored linen suit, gold stud earring. The shot had good composition, with the camera pulled back far enough to take in the intercom and speaker phone, two long-stemmed cocktail glasses, five-inch video monitor, and cobalt blue vase with a spray of birds of paradise on a large glass-topped desk. Very trendy. Behind him was a bank of video monitors—some with scenarios showing different floors of the club where workers were putting finishing touches on the renovation, some with rock videos, two or three with movies, and the rest occupied with the profile, frontal, and overhead views of the smoothie with the rough complexion. His eyes were big, blue, and animated.

"You haven't said anything, Martin. Go ahead, I can hear you. The bar's wired."

Bud Salvador was behind one of the glass-tiled and stainless steel bars of the 123 Club, fixing himself another José Cuervo and grapefruit. It seemed like everything in the old deco theatre was now either stainless steel, glass tile, or black. There were video monitors and cameras everywhere, instead of mirrors. There was a DJ/VJ booth big as the Queen Mary and a maddening array of fixed and rotating lights were aimed down at the dance floors, computer-controlled, no doubt.

"Nice," I said.

He seemed amused. But just for a second. It was time to get serious. "Martin, I saw Frankie today."

"So what?"

"So I just wanted to thank you. I know you've been to the police and I just wanted to thank you for leaving me out of it."

"That's why you had this goon of yours drag me down here, so I could watch you on TV saying thank you for not mentioning your squirrelly deal with Johnny and the critics? Man, I have trouble enough thinking about it without laughing, let alone going around talking to the police about it. It wouldn't hit their funny bone right."

"Nor would it strike some other people as being funny, Martin. And that's why it's just as well you didn't shoot your mouth off, OK, because actually I have very little stake in the whole thing. I just made a call and arranged a line of credit, if you will, and so there's no use assuming that I'm to blame in any of this . . ."

"I guess you didn't have much riding on the people who've been killed, either."

"Oh, Martin . . ." he shuddered, "let's just try to get over all that, will you? Now I just wanted to say that I appreciate what you've done so far and now if you'd just bring the coke to me I could straighten the whole thing out. Some people have gotten out of hand over this thing and I hate it, I really do, but if you'll just let me handle it from here on out it'll all be past us."

"What do I get out of it?"

"What do you want?"

"How about $60,000?"

He laughed. It was nauseating. The hard lines of his face weren't suited for it. "Let's say one tenth of that," he said.

"That might be OK."

"I like you, Martin, you can be reasonable. I . . . just a second." He paused because of a red light beeping on the small monitor on the desk. He pressed a button and a voice said someone wanted to talk to him on line two.

Frowning, he shook his head. You could tell it was about money. "No, I'm not in, take a message, babe."

I spoke up when he looked at the camera again. "But that price would be cash in advance."

"Now, Martin, I object in principle to that. You know the money is no problem but the thing is, it isn't your coke to bargain with in the first place. I'm doing you a favor by taking it off your hands. And I'll do you another favor, I'll give you a chance to make a lot more than just six grand. I'll give you a job."

"A job."

"That's right, Martin, a job. See, I do respect you. Let's cut the crap. You've been checking things out for the past few days, OK. And you probably have things figured out for yourself. You're a genius, all right? Is that what you want to hear? Let's get that out of the way because I don't have time to bullshit and I don't have time for people who bullshit me. You were out at the storage warehouse and I don't have to tell you what's going on. You're a fucking nuisance and a smartass but you've got a couple of good attributes, too. Like how you think you're tough."

"Think?"

"That's what I said, Martin. As long as you think you are, you've got more going for you than most people. I'm willing to gamble on you even though you've tried bullshitting me because I respect you, Martin. I mean that."

"What's this about bullshitting?"

"You're hanging around with Johnny, you're hanging around my warehouse and my campus operation, you're hanging around my fucking neck. Do we have a deal or not?"

"Nother drink while ya decide?" asked Bud Salvador, not sounding anything like a bartender, just a hood with an ice scoop in his hand.

I was in a bad spot. I wanted to ask some nasty questions, but when Ward said I obviously knew what was going on, he put me in a category I wasn't sure I belonged in. He thought I had the coke, he thought he needed to offer me a job. I downed my drink and slid the glass over to Bud, then said:

"The money's OK, the job might be OK, but when you put it up next to the cost in blood, it doesn't sound so great. I just don't like giving up my bargaining chip when three people I know got themselves dead over it because they crossed Jake Ramirez." There, I got it out. It was pushing my luck, but I did it anyway.

"Oh, Martin," blurted the clubowner. "Did I say that? You know I didn't say that. I didn't say anything about Jake Ramirez and don't ever say I did."

"I definitely caught the implication . . ."

"You know, Martin, when I was a kid I'd lie awake at night wondering just how big the universe was and if it went on forever, well, what did that mean? How long had it been here and what was here before that?" He paused, took a drink from the long-stemmed glass, looked at the birds of paradise as if to say, don't they look expensive, and went on. "You know when you're a kid things like that hurt your brain, these questions, these terriying questions, they don't seem to have an answer, but you're at an age when you still believe there's an answer for everything."

"That must have been tough on you."

"The point is, when you're a kid, all those terrible questions can do is make you lose a little sleep. The questions you're bringing up can lose you a lot more than that."

I got the message. His wordy essay really boiled down to one thing: I was supposed to get the impression that Jake had done the killing, though Ward wasn't going to be the one to tell me. "So next time I wonder who killed my guitarist and a couple of writers, I should just lie in bed and count the stars?"

He cackled. "You got it, Martin. Now, how about our little business deal? The money's no problem, of course, but I'd rather have you work for me instead."

I gave it a dramatic pause, and got a little more time when his red light blinked again and the clubowner told his assistant that no, he wasn't in for that person, either. There definitely was a red tint to the man's cheeks now, I decided. He talked fast and philosophical when the subject of murder came up and he turned red and laconic when people called him on the phone. It wasn't video distortion causing that, and it wasn't video distortion when I noticed the shine on a pair of green Springolators at the side of the desk.

She must be barefoot again.

"Well?"

"What does the job entail, anyway?"

He snorted, irritated, pushing himself back from the desk a few inches. "Use your imagination, Martin, OK? You gotta pretty good idea what I do here, I gotta pretty good idea what you can do, all right. Bottom line is, you do what I say. OK? So what's your answer?"

"You know how to reach me?" I asked.

"No, I don't." Another lie. "I assume you haven't been staying at home."

"Good. Then don't bother me there. I might be looking at the stars and lose count."

"Just make it snappy, OK." The red light was blinking again when the screen went dark.

We were in the Ranchero headed east on 7th Street, going under the interstate, past the state cemetery and the French Legation. Rush hour was past and the traffic was almost leisurely. The clock in the dashboard said it was 6:35 but it felt later. It had been an interesting, illuminating day. I was thinking about Ward's expression when he told his assistant to tell people he wasn't in, trying to figure it out. And that was probably why we'd gone so far before I noticed.

"Hey, this isn't the way back to my car."

"Ya wanna ride, I gotta couple of errands I gotta run first. Ya already fuck me up and some these people don't like to wait." He spit out the window and wiped his mouth on his shirt sleeve. "Just take a minute," he said as we pulled up at the Glass Key.

He took his keys and the ice chest with him, ducking into the little lounge. In less than a minute he was back and we went further east, this time circling over to 12th Street to Sam's Barbecue. He made another drop there and then went west, passing the Untouchables Lounge, the Groovy Bar, and King Tears Mortuary without stopping.

Around the capitol, then Lavaca up to 15th toward Windsor Heights. I wondered what the corporate types working overtime up in the looming monoliths of mirrored glass and Texas granite would think of a couple of guys making their rounds, taking in as much money as they ever did, off the books, underground.

We eased up the tree-lined drive of a French colonial-style mansion off Windsor, where a black man in a chauffeur's uniform waited for us in the porte cochere. Bud handed him a packet, said "Later," and we were off again.

"Guy's a dentist," said Bud, negotiating the curvy street. He took note of the big houses with their acres of green lawns and expensive cars with tinted glass, saying, "Purty effluent digs, eh?"

I started to correct him, then let it stand. "It's bad when dentists have to sell dope."

"Sell dope?"

"I know you didn't ask for my opinion, but if you guys want me to work for you, stocking your Colombian 7-Elevens, it seems like there might be a less conspicuous way to make the deliveries than in this thing, driving up in their driveways and dropping it off to their servants."

His grin turned into a toothy smile, then a chuckle that turned into a guffaw. He turned onto Lamar, downshifting, then slapped the dashboard with the heel of his hand, laughing so hard that tears came to his eyes. "Dope? Ya really think that's whut's goin' on here?"

I nodded.

"Boy howdy. An Ward thinks yer a brain. Whooee. That's a good one. *Dumbass,*" spitting out the window, barely missing a passing car, "we're *ticket brokers.*"

"You mean all the places we've stopped, the frat house, the bars, all these places scalp tickets for you?"

"Frat house is one of our outlets," he corrected. "But these guys I been payin today're investors, stockholders. Reason I'm doin' these personally is, well . . . we got sort of behind paying some of these fellas, an' they been gettin' little hot under their Polo shirts."

"Having a little cash flow problem?"

"Plenty a cash flow, in an' out, but with these goddamn guys addin' concerts, an' that one bimbo cancelled her whole tour 'cause her voice give out, that put a little pressure on the corporation."

"You're incorporated?"

"Sure. First thing Ward did. See, I git onto this couple a years back, since I had connects at Autoticket. Lemme tell ya something, it's the best racket I've run. Better'n hot cars, better'n runnin dope an' whores. An' it's legal. But I got into a bind last year. Fucked up with the same kind of thang's happen this week with that Purple Rain guy and Springsteam, addin' dates all over the country in cities where they sell out. Just when we git a million profit showing on a show, they add dates an' we have to spend what we made on the last batch a concerts, an' we have to recruit new investors to pay off the old ones. That's where Ward come in—he knew all these guys with loose money that he's been taking off their hands with his stupid clubs an' stuff. Now the fucker is taking their money an' telling them 'stead of giving em a write-off or laundering it, they can have 500 to 1,000 percent return on their investment."

I just shook my head. "Like a Ponzi scheme."

"It ain't a goddamn Ponzi scheme. We're payin' these guys back. We're just a little behind, is all."

"I still don't believe it."

"Better believe it, bub. Hell, we sell more bonds than Uncle Sam, an' I get more ass than a toilet seat. Sure would like to get a taste a that redhead been hanging around Ward. You seen that stuff?"

I nodded.

"Man, that chick is pussy on wheels. Whooeee."

"What's the name of your corporation, Bud?"

"Hell, I don't know. An' I don't *wanna* know. Ward handles all that shit an' gimme my cut. He's got some lawyer friend draws all that crap up."

"It isn't the Futura Corporation?"

He paused. "I tole you just now I don't know, didn't I? Far as I can tell, they got half dozen outfits drawn up. I mighta seen that name, I don't know. I trust that skinny little prick cause he know I whup his ass he tries to fuck me. He shows me some paperwork now an' then, an' I just tell him that—what I said—I trust you Ward 'cause you know I'd rip yer arms out an' beat ya to death with em you try to fuck me."

"So what were you doing out on Noon Street today?"

"I thought I recognized that little car a yers. Hell, I was just escorting some Mex. Sposed to meet him, point out what direction he was looking, cause he was looking to buy some land out there."

"And you dropped a deposit off at Stubbs' office."

"Man, ya do get round. Yep, that's right."

"And Ward sent you on these little errands?"

"Hey whut's this now, a quiz show?"

"I was just wondering what your cut of five million dollars would be."

"I don't know what the hell yer talking about an' I don't think you do either."

We were back in Casey's parking lot where my car sat with its new sun roof, and, hopefully, KC's guitar still in the back seat. He got a can of Skoal out of the glove compartment as I got out. I tested my luck one more time, saying: "I suggest you go take a closer look at some of the paperwork for your little ticket scam."

"Man, the day I start takin advice from you. . . . I s'gest you quit sittin on that kilo. Ya habbem't moved it yet, have ya? I *know* ya habbem't. Cause somebody moves ounces in this town

I know 'bout it. Ya gonna be in a world a shit ya don't wise up."

"Meaning what? You going to kill me?"

He laughed. It was an ugly sound. "I habbem't kill nobody." He revved the engine and shifted gears, adding a qualification as he packed a wad of snuff in his lower lip.

When he smiled, his teeth were covered with black flecks of tobacco. "Not lately, I habbem't."

26

It was pretty late in the game and I didn't have a plan. I just sat in my car for awhile thinking, tracing the circular brand on the tip of my middle finger. Fifteen years' thick skin from playing round wound bass strings burned off by my own cigarette lighter. I pulled the lighter out of my pocket and tapped it on the gear shift. A black chunk of me fell out onto the floor mat. Do the do.

I'd been so passive the last few days, just getting tugged along by the stupidity of everything—the reunion gig, the burned-out guitarist, the burned-out guitarist's girlfriend suddenly in my bed, him suddenly dead. Knocked in the head, questioned by the cops, tortured by a clubowner's gofer, given an ultimatum by the clubowner.

As much as I despised the clubowner, what did I have on him that I could take to the cops? The fact that he arranged the screwiest coke deal in history? The fact that he was engaged in a parasitic enterprise that forced thousands of fans to pay ten or twenty times the posted price for tickets to see their heroes? As much as the public disclosure of that last one would hurt his standing in the music scene, it wasn't the kind of crime that landed anyone on a "most wanted" poster. I knew he and Bud Salvador had to be in on the land deal, too, which gave them all the more motive to kill the critics, but I had no proof.

I wanted to hit something, to scream at somebody. I wanted to walk in on the redhead while she was screwing Ward and give her hell for it. Suppose she *had* had it rough with KC— her hanging out with Ward still felt like a betrayal. She'd used me. Like a guitar pick. Like a piece of furniture. Like she'd probably been used at various times in her life.

Damn, I was in a foul mood. If it were a TV show instead of real life, they'd have a suitably emotive set to wrench some melodrama out of it. But there were no hazy rock-laden hills looking like tombstones in front of the setting sun, no big city backdrop smoldering in its own noxious gases. Just South Austin—dirt yards with spare tires and cats out front, squat frame houses with dirty preschoolers fingering the screen doors, hanging there like cicada shells. A cheesy coffee shop that—by the smell of it—served bad coffee, a body shop across the street, and the generic concrete bunkers of the self-storage warehouse, now deserted and locked up tighter than a Sunday morning alibi.

In the midst of all the cursing and mumbling I started driving—down West Mary, then down Congress towards downtown. The capitol sat downhill at the head of the avenue, looking austere and self-righteous. I kept driving toward it, aware that police headquarters was the same direction. I could still hook it over east once I hit Riverside and go back to Ladonna and Johnny, but what would we do? Sit around and talk about doing the right thing? Try to avoid Ward and who-knows-who-else until Monday when Ladonna could try to dig up something on paper that would link Ward, the land deal, and the critics' murders? We could hide and rationalize. No. To hell with Monday. It had been nothing but a bad week and I was either going to make it a little bit better or a whole lot worse.

Because what good had I done so far? I'd just been driving around in circles. Following somebody else on his little circuit of greed. Martin Gandhi, I was. I hadn't done any more good than picking on a scab with dirty fingernails. If I was going to be a passive stooge, I might as well go all the way.

And I might as well admit it, my head felt a little clearer as I took the steps two at a time up to the front doors of the Austin Police Department, taking KC's guitar with me.

"This is not a conversation, Martin," said Lasko, tugging on an earlobe which—I noticed for the first time—was pierced.

He leaned back in his swivel chair, annoyed. He was wearing a loose rayon shirt with grand pianos all over it. "And it's not a dialogue," he added. "When two people are talking but they're not talking about the same subjects, it's two monologues."

"Like if David Letterman and Johnny Carson were both on at the same time?" I said.

"Like if I'm talking about people going tits up because of drug deals and you're talking about a sudden upswing in funeral home stocks because of real estate. I can't get a search warrant or arrest somebody because you shuffle in here saying that somebody's using the money they make off scalping tickets to make land deals. I'd be tickled to look into this secret corporation shit, whatever it is, but you know damn well all the state offices are closed till Monday morning. Meantime . . ."

"What *are* you going to do?" I said.

"Maybe I'll convince you to tell me what you know about people you know who sell drugs, and how it might have contributed to these deaths."

"You're not even used to calling them murders yet. I can't see that you guys have done a damn thing."

A big vein in his temple seemed to react to that. But he kept his cool and only raised his voice a little, like a patient father talking to an errant son. "Like I said, we've found that KC dealt some. His old lady has a sneeze habit. Cole Slaughter had three packs of baby laxative in his kitchen—which you may happen to know people cut cocaine with, even if you don't know anything about them having a drug deal working—and not a baby turd in sight. Maybe you know Cole and Neil had been hanging out with Johnny, who hasn't filed an income tax return since 1977, even though you don't know anything about any drug deals. You don't, do you?"

"No, not really." The guitar case was leaning against the front of his desk. I propped my foot on it.

"So maybe these guys just got in over their heads in some deal and knew they were gonna get hit so they just decided to do the Dutch act instead of letting someone else do them."

"You're pissing me off when you act that stupid. At this rate we'll still be in here come next Mardi Gras, saying, was it suicide or murder, suicide or natural causes?"

"You're pissing *me* off, Martin."

"OK. Just don't bring up this suicide crap again. It was obvious to me that it was murder when I got there. Like, what about the bump on the back of Cole's head?"

"Coulda slipped in the tub when he was cutting himself. Serious wrist-slashers get in a tub of hot water to keep the blood flowing, you know."

"What about the pizza Neil ordered right before he died?"

"I thought it was too salty. I hate anchovies. Gross little fuckers."

His phone lit up and I just sat there getting mad while he answered it. While he responded to the questions on the other end of the line, he opened his desk and got out a cigar, unwrapped it, rolled it between his fingers by the free ear, and stuck it in his mouth and lit it. He left it there through the rest of the conversation, which was the kind of conversation you didn't need to take your cigar out of your mouth to conduct. When it was over, he looked at me and sighed. "Look, Martin, I'm not gonna bullshit you."

"You're not going to make me sit in that little room by myself again, are you?"

"No. But I'm supposed to keep you here awhile."

"Great."

"You got a gig tonight?"

"Yeah. One I don't want to miss."

"Where?"

"Why, you have a date you wanna bring? Look, Lasko, I'm glad you like my work. But I'm not that fond of yours. How about telling me what's going on. Am I under arrest?"

"No. But you could be, it's up to me. And we need to get a fresh set of your prints. I guess you can imagine the kind of things we want to compare them to, even though the ones of yours we got from D.P.S. are OK."

"Aw, come on."

"Come on, my ass, Martin. I know they weren't suicides. I

just been trying to get a rise outta you. You said to give you a little space, that you were close to this thing. Lemme ask you something, did you know anything about this land deal stuff when you went over to Neil's house?"

"No."

"Then what'd you tromp over there for?"

"I don't remember exactly saying that I did."

"But you know I know you did."

"Come on, Lasko, just because you got an anonymous tip . . ."

"Well, it ain't so anonymous now. I can't give you no more space, it's priced itself out of the market. Pizza delivery boy just ID'd you."

"Mmmm."

"You wanna talk about drugs?"

I shook my head. I could see it wasn't going to work. There was no way I was willing to just waltz in and incriminate Johnny and get nothing in return. And I knew that was what I'd get: nothing.

"You said give you some slack. You got slack, I got shit. Come on, let's go." Pushing his chair back, getting to his feet.

"I know it looks bad . . ."

"For you to have been hanging around all these dead people? Aw heck, it's OK, you've only been on the scene of three murders."

He had a point. I followed him out of the room, taking the guitar with me, down the hall, into another room that was too brightly lit and too well air conditioned.

No one was in the fingerprint room. Lasko picked up a phone and dialed the intercom. When he put it down, he said: "Actually, this could wait. If you *were* willing to give me a hand . . ."

"What, for example?"

"Get Johnny to come in. I'll let you in on a little secret: we're not quite as befuddled up here as you might think. We do know a thing or two about Bud Salvador, Ward, and Johnny. If you could get Johnny down here for an interview . . ."

"I could try," I said.

"Another thing, about KC. The whole reason I've been flexible with you is because I've felt funny about this from the start."

"The start? You mean KC?"

"Yeah. Like I was saying at first—was he really gonna do the gig? Why wasn't there a guitar in his room? His girlfriend sure seems to either love you—yeah, you, Martin—or hate you, I can't decide which. I get to wondering, what's really put a burr under my saddle here? I think over the scene at the ranch: He was bummed out, maybe burned out, an alcoholic. The gun's right there on the floor under his right hand. His old lady is conveniently not in the room when he does it. Maybe she's got a case of sleepwalking . . ."

"What's that supposed to mean?"

"It means it's perfect. Too perfect. A .38 has a bit of recoil, you know, Martin, especially when you stick it up against your head. It could've happened that way. Or he could've fallen over. The gun could've been all the way on the other side of the room. I've seen suicide scenes aplenty. There's just no telling about them. But this one's right out of the movies. And the critics, well, hell, those were just flat out weird. I know something's going on, but I don't know these people."

"What are you trying to say?"

"It's like this, Martin. These killings—I sure as hell don't want them to get away from us. You might think I don't give a damn, but I do. I damn sure do give a damn. Most murders are easy. It's the wife, the husband, the brother-in-law, the guy you lost your money to at the cockfight. But when you don't know the guys and can't really tell where they're coming from, and you can't put a motive together—that's the kind of killing that doesn't get solved. No connection between the victim and the suspects. You just pray you get a break. Or you depend on people to help you out. I gotta talk to Johnny. Dope is the most likely connection, I figure. And I'm not finished with you."

"I'll do my best to bring him in," I said.

"You save your best for playing the blues. For me, you just do it, OK?"

"Johnny's a strange guy, Lasko. What if I can't find him?"

"Lemme put it this way, Martin. If you don't have him down here in a couple of hours, I'll have a warrant issued for both of you. What do you think of that?"

I told him. It was completely negative.

If the clubowner had been crossing the street, I would have run over him. That was how I felt about it.

There didn't seem to be any way I could nail him unless Johnny came in and told Lasko about the drug deal. I could imagine the deal they'd try to cut with Johnny. They'd want him to set up a deal with Ward and let them videotape it or tape record it. Then they'd nail Ward. But they'd let Ward off, too, so they could build a case against Jake Ramirez. Meanwhile, no one would understand why the critics got killed. And it would just look like KC got caught in someone's crossfire. Or something.

What was it about drugs that always captured everybody's attention?

A city can let a whole neighborhood go to hell because of zoning and disintegrating economics and when it's so bad off, a no man's land where no one can stand to live except for the poorest of the poor, and the only people who make money there are drug dealers, what does the city say about it?

Go after the drug dealers.

That was why I hated Ward. Not only was he central to the screwball drug deal, but he managed to divert all the attention from himself, make it look like all the danger was coming from another party—Jake—and meanwhile his land deal and ticket scam went unnoticed.

He'd told me, in a circuitous way, that Jake was responsible for the killings. But that was a lie. If Jake was the kind of man who'd order a killing or two to publicize what happened to people who crossed him, it wouldn't do him any good to make their deaths look self-inflicted.

But Ward was trying to make it play that way and confusion was his playing field. I could buy his scenario, and maybe I'd live, or I could sell out Johnny and then he'd order Bud Salvador to kill me anyway. Johnny, too. But maybe he wouldn't have to. He'd just let Jake know that Johnny had lost a kilo of his merch. And that would be the end of the fun for both of us.

Ward was one chilly bastard. I thought about the little charade with his hood, Bud Salvador, showing off their operation— *"Money's no problem."* I was guessing that money was a big problem to a guy whose empire could implode when a couple of shows were added in one week, dumping two to three times as many tickets on the market. The sleazy bastard couldn't buy everything.

Now it was starting to make sense to me. Thinking of all the concerts that had been added, Bud Salvador running around like a delivery boy trying to play catch-up, Ward turning red when people called and wanted to talk to him about green. If I could show that Ward's speculative empire was under the kind of strain that only the five million dollar land flip could alleviate, if I could prove that Ward was the Futura Corporation . . .

If, if, if . . .

And if *"Money's no problem . . ."*

Then what was the big deal over 2.2 pounds of coke?

27

When I got back to Travis Heights, I drove around in circles for awhile to make it harder on people who might want to shoot me. Ward's job offer seemed to imply a short grace period, but I didn't want anyone to follow me to Ladonna's, just in case Lorraine hadn't told them where we'd been hiding out. Naive? Maybe, but the redhead had to be good for something.

The aroma of Ladonna's Italian cooking drifted around the parking lot when I pulled in. I got the guitar out of the back and covered the Ghia with its raincoat. It didn't disguise the shape but it was better than a billboard with my name on it.

They were glad to see me. Me and my tire iron. Johnny actually looked up from the TV and waved at me with the baseball bat, and Ladonna led me to the couch and hung up my jacket.

"Are you hungry?" she said. "Where've you been? Mother called, Michael's having a good time. Martin—" a look of repulsion came over her when she started to hold my hand, "What happened to your finger?"

"Bud Salvador tried to smoke it," I said. "Yes, I am hungry."

She hurriedly walked off to the kitchen shaking her head. I heard her open the refrigerator door and take some dishes out. "You'd better do something with that or it'll get infected. And you'd better tell me what's going on."

"Yeah," piped in Johnny. "And what's with the guitar?"

"KC pawned it on Tuesday," I said, opening the case. "The ticket was inside that Howlin' Wolf album—the one with a song on it called 'Do the Do.'" I lit a Camel and basked in the moment. Johnny covered his mouth and looked over the guitar with a gleam in his eyes. Ladonna said something we all felt: We should have known.

Johnny took the big white guitar out of the case and checked the tuning. He strummed it a few times, frowning at the tone it produced.

"Sounds like it's got a cold. Maybe it's been doing too much coke," he laughed. He turned it over, looked at the back, then over again, and peeked in the f-holes.

"I'm not in the mood for coke jokes right now," I said. "I've just been read the riot act by Ward. He wants this kilo and he offered me a job with his ticket service. They buy out all the good seats for concerts all over this part of the country, and set up shop at places like the frat house where I was looking for you, Johnny. I tailed Bud Salvador out to a little warehouse where they were counting money. Lots and lots of money."

"Interesting. Very interesting," said Johnny, but I couldn't tell if he meant my revelations or the guitar, which he was paying more attention to. "Donna, you got a Phillips screwdriver?" He went into the kitchen and came back smiling. She was behind him, with a plate of linguini and clam sauce. She set the plate and a can of beer down on the coffee table.

"Don't touch that yet," she said, and walked back into the kitchen. She came back with a bottle of alcohol and a piece of aloe vera. She sat on the couch by me and went to work on the finger. Her hands were soft and nice. The alcohol was cold, the aloe vera wet, slimy. "It'll make it heal," she said, daubing the cactus juice over the wound.

"You're an angel," I said.

"I know. Now eat."

"Hey," exclaimed Johnny. "Look at this, will you?" He'd unscrewed the back plate of the guitar, which had apparently been installed to give easy access to a customized wiring job. Johnny pushed some of the electronic nest aside and delicately removed a clear plastic bag with what looked to be 2.2 pounds of cocaine, give or take an ounce or two.

"I knew that guitar felt a little heavy," he said. "Did you know?"

"I knew," I said. "I knew when I heard 'Do the Do' and I knew when I picked up the guitar. I knew when I went to the police to turn myself in just to try to get to those bastards."

"But you're back," said Ladonna.

"And you didn't tell them about the coke," said Johnny.

I looked at them both. They *were* glad to see me.

"Wanna bump?" asked Johnny.

"No," I said, "and you don't either. You want a bump on the head? Look at how much trouble this powdered money has caused. Lasko wants to see you and he doesn't mean maybe. I promised to bring you in. If I saw you."

"Well OK, OK. You through sermonizing? Because I've got something to tell you."

"What?"

"You know I burned up the phone lines while you were passed out? And then I tagged along with Donna and checked a couple more of my contacts. Just about an hour ago, I did some follow-up. And guess what?"

"What, Johnny?"

"Bud Salvador is looking for you. He was looking for me all week, and now all a sudden he wants to talk to you. What do you think of that?"

"I don't get it," I said. "I just talked to him a couple of hours ago."

"Maybe something has changed."

"Yeah," I said, mouth full of pasta. "This is great, Ladonna. I'm taking you out to dinner as soon as we get all this settled." To the cat, getting more aggressive about getting an angle on my plate, I said, "And you, too," but she wouldn't hear of it, didn't believe in men's promises. She lunged.

"Stop that, Betty," scolded Ladonna. She grabbed the wiry black and white ball of trouble and locked her in the bedroom. Then she came back and sat down again.

"I just wish I knew more about this corporation. I couldn't

really ask Ward because he thought I knew a lot more than I knew and I didn't want to disappoint him."

"I thought you weren't too excited about the corporation angle," said Ladonna.

"The thing is, I like it better all the time. I can sure understand why a clubowner would want to keep secret a corporation that makes getting a decent seat at a concert cost an arm and a leg. Not good P.R. But it's too haphazard. Like, Bud acted like he was nothing more than an errand boy on the land deal and he didn't seem to know anything about any five million dollars."

"Like I said, maybe something's changed," said Johnny, staring at the coke, smoking a cigarette, rattling the ice in his drink, looking over his shoulder toward the window.

"I'll call him when I'm through eating," I said. "Maybe he wants to give me something that'll light a fire under the homicide squad's butt."

"If he doesn't, maybe Jack can," said Ladonna, "the friend of mine who's meeting you at the Continental Club tonight." She got up. "Had enough to eat?"

I nodded. "I'll take care of this," I said, indicating my plate.

She shook her head. "Do me a favor. Don't spoil my image of you. I just can't see you washing dishes."

"And I can't see you asking Bud Salvador for a light again," said Johnny, breaking into laughter.

I dropped a Camel out of the pack for dessert and leaned back for a smoke and a little brain-fest. My friends.

"Just stay out of that bag, Johnny," I said.

28

There was no answer at Bud's apartment. I called the Cedar Door, the massage parlor, and some other numbers Johnny gave me, and the 123 Club, too, but he didn't seem to be around.

I got my bass out of its case and tuned it up. Johnny was watching TV and reading a book, *Rock and Roll Babylon,* or maybe he was just holding it up in front of his face. Whenever I wanted to talk to him I had to hit him or I'd end up just talking to myself. Ladonna was in the kitchen, transplanting a plant with big pink blooms into a larger pot. Once in a while she'd look up at me, standing by the sink, her hands covered with dirt, and she'd smile. Then she'd bite her lower lip, and shake her head.

It was pretty tough playing bass with one of my plucking fingers out of commission. After stumbling through some easy walking patterns, I found that I could take up some of the slack with my thumb, using it for the downbeat, and the index finger for the upbeat. That worked well enough sitting on the couch, improvising, but it would probably earn me some cramps over the course of a three or four set gig. I wondered if I'd still be able to do the session with Billy.

I called him at the studio. He sid I should come by tomorrow and try a bass line on the song he was working on. "You any further along in your little investigation?" he asked.

"A lot of things have happened, Billy. Why?"

"Well, I hate to be the one to tell you, but the word out on the street is that you and Johnny ripped off the critics." Rumors like that sound even more worse when they're shouted over a background of loud guitars and drums. Phones aren't made to broadcast loud music, and some of the more dynamic sounds, like effect-laden drums, came across tinnily. Like little firecrackers. It was funny. The rumor ended up sounding big, the music small.

"You don't believe that, do you?"

"Of course not, Martin. I just wanted to let you know."

"Thanks. I'll be by tomorrow."

I hung up and went back to the bass. A couple of minutes later, Ladonna was done in the kitchen and joined me on the couch, but didn't sit close because of the bass. I said "Hello, gorgeous," and kept thumping the four strings.

"What song is that?" she asked.

"No song in particular," I said between riffs. The action was good, but a couple of the frets buzzed from always going back over the same ground. Blues in B, rock and roll in E. Probably because I hadn't played with enough black people. They aren't afraid of the black keys on the piano, the sharps and flats. White folks tend to stay on the white keys, and so my frets wore out. Blame another one on unhip white people. I was just the bass player, so it wasn't my fault. If the song starts to speed up, or the groove gets ahead of the backbeat, then give the bass player a dirty look. But the singer or the guitarist usually chose the key for the song, saying, that key's not good for me, let's try it in another key. Never the bass player.

"So are you playing, or just playing around?" she asked. "Or just thinking?" Betty was back in the room, staring with bewilderment at the buzzing wire and walking fingers.

"Thinking. But I wouldn't mind playing around." Betty leaped on me and gripped my leg with a set of sharp claws.

Ladonna grabbed her and held her down in her lap, stroking her head. "Bad girl. Leave the man alone. Can't you see he's thinking?"

She wasn't looking at me, only at the cat. I stopped playing.

"Do you realize you've done nothing but eat, sleep, and play that thing while you've been here? Maybe you should try to relax." The cat jumped off her lap and ran under the TV.

"Yeah, Fender. Relax," said Johnny. "You're making me all stressed out." He put the book down and turned up the volume on the TV. Clear signs of nervous anxiety.

The ten o'clock news was on. The lead story was the heat wave. There wasn't much to say about it, except that it was hot. So hot that two people had died from it today, three yesterday. And it would get hotter before it got cooler.

"I'm sorry I haven't been a barrel of laughs, guys," I said.

Ladonna slid over to me and took the bass out of my lap, handed it to Johnny, who leaned it against the wall without spilling any of his drink or losing any ash off the cigarette in his mouth. Ladonna put an arm around me and laid her head on my shoulder. "Put your feet up, Martin," she ordered. Softly.

"Fender, you'll be up there someday," said Johnny, pointing at the TV screen. It was a close-up of a Big Mac. A pair of feminine hands clutched the hamburger and squeezed it till grease ran out, then a big happy mouth took a big bite out of it. "You need to record a song and get with a band of good-looking guys and do a video. I can help, man. I can get the equipment for nothing. I've done videos and got them on TV with a lot of guys that have less talent than you. Rock and roll is what they want, man. Rock and roll, and video. Guys in undershirts and tight pants, that rough, unshaven look . . . you've got it, Martin. Give it to 'em." He popped the top off another Diet Coke and poured it over a glass of Bacardi and ice, then flicked the channel changer past MTV.

"Look Martin," he continued, "all we've got to do to get out of this deal is this: We go give the coke to Ward and say, sorry this deal didn't work out. After all, it isn't my fault and it certainly isn't yours. Then we call the cops and have him busted. See? Simple as MTV."

"No, not so simple," I said.

"Why?"

"Sure, Ward would be happy to get the coke back. But why?

Why does he want it? What happens after he gets it? What happens when he finds out for sure we have it, Johnny?"

"What do you mean?"

"This stuff is our leverage, somehow. But we need to really get the goods on this Futura Corporation to stack the deck. We won't have a winning hand till we do."

"Well that just puts us right back where we started," said Johnny, "chin-deep in shit and tired of standing on our toes."

"Look what your boneheaded attitude has done for your sense of perspective, though, Martin," said Ladonna. "You thought these frats were selling drugs when all they were doing was scalping tickets. You're a musician, not a detective. Why don't you just lighten up instead of trying to be a hero?"

I started to open my mouth, but she put a soft fingertip on my lips. She said: "Don't get me wrong, Martin. That's one of the things I like about you. You're so stubborn. Sometimes you're mean, but just because you feel things differently than other people do. That's why I've been thinking . . ." Her arm was still around my shoulders, her hand playing with the collar on my shirt. Her face, with its strong bone structure and exaggerated eyes and nose, was close to mine. I could feel her breath coming out, see her nostrils flare just slightly as she breathed.

"I've been thinking," she said, "that you could move in here. You could quit that stupid skiptracing job before they fire you. Concentrate on your music. That way you wouldn't be forced to take jobs with bands that you don't care for, for the money. You could concentrate on your songwriting, do some recording, and you could start a band, really get somewhere."

"Just you and Michael and me," I said.

"Yes, you know he really likes you. And so do I."

"And I you. And Michael, too. But I wouldn't feel right, staying here, you working. While you were at work I'd feel like I had to do the laundry, go to the store, that sort of thing . . ."

Maybe she saw it coming. Johnny did, because he left the room.

"Well, if you wanted to," she said.

"I could wear an apron, and be the little man," I said.

"It wouldn't have to be like that, Martin. I meant just till you get on your feet with a new band." Her arm came off my shoulder.

"You wouldn't like living with me," I said. "I've got bad habits. I smoke in bed. I eat Cheetos for breakfast sometimes. I don't necessarily think night time is the right time for sleeping. Sometimes I don't comb my hair for three days. So what's the use in shaving? I never use a coaster for my beer cans, and my cat doesn't like other cats."

"You're the cat that doesn't like other cats. Just forget it. Forget I said anything, Martin. Just forget it."

I switched the channel back to the news and drank my beer without tasting it. Ladonna took a couple of sips from hers, then placed the can down on the coffee table purposefully. She lit a cigarette and smoked with her arms crossed over her chest.

"Martin, what happened with Big Red?' she said. "I thought she was going to stay here."

"I don't know. Nothing." I glanced at the TV. The news was over. That meant it was 10:30. "Can I take a shower? Johnny and I need to get ready to go out."

"Sure," she answered.

"And, I was wondering . . ."

"If you could use my car?"

I nodded.

She sighed. But it was from nerves, not fatigue. Then she nodded, without looking at me, and said, "I guess Betty and I will stay here."

"I think that's best," I said on my way out of the room.

29

The Continental Club was a funky little beer and wine joint with a faded, tattered candy-stripe awning out front and a checkered past behind. On South Congress across the street from a couple of cheap motels, the dimly lit, poorly ventilated nightspot provided a small stage for Austin's lesser knowns and a cushioned bar for the neighborhood's elbows. It was too funky for yuppies, too low tech for college trade, but it had a cover charge that managed to keep out the cut and shoot crowd. Despite its reputation for being the spawning and even foraging ground for some of Texas's premium exports like the Fabulous Thunderbirds, Stevie Ray Vaughan, Joe Ely, Charlie Sexton, the Leroi Brothers, and Lou Ann Barton, and as a drop-in spot for big name touring rock bands who came to jam and rub shoulders with the South Austin cognoscenti, the club neither thrived nor ever completely folded. It just smoldered like a slow-burning fire in a garbage dump, never quite ablaze, never totally extinguished.

Johnny and I were on the back door guest list, let in by Scooter Schmidt, an old friend of mine who happened to play bass with Johnny Reno and the Sax Maniacs, a position that I'd procured for him with a timely phone call. He was in the middle of changing the strings on a '63 model sunburst Precision—tortoiseshell pick guard, wide, flat neck with a rosewood fretboard, just the way they made them that year. I told him we were trying to keep a low profile and he said he couldn't imagine why but wouldn't ask. He said Reno was still over at the Imperial 400 trying to decide what shirt to wear first, since the indoor temperature of the club had determined that it would be a three shirt set.

"Martin," he said as we were leaving the dressing room, "something wrong with your arm?"

I said no, there wasn't. But you try going around with a tire iron up the sleeve of your jacket and see if you get away with it.

The club was packed. The opening act, just finishing up, weren't tight, but they were intense. The guitar players chugged away with barely controlled abandon. The bass player used a pick, something akin in my book to putting ketchup on enchiladas. The drummer was hidden behind the front line of the group on the tiny black and white tiled stage, thrashing away.

The singer had his eyes closed, his lips kissing the microphone, and though I couldn't understand a word he was singing, critics rimmed the dancefloor, bobbing their heads up and down, patting each others' backs, hanging on every word. They were also obscuring the view for most of the seated customers, mostly members of the South Austin blue jeans and T-shirt constituency.

There was a bottleneck forming at the door as Johnny Reno and the Sax Maniacs' more uptown crowd arrived and the rock critics and T-shirt crowd filed out. The warm-up band's set was over. Reno had arrived.

The bandleader had the hollow cheeks, Clint Eastwood squint, and self-possessed cool of a born matinee idol. He had a vintage clothing collection that put mine to shame, and was thin as paper. He could blow a mean saxophone, was a great blues shouter and crooner both, was a shoe-in for the remake of *The Man with the Golden Arm,* and always had a crackerjack band. He was glad to see me, too.

"Hey, man," he beamed, pumping my hand, "how's tricks?"

"It's been a rough week," I replied. "I thought I'd better shake hands with you before you get all hot and sweaty."

"Ain't that the truth," he said. "It got up to 115 today in Ft. Worth. Christina and I for once talked seriously about moving."

"You know my pal?" I asked, indicating my companion in

the white dinner jacket, with matching double-pleated pants, fresh lavender silk shirt, and Stacy Adams.

"Like my own brother," he said. The two Johnnys shook hands.

The Johnny I'd brought broke open a fresh pack of Pall Malls, non-filter, and said, "Reno, you know where we might find that other Fort Worth native, Jake Ramirez? We need to talk to him."

"Yeah," he answered. "Whenever I'm in town I run into him at Matt's El Rancho. We both order the same thing, every time. That number four dinner is something else, man."

"And?"

"Well, Jake's a real entrepreneur, always looking to the future, you know, and he's onto the fad with Ecstasy. The word is that all the preppies and sorority girls who'll barely smoke a joint and wouldn't drink anything stronger than a strawberry margarita are nowadays popping Ecstasy like crazy, man. Tonight Queen Bee's having a TGIF blow-out over at the Sindrome to take some of the steam out of the 123's grand opening tomorrow, so Jake's gonna be there mapping out his territory."

"Probably have an accountant with him," I said.

"Right," laughed Reno. "That's Jake. He'll have a couple of monkeys at the door and whenever your disco deb or limp-wristed lifeguard inquires about the stuff, they'll point out their man working the floor."

"Barbie and Ken on acid-speed cocktails," snorted Johnny through a cloud of Pall Mall.

"You got it, man," said Reno. "Jake's gonna be there, laughing all the way to the bar. He's a happy man. It's legal, and at twenty bucks a hit, it's still cheaper than half a gram of coke."

We thanked him for the tip and headed for the bar. I bought us some Coronas since they didn't have Labatt's. I raised my glass.

Johnny shook his head. "I just want it to be over. I'm tired of being holed up. I can't even take my suits to the cleaners. I don't know how much longer I can hold out." A brunette slinked past as if to accentuate the problem. "Why don't we blow off this friend of Donna's and just go home? I don't see what he'll be able to tell us that'll make any difference. I'm not looking forward to talking to Jake, either. Even if he's a happy man, he still might not be in a good mood about the coke."

I lit a Camel. "Don't worry. I'll do the talking. And it's still early."

"So?"

"We've still got to break into Ward's office at the club after hours if this friend of Ladonna's hasn't come up with anything."

"You're nuts, Martin. You know that?"

"No, I'm not. I brought my big screwdriver with me. That gets me in more places than this semi-legendary face ever has."

"Excuse me," said a voice, as I felt someone tugging on my jacket. I turned around. It was a short guy with wrap-around shades and a pug nose. He had a big gap between his two front teeth and another one between the bottom of his Izod shirt and the top of his jeans.

"Excuse me," he repeated. "Are you Martin Fender or Johnny Craft?"

"Hi," I said. "I am, he's or." Johnny acknowledged the kid, looking at him a little suspiciously. "You're . . ."

"A friend of Ladonna DiMascio," he said. "My name is Jack." He smiled, showing off his gaps.

"Want a drink?" I said.

"No thanks," he said. "The information you wanted—I found it. On file at the secretary of state's office here, where they keep trademarks, things of that nature. I found the articles of incorporation for the Futura Corporation, which is something that has to be filed for any corporation, whether they're public or not." He smiled a little jerky smile and went on. "The articles of incorporation . . . well, the main thing is that the registered agent is a lawyer by the name of George Walters. I don't know if he's a member of the corporation, or just the registered agent. It doesn't say. It isn't required. A lot of groups form 'S corporations' and just name the registered agent and a mailing address. That's all they *have* to do. But on this one, there *is* a name, and address . . ."

"Well . . ." I was getting impatient.

"Henry Maxell," he said.

"Also known as Bud Salvador," I said.

Our informant nodded. "I hope that does something for you."

"Oh, sure," said Johnny. "Makes my day. Here," he said, handing him a twenty dollar bill.

"No thanks," said the little man. "Really, it's OK, don't bother," he went on, making a small fuss over refusing the money. He stood there for a moment as the Sax Maniacs fired up, then bit his lower lip, took another look at the bill, and snapped it up. "Thanks," he said, and disappeared into the crowd.

"That answered some questions," said Johnny.

"Yeah," I shouted over the music. "I wonder if Bud is asking any of them. I wonder if that's why he called me, wondering about some of that paperwork Ward shoves in front of him from time to time."

"I don't know, but I think you'd better talk to Jake after this next beer."

"The next one?"

"Yeah, the one I'm ordering," he said, waving at the girl behind the bar. We had another round and absorbed the music. I looked over the crowd again. The warm-up band was loading out their tattered equipment with the help of a couple of roadies, looking sincere and proletarian. Their guitarist walked by, cigarette limply dangling from his mouth, the slack, sallow face of a loser. He was more bloated than KC had been, and had less to lose. I became aware that I was despising the band, just a bunch of no-hope jerks peddling their own despair.

Johnny Reno and the Sax Maniacs, on the other hand, were vibrant and full of soul. Reno dedicated "Harlem Nocturne" to me, which we listened to as wistfully as a couple of guys in thriftshop suits can, waiting for Philip Marlowe to walk in the door, but he never did so we left.

On the side street outside the club, next to the bamboo jungle taking over the sidewalk, amidst the fluttering moths and june bugs, swapping stories and hits on a smelly joint, were members of Austin's literary elite.

"Well," boomed the baritone of the barrel-chested, moon-faced Gerald Ruby, who was obviously holding court, "if it isn't the hardboiled dickhead and his sidekick, Johnny Pinstripe."

"Gee, I hope you guys aren't selling cocaine out here," lisped Hilly Burns, the film critic. A big black mustache fringed a somewhat frozen toothy grin. "Because we don't mind our coke being cut with ether or even speed but not blood."

Also in the assemblage were Leonard Oswald and John W. Booth. Oswald, a free-lancer, was an owlish-looking character with thick glasses and stooped shoulders. Booth, the rock writer for the *Statesman,* was a hard-drinking chainsmoker who could quote Tolstoy in his West Texas twang better than anyone I knew.

"You guys are as corny as that opening act," I said. "You ought to learn some new clichés."

"You guys didn't like them?" asked Burns.

"Not much," I said, "but I can see you guys are about to set them up as the next big thing."

"Too much like the Velvet Underground, exept with a phony country accent and no heroin," said Johnny.

"Sour grapes," said Oswald, looking away.

"Don't you guys have a movie review or something you're supposed to be doing?" I said. "A restaurant or band you've been wanting to trash?"

Ruby passed the joint, blowing the foul smoke our direction. "Don't *you guys* have somebody to rip off? What happened to your finger, Fender? You break it when your pal here sat down all of a sudden?"

They cracked up.

"What a sapient bunch of saps you guys are," I said. "What makes you think Johnny and I have that kilo?"

Booth tugged on his beard and talked out of the side of his mouth: "This ain't nothing but a small town in a small world, Martin. Word travels faster than fire in a grain silo."

"It's common knowledge, guys," piped in Burns, adding,

"Nobody's saying you two killed them. Don't get me wrong."

"But people are saying that what goes around, comes around," Ruby said.

"Yeah, Manson believed in karma, too," said Johnny.

"What's that s'posed to mean?" said Booth.

"It means we'd love to stay and rap with you, but Johnny and I have a prior commitment."

"You better hope you don't have another kind of prior," said Oswald. "Or the only playing you'll be doing is the old drop-your-soap routine at Huntsville. Or maybe if you're lucky you'll get sent to Big Spring. I hear they have a house band there with a bunch of Austin all-stars."

"Up yours, twerp," spat Johnny, collaring the little man. He lifted him off the ground. Johnny looked like he was ready to beat his face in and Oswald looked like he was ready to have a coronary.

I pulled him back. "It's not worth it, Johnny." He let him go and we started to move away.

"It's the same old story, the writers don't have the facts but it doesn't get in the way of them turning in their stories," I said. "They'll get them soon enough, if things work out. Come on, Johnny."

We moved away, towards the car. The critics were snarling, grumbling, still passing the joint.

I turned back and said over my shoulder, "And if things don't work out, just make sure they play 'Wang Dang Doodle' at my funeral."

30

We sped down Congress with the windows down, keeping an eye out for cops. Johnny whistled nervously and adjusted his collar, which tended to flap against his lapels. He lit a Pall Mall.

"I guess they're just doing their job, Martin," he said. "Being assholes and looking out for a couple of their own."

"Nobody's doing their job on this, Johnny. Everybody's just fucking up, acting and reacting. There's no job to it."

"Is that what we're here for, then—to tank up on some liquid antispasmodics?"

"Here" was the Sindrome. I'd taken the alley route off Lavaca and parked in the dark shadow of the disco. We went in the out door, past the flush-faced trendites and Reagan Youth chatting, giggling, and dancing as they waited in the line that snaked out to the street.

We were nodded in without much ado.

Johnny went ahead to the bar while I leaned on a pole near the DJ booth, watching the people come in, keeping an eye out for men who were keeping an eye out for us. We had decided that the tire iron would be a problem in the crowded disco, so I'd lightened up, carrying just the big screwdriver in my back pocket, and Johnny still had his switchblade. Reno was right. Just past the box office stood a couple of faces bearing no expression in particular, faces that belonged to men that belonged to Jake Ramirez. They had their hands in their pockets and their eyes on the new customers' lips that mouthed the abbreviated name of the drug.

"X."

Was there a tie-in between Jake, Salvador, Ward, and the Futura Corporation? It seemed a little too grandiose. But we had to wonder, and we'd have to ask. I had to know.

The club was cold. From the icy glass tile walls to the cold brushed steel balustrades around the upper balconies, I couldn't escape the feeling I was in an art deco meat locker.

I didn't see Queen Bee anywhere. The door men didn't know where she was and it was probably part of their job not to. She wasn't in the ladies' room, not in the men's room. Nor the downstairs bar, nor the patio where it was hot and sticky and smelled like butyl nitrate. Poppers.

I bumped into a few people on my way to the bar. I didn't have time to order before Johnny jostled my elbow and handed me a peach schnapps and a beer. Then I saw him. Maybe the gleam from his Italian loafers caught my eye. He was medium height, muscular and blocky, in a sharp shiny suit with a silk shirt and no tie.

"Hey," I said, poking Johnny in the ribs.

"Yeah, I see him."

"Let's go." We followed him into the men's room.

He stood by the mirror, sniffing a lump of powder out of the inch-long nail of his little finger—the one with the ring. The powder came from a glass vial snuggled in his fist. After servicing the other nostril, he ran some water on a finger and sniffed that too, as a chaser, and checked his reflection for signs. That was when he acknowledged us.

"Hola, muchachos," he said.

"Hello, Jake," said Johnny. "Good to see you."

He held his chest up high, like a rooster, and it was impossible to tell if he was twenty-five or forty-five. "I sure hope they sharged you at the door, Juanito. I hate to see them let riffraff in for free."

"Aw, Jake . . ." groaned Johnny.

The Mexican's face broke into a grin. "Don't take it so seriously, Juanito. You must have guilty conscience." He offered me his hand and we shook. "Hello, Marting. You playing around?"

"Not lately, Jake," I said. "We need to talk about something."

"Go ahead, talk. Mind if I piss while you talk?" He didn't wait for our answer.

"You fronted a kilo to Bud Salvador," I began.

His lower lip suddenly curled inward and a whistle came through his teeth. A thin young man with a very bad complexion, dull eyes, and a big jaw stepped out of one of the stalls and said nothing. "Maximo, what do these boys want?" said Ramirez.

"No se."

"Are they wearing a wire?"

There was a grip on my arm, not like a steel vise, but like a doctor checking my blood pressure. Nothing more, no frisking, no head to toe inspection. Just face to ravaged face with the wiry man and his dead eyes. I spread my fingers out in the air in front of my chest, then slowly reached back and took the foot-long screwdriver out of my back pocket, showed it to Maximo, then put it back. Johnny did the same with his switchblade.

"Should I talk to them?" asked Jake, turning around, smiling smugly, zipping up his pants, making sure we saw his cock.

Maximo shrugged. *"No importa."*

Jake nodded. Maximo stepped out. And no one else came in to use the bathroom.

"What business is it of yours?" he asked.

"You fronted the kilo to Bud, for Ward," I began again. "And I was wondering if you were expecting to get paid for it."

"Of course I am, Marting."

"So you might have to pay a visit to Bud pretty soon, since no one's dropped off the money, right?"

"I don't go knocking on doors, Marting."

"Maybe you and Ward have some kind of special something going, Jake."

"What are you trying to esay?" Getting more irritated. The steely eyes stayed that way, but the muscles in his jaw began to pulse.

"Maybe I'm out of line, Jake, but some people I know have been put away and I want to know why. The work is sloppy, so I just wondered if you're slipping or maybe you've got nothing to do with it. Because if you and Ward and Bud aren't getting to be hot and heavy in cocaine and rock and roll and real estate . . ."

"Wait just a minute, *pendejo*," he said, waving a finger at me. "Ward may do some business with me, but I don't go partners with white boys. I'm a family man, muchachos. A *cabrón*. My father and his brothers and their father, they make lots of Ramirez, you dig? So I don't need to make partners with *los putos* like Ward."

"OK, OK," said Johnny. "Look, we'd just like to get to the bottom of this. I know you want your money, but I think you might want to keep a low profile for a bit. Martin seems to think there's some kind of a setup in the making."

"Oh, a setup." He seemed to think it was funny. "A *setup*, eh?"

"Yeah," I said.

Jake's gaze shifted from Johnny to me, then back to Johnny again. "You have the cocaine?"

Neither of us said a word. He pulled his vial out again and waved it in front of our noses. We declined. He popped the top and boosted himself, repeating the ritual with the water and the finger and the mirror, then said: "Tell you what, muchachos. I give you till Monday. Then you are going to pay me for the cocaine."

"Wait a minute . . ." stammered Johnny.

"Hey, *estoy hablando*—I'm not finished espeaking," he said coldly. "You listen to what I'm esaying. You axe me if I kill somebodies. I don't have to tell you nothing. I need to kill somebodies, I don't have to go round splaining it to you, you dig? And if I make a deal, I get paid. I am not sharity."

"But Jake," I began, firmly, reasonably.

"Fifty grand," he said.

And it was good-bye and have a nice day. The two of us stood there, looking at the door swinging after he'd gone back into the club. We'd been brushed aside like two pieces of lint on a thousand dollar suit.

We split.

"I don't know about you, but I feel a whole lot better now," said Johnny, fumbling nervously with his seat belt as we rounded a curve a little too fast.

"You don't think we learned anything?" I said.

"Sure," he snarled. "Jake's a simple coke and Ecstasy dealer. No white parners."

"The way I see it," I said, "we're a lot closer now. We're part of a very small group of people who know the coke deal and the land deal and the murders are connected. But people think we have the coke and kind of want to hurt us because of that."

"But we do have the coke."

"That is a problem."

"You know flies need meat?" I said as we sat idling at a red light. "Feed them nothing but sugar and they can't lay eggs."

"Bet it rots their teeth, too."

"You know you can't get a male cheetah to mate a female cheetah in captivity unless you put another male in the cage for competition?" I waited for his answer a couple of seconds, then ran the light at East 1st and Guadalupe.

"Come on, Martin," he protested, slapping the dash. "Trying to get us arrested?"

"Might not be a bad idea." I ran another light, then sped up.

"What's on your mind, man?"

"Nothing."

"Come on, spill it."

"Nothing. But maybe I should be more careful. I'd hate to get us arrested and Lorraine's car impounded."

"*Ladonna,* you dickhead," he spat. "It's *Ladonna*'s car. You're so hot for that redhead you're getting the names mixed up. If that doesn't take the goddam cake." Out of the corner of my eye, I could tell he was nodding his big square head, trying to fold his arms across his chest and keep a grip on the arm rest at the same time. "Go ahead, Martin, call her. But don't get us thrown in jail. I'd rather take my chances out in the open."

"You should have thought of that when you picked up that kilo in the first place."

The next light was more red than amber, but we were making great time.

"Come on, pal. Knock it off. I know you wanna call her. And you know where she's at, don't you? Maybe you can rescue her, make her look in the mirror and see something besides a dusty road to numbsville." He flicked the ashes of his cigarette on the floormat, glaring at me.

"You really think she's got a serious coke habit?"

"Man oh man, love *is* blind, ain't it," he growled. "She's got a jones so big that if sticking you up her nose would get her through the night there'd be a vacancy sign on your apartment instead of your forehead."

"Very funny. I can tell she does the stuff, but I never thought much of it."

He snorted disgustedly, then breathed a sigh of relief as I stopped at the next amber. "Brother, you need to start looking at her with your eyeballs instead of your balls."

"Screw you."

"Same to you, brother. But what pisses me off is that we've got the coke and you don't wanna sell it, but you don't want to give it back, either. You started looking for the shit because of her and now you've got it and I wish to hell I'd never laid hands on it. Just where in hell are we going?"

"Did you forget? We still need to talk to that other Romeo, Bud Salvador."

We headed up the hill on Academy Drive into an apartment complex which, back in the 1940s, had probably been a pretty nice place. The compound of courts and swimming pools had been thoughtfully woven into the hill above South Congress. Now it was just another dilapidated, quirky nest of drug dealers and musicians and the people who didn't mind living next door to them.

Bud Salvador's black Ranchero was parked in front of his apartment, but no one answered his door. Behind some other door a man was yelling at his wife, and somewhere, a crowing voice called out for someone or something named Sparky.

"I've got a bad feeling about this," said Johnny, looking up at the bats circling around the street lights.

The door was unlocked. The trail of blood began in the living room and we followed it to the bathroom. Bud was sitting on the toilet, a big black revolver in one hand and a roll of toilet paper in the other. He was wearing only his boxer shorts and an undershirt, the front shiny with red blood. Blood also ran down his forehead and circled his eyes, making a kind of red raccoon mask of his scowling face.

"Sumbitch shot me," he said, lowering the gun.

He hollered and bucked on the bathroom floor while we tried to stop the bleeding, mopping up the blood around the purple-black traumas, trying to figure out just how bad things were.

The wounds, one on the belly just to the right of where Bud's big cowboy belt buckle normally dug into the overhanging flesh, and one on the top of his head, gave off a meaty smell that the alcohol and peroxide didn't take away. There was also the scent of gunfire in the apartment which should have reminded me more of the scene in KC's room at the ranch house, but didn't. And I wasn't sure why.

"I'm gon' take care that cocksucker right now," he was yelling. *"Those questions aren't appropriate right now,* the asshole says, after I axe him what the fuck was with the five mil. Then comes over an' shoots my ass."

"You're just lucky this low shot hit that cowboy belt first and the high one just took some of your scalp off," I said. "Now be still, I can't tell if this other one's in your belly or not. If it is . . ."

"Fuck it," spat the hood. "Call Truman, tell him git his ass over. Then I'll go take care that cocksucker, teach him to shoot my ass an then not check an' see I'm playin' possum or not."

"Who's Truman?" asked Johnny, rinsing another towel.

"A doc who can keep his goddamn mouth shut," said Bud.

"Nope," I said. "Put your pants on."

He balked, then flailed at me and knocked me aside, wallowed on the floor and managed to kick me in the groin.

"Don't you fuckin' tell me what to do, faggot," he bellowed, getting to his hands and knees, crawling toward the revolver by the toilet.

I held him back until Johnny picked up the gun and handed it to me. To Bud, I said: "Where's your pants? We're not sticking around for the cops to get here. We'll call your friend from the motel."

"What the fuck you think yer doin'?"

"Whether that slug is in you or not, I know where it came from."

"From that hemorrhoid Ward, I tole you."

"Using *my* Beretta, Bud. Just don't die on me." We grabbed some clothes that were lying around the dark apartment that was humid with perspired tequila, cordite, and bodily fluids. And on the floor, several ejected 9mm casings.

He gurgled on our way out and dropped a wad of phlegm at my feet.

"Welcome to frame city, faggot."

31

"I'm sorry about your car. I'll get the blood out, somehow, and I know you think I should have called the police." I was talking to Ladonna on the phone from a dingy double at the San José Motel on South Congress. Truman had just left. Salvador was out, a big bandaged heap, snoring under a sedative. Johnny was leaning heavily on his elbows on the other side of my bed, casting a big, troubled shadow on the wall. "What did Lasko say?"

"What do you think? He said you were in a lot of trouble. I still don't know how he found me."

"It doesn't matter. How many times has she called?"

"Just twice," she said. "I still don't think you did the right thing."

"The fact that she's been calling proves we did, I think," I said.

"Maybe she just misses you," said Ladonna. "You know where she is, I suppose. Are you going to call her back?"

"I don't have a choice."

"Well, go ahead. But call me back before you do anything else stupid."

I promised as I said good-bye. Then I dialed the 123 Club.

"Martin. Is that you?"

"Yes, Lorraine. What's going on?"

"I wouldn't tell him where you were staying, Martin. But I promised to get in touch with you." She hesitated, then said something that I didn't catch. There was something in her voice. Regret?

Ward's voice: "Fender, are you there?"

I said I was.

"Listen and listen good OK. The stakes have gone up. You bring the coke to me here at the club and I'll give you a little present."

"What might that be?"

"Your 9mm Beretta. Still smoking."

"Bud Salvador catch some slugs tonight, did he?"

"With your gun, Fender. Consider it a little voodoo to help your finger heal."

"Sounds like a helluva deal, Ward. You must have read this one in a Mickey Spillane."

"Believe it, Fender. It isn't fiction. Oh yeah, you want this cunt, you can have her too."

"All right, Ward. I'll take your deal. But I can't get the coke until Saturday night. You'll have to take a break from your grand opening festivities to do business."

"It's already Saturday and I'm gonna be busy, Fender. That's not a good time for me."

"It'll have to do. And this will square us, right?"

"Sure. I don't see why not."

"And Johnny, too. That's part of the deal."

"What're you consorting with that burn-out for, Fender?"

"You wouldn't understand."

"OK, OK. It'll work for me, I guess. You know, you don't have to make a big deal out of it. I don't hold grudges against fuckups like Johnny any more than I hold a grudge against a dog that pisses on my carpet."

"Yeah, right. So he'll be in tonight to handle the video and I'll be in sometime later to deliver the key."

"Wait a minute here, OK? Tell him to come in early in the evening. I've got the most sophisticated club video system in the country on line here. He'll have to come in early for a run-through."

"Will you be there?"

"I don't have to be. I've got managers for that kind of shit. Ricky will show him the ropes."

"You'd better mean that figuratively, Ward."

"Of course I do, Martin. Like break a leg."

"I don't like that, either."

"You're too sensitive is your problem," he said and hung up.

"He wants to give my gun back, all right," I told Johnny. I put the phone back on the rickety nightstand and lit a Camel.

"I hate this," said Johnny. "It doesn't seem real and we don't even have a damn thing to drink."

"Cheer up," I said, raising my glass of water, "you got a job."

"What the hell are you talking about?" said Johnny.

"You know, your VJ job at the Club 123. Aren't you supposed to be Mr. Hot Shot with videocassette systems and stuff? Aren't you supposed to be a cross between Einstein and Jesse James with a soldering iron?"

"Quit fucking with me, Martin," he complained. "You know I kept that old Bassman of yours working through all fifty states. Sometimes with nothing but a paperclip, some duct tape, and a prayer."

But I wasn't listening. I gave Johnny a look that seemed to scare him. "Johnny, can you hot-wire a couple of the cameras in Ward's office at the club?"

"Of course I can, man. Why?"

"I know you know what I'm thinking."

"I sure as hell don't. What are you talking about?"

"Just this: a simple live broadcast from Ward's office when I give him the coke. The whole thing has to be blown open right then. Because there's one thing I know for sure."

"Let me guess," said Johnny. "Either Ward leaves that office with a gun at his back or you leave it with one at yours."

"Yep," I said. "When you know everything, you know too much."

I looked up Lasko's home number in the phone book, then called him. He answered, his voice strained and his manner abrupt.

"Guess you think you're real cute. You've gone from bad to

worse in a big goddamn hurry. I'd like to know why we found your wallet in Bud Salvador's Ranchero and lots of blood in his apartment."

"Nobody home?"

"Nobody home," he answered, mockingly, "no body. Where you at?"

"Between a rock and a very hard place, Alaska. I've got Johnny, and I've got the big fish, or will have. I know you're pissed but you'll be glad when I get this worked out. You'll see. Meet me at the 123 Club grand gala tonight. And bring some of your friends from work. And some guys from the Texas Alcoholic Beverage Commission."

"They'll already be there. They always keep tabs on Ward's clubs."

"Bet they have tabs in them, too. Sorry I can't put you on the guest list, but I know you'll get your money's worth."

"Fender . . ."

"Says good-bye," I said, and hung up.

Then I called Ladonna. It was rough, trying to sound like everything was cool, everything worked out. I told her I'd talked to Lasko and that gave her a bit of relief, relief that was diminished when I said I didn't think it would be a good idea if I came over. Diminished even more when I asked her if she thought she could drive that rental van Johnny had stashed at his mother-in-law's house. We arranged to meet in the H.E.B. supermarket parking lot at four-thirty the next afternoon and work the rest of it out.

It was a screwy, unbalanced plot. It was as screwy and unbalanced as the people we were going to inflict it on. That was why, after Johnny and I talked some more, I took a cold shower and slept like a baby, knowing that it just might work.

32

"Oh man," rasped Johnny, squinting his eyes up at the ceiling. "I feel like I made a big mistake last night." He rubbed his eyes, then scooted up against the headboard. When he saw me, sitting on the armchair by the TV, he started to laugh. When he looked over at the other bed and saw Bud Salvador, swollen, whiskery, and bandaged, a look of horror came over Johnny's face.

"Then it wasn't a dream?" he said.

"Fuck no," belched Salvador.

"Bud's ready to cooperate," I said. "You'd better go on down to the club," I told Johnny.

"Man, I'm not feeling anywhere near ready yet," he protested.

"They'll have coffee down there," I said, slapping his leg. "You've got time for a shower if you make it snappy. I'll call a cab. And your beeper, Johnny. Is it at Ladonna's?"

"The batteries are dead."

"So she'll buy some new ones. She's going to need it."

He stumbled off to the bathroom moaning and mumbling pitifully. But fifteen minutes later he emerged, half-way slick again.

"Cab's waiting," I said. "You sure you can handle it down there?"

He nodded and said, "You'll be the first to know if I can't."

"That's very considerate of you. Make sure I can get in the back door and be ready at midnight."

He was at the door, his jacket under his arm, an unlit cigarette hanging from his lower lip. "What are you going to do, kiss me good-bye?"

"No," I said, going over and patting him on the cheek. "Let's do it, then."

"Do the do," he said. "You bet." And he went out.

I put my shoes on. Bud Salvador was quiet, almost somber in a seedy way. Before I left, I paused at the door and started to say something.

"Don't worry 'bout me," he growled. "I ain't goin' nowhere."

"Hi, Martin," said the animated young voice. "You left your guitar at our house."

It was Michael. Ladonna had brought Michael along.

He sat there between his mother and me in the front seat of the big Oldsmobile that belonged to Ladonna's mother. He had dark hair in a Beatle cut and Ladonna's huge, dark eyes. He wore a Los Lobos T-shirt and little blue jeans that were going to get their knees ripped out the next time he rode his skateboard. "Thanks for bringing it, Michael," I said.

"You're welcome," he said, innocent and proud as a six-year-old could be, knocking his tennis shoes together.

"I'm sorry about the Springsteen concert tonight," I said.

"It's OK," he said. "Grandma and Grandpa are going to take me."

Ladonna squeezed my hand. We'd already had our big kiss, when I first got there and saw the two of them waiting in the H.E.B. parking lot. "While I'm here I might as well pick up some charcoal and chicken and plan to barbecue Sunday afternoon," she said. "Do you think everything's going to turn out OK?"

I looked at her. She was cool and calm and not in the least bit naive. I'd be willing to bet that any of the single young professional upwardly mobile Volvo-driving guys she worked with would gladly take her up on any Sunday afternoon barbecue invitation and anything else she wanted to do, and she'd be able to depend on them following through with it. On the other hand, while they were out at the lake skiing or maybe playing tennis, I was here with her, planning something wild and unpredictable and vital as hell, and while their futures might be already printed out on their stock portfolios and their life insurance plans, I had a deep appreciation for velvet Elvis Presley paintings.

"Will you stop staring at my boobs long enough to tell me if you think things are going to turn out OK, Martin?"

"As long as we let the coals get white before we put that yardbird on the grill," I said. Michael leaned forward so I could kiss her. She didn't help any, but afterward the pursed lips began to take on a smile.

"I hope you know what you're doing," she said.

"I'm not so sure it would help if I did," I said. "Sure you can drive that van?" She nodded. "All right. Johnny will beep you when your part in the show comes up. I won't see you again until tonight at the club, and I don't think there's anything to worry about, but I want you to keep this within reach at all times."

"Martin, a gun?" Bud's revolver was big in her delicate hands. "It's heavy."

"Just in case."

"Martin, I'm not going to shoot anybody . . ."

"Unless you have to?"

"Or if they don't show up on Sunday and leave me with a bunch of leftover chicken."

"No jury in the world would convict you," I said.

And kissed her good-bye.

33

Echo Sound was a studio in the basement of an old brick produce warehouse on the East Side. The Budweiser clock on the wall said it was 5:05.

"Bob's setting up the automation track now," said Billy, who sat in a swivel chair behind the console. Bob, the assistant engineer, was leaning over the console, studying a fluctuating needle on a V.U. meter.

"There it is again," he said. "I don't know where that could be coming from, except your doctored-up drum track."

"What's the problem?" I asked.

Billy shrugged and said: "There's a couple of phantom drum beats on the recording I did out at the ranch, apparently. You could say that they add character and a human feel to it, or you could say . . ."

"It's a goddamn glitch and there doesn't seem to be anything we can do about it," said the assistant.

"Not a mistake on the master drummer's part?" I asked.

Billy chuckled. "Well, it's possible, but . . ."

"Is it on the original track?"

"One way to find out," said the assistant. "We've still got the original drum part here, on tracks 5, 6, 7, and 8. The 'effects' tracks with the hacienda room echo are 11 and 12. What we wanted to do is a sub mix of the natural tracks and the echo tracks."

"So why don't you pan the natural tracks over to the left side and the room echo tracks over to the right and we'll see what we've got," I said.

Bob turned to the board, made a couple of adjustments, cued up the tape, and let it roll. We sat and listened to the sounds coming out of the massive monitors.

The drum tracks were impressive. The natural tracks were aggressive in their execution, awesome in their tonality. The room echo was wild. The dancers at the trendy discos in town would really shimmy and shake to these sounds. The kick drum sounded like an elephant stomp, the snare like blasts from a rocket engine. At the end of a particular passage there was always a drum roll that sounded like a truckload of bowling balls dumped on a tin roof.

"There it is," said Bob. He stopped the tape and rolled it back. The three of us listened again, nodding in agreement: The phantom rim shot was only on the "echo" side.

"The next one is during this end section," he said, letting the tape roll on. And there it was. He rolled it back over the spot twice to make certain, but there was no doubt. Two glitches on the tape, both on the recording from the ranch house, one of them about ten minutes after the first.

"I can't wipe it without there being a blank spot on the echo track," said Bob. "We can add some digital delay there, maybe splice in another section of the tape."

"No splicing," said Billy. "Each verse of the song is different. I subtly changed the hi hat patterns as the song progressed, to give a feeling of momentum and climax. I never thought I'd run into a problem like this."

"That's a shame," I said.

"Let's give it a rest," said Billy. "Think it out. You guys want some pizza?"

Bob and Billy negotiated on what kind of pizza to order while I smoked a great deal and walked around the studio. It had an old, musty smell to it, and a lot of memories. My bass case, heavier than usual, was propped in the hallway by the racks of amplifiers that powered the monitors.

Bob was on the phone ordering the pizza, smoking one of Billy's Kools, twisting the cap off a fresh liter of diet soda.

"Billy," I said. "Do you remember what time you did this drum track at the ranch?"

"Of course," he said.

"You sound pretty certain."

"Martin, I'm a studio musician. I get paid by the hour, most times. You learn to watch the clock. Gets to be a habit."

"So you finished recording this track when Lorraine asked you if you could knock off for the night?"

"No," he said, flipping through one of those magazines you only see at recording studios, because no one anywhere else would get bored enough to read one. "The track is twelve minutes long. After I did this version, I listened to it one time all the way through on the speakers. That's when she came in and respectfully requested that I knock off."

I looked around the room. Things were getting clearer. The tape had the sounds, but it smelled like hot tape. The glitches sounded like muffled gunshots, but the smell in that room hadn't smelled exactly like them.

"Thanks, Billy," I said. "I'll have to come back on Monday and do the bass part. That all right with you?"

"Sure. I'd rather do it sooner, but I can wait. Aren't you going to stick around and have some pizza?"

"No. I've got to go buy some firecrackers. Would you make me a dub of that drum track? Sorry about the glitches, but I wish you'd leave it alone. I think it has real personality."

"Sure, I'll run you off a copy. That was what I was hoping you'd say. It's gonna stay the way it is, glitches and all. You get an idea for something like that, it's a shot in the dark, you go with what you get or shit-can it. No guts, no glory."

I was already up the studio stairs, door open, bright early evening sun and hot breeze pouring down the dark stairwell that I left behind. I got in the car and followed I-35 north to 290, got off and headed east till I spotted a fireworks stand. I bought a couple of bucks worth of Black Cats, turned around, and drove back the way I came.

I stopped at a roadside rest stop and practiced an old trick, one that had been around as long as firecrackers and cigarettes had been around. But I got no satisfaction out of it past the first time, and quit while I still had some cigarettes left.

So I took off and drove some more, squinting at the skyline, wondering how the Tonkewa saw the area when they lived here, sixteen thousand years ago. And I drove by the Erwin Center, looking like a giant concrete drum, where people were paying fifty, a hundred, two hundred bucks to scalpers to watch performers that looked the size of ants in a room with the acoustics of a giant concrete drum.

My bass was in the hot back seat, bouncing around, with a kilo of cocaine inside that was bound to be getting too gummy to put up your nose without a mortar trowel.

I finally circled back and ended up at the studio again. Bob and Billy were washing down the last slice of pizza when I came down the dank staircase. I shut the soundproof inner door behind me, set the bass down on the ratty couch in the control room, and said:

"I got nowhere else to go."

34

The song was easy. The drums seemd to dictate a melody of
their own and I just played off of them. I kept the idea simple
and lean in the key of E. Once we had the basic idea laid out,
I went in and put down a rough track. The feeling was there,
the tone and levels were perfect, and we all liked first takes,
so we called it a keeper and I went back and punched in the
rough spots.

Meanwhile Frankie had arrived and brought a six-pack. We
listened to the playback and liked it. Frankie was scat-singing
a melody and Bob mimed a guitar part. Someone asked: "What
do we call it?"

I said, "How about 'Betrayal'?"

It was a keeper. That was about seven.

We killed about all the time there was to kill between then and
midnight. When I left there, the stars were twinkling overhead
and the air was almost cool, though it had a damp, used feel
to it. In my pocket was a cassette of the rough mix of the
complete song. On the B side was the stereo drum track. Pretty
soon I was listening to it through the Walkman headphones,
driving up Congress Avenue. I circled the capitol grounds once,
then headed over to the club.

Sixth Street, from the Mid City Roadhouse and Waterworks
Hot Tub Rental at Waller Creek, to the Driskill Hotel on Bra-
zos, was a honking, cruising, partying mass of humanity, almost
all of it under thirty. At least half were under twenty-one. You
couldn't walk more than ten steps without being at the door of

a new place to get drunk and you couldn't walk more than two without running into someone who'd just stumbled out of one. Street musicians, magicians, panhandlers, frat rats, yuppies, fajita vendors. Break dancers, tourists, punk rockers posing in front of the Ritz, cops. The smell of Giorgio, vomit, sex. Music from *The Big Chill*, patronized by people who didn't remember the day Kennedy died.

The line stretched from the front entrance of the 123 around the block. A six foot transsexual stood glaring at the faces of the hopeful like a Marine drill sergeant, prolonging the humiliation of those on the wrong side of the velvet rope. Two buffaloes with suits and little pig eyes stood by the entrance. One looked like his mother had just died, the other looked like a possible reason. The facade of the club had no sign or marquee advertising its identity—the ultimate in chic anon.

I parked in the alley behind the club, next to the kitchen entrance of Jorge's Enchilada Bar. The alley reverberated from the blitzkrieg inside the disco. I pulled the bass case out of the back seat, locked up, and knocked on the back door.

A hatchet-faced kid with a flattop regarded me with indifference through the crack he opened in the door. I held the bass case up and pointed at the name plate. He nodded and I was inside.

It was wild. From the entrance at the back, you could see all three levels, making the view a triple decker sandwich. Strobes and flashes of pastels went on and off, giving brief snapshots of a sea of flesh—waving arms, leather, lipstick, drinks, bright orange blurs from dancing cigarettes, faces with open mouths and half-open eyes. There had to be thousands of people just on the dancefloors.

A few minutes later, the doorman ushered me into a men's room around the corner. I went inside. It was a one-stall outfit, probably there to service the employees, I figured. I didn't need to use the facilities, and there was no one else in there, so I went over to the mirror, dropped the tire iron out of my sleeve, laid it on the sink, and got out my comb. Only it wasn't a mirror. Set in a chrome frame just below a tilted camera lens, it was a video monitor. The glass tile walls, girls dancing in cages outside and chrome toilet seats weren't enough for him, he had to have TVs instead of mirrors. I combed my hair.

"Shouldn't use that greasy kid stuff, Martin," said a voice from the monitor. Then my face was replaced by the chiselled-out cheeks and weak grin of the club owner, eyes wide open and full of cathode-like energy. "Did you bring it?"

I blinked my eyes and glowered at the screen, unhappy with the way my reflection was superimposed on top of his, or was his just bubbling underneath mine? Ward was sitting behind the glass-topped desk again next to those birds of paradise.

"I did," I said. "But you try to take it away from me now and there's gonna be a snow storm inside the 123 Club, Ward. I swear I'll rip the bag open and toss it up for a free throw."

"Now why would I do that, Martin? You don't think I want to keep your little blow dryer here, do you?" The screen flickered and focused on the Beretta, a gun I had never fired since buying. It was doing a great job of protecting me. I'd have to write *Guns and Ammo* and give them a testimonial. "I'll have it brought down to you, OK?"

"No way. If I wanted to watch TV I'd have stayed home. I'm coming up."

"You are such a hothead, Martin," said the video screen. "Just follow the stairs around the corner. The office is in the same place it used to be."

It was a nice office if you like gun metal gray and bloodless pink, if you like sound-proofed rooms quiet as the inside of a pillow, if you aren't picky about the company you keep. The charcoal gray carpet made no noise as I walked across it, and no expressions changed on the mottled face of the wiry man behind the desk in the unconstructed suit with too-padded shoulders or the big redhead poured into a chaise lounge, zebra-striped stockings on the long substantial legs, a noose of pearls at her throat, a hugely oversized shiny black shirt draped over her torso like the flag of some defeated nation.

It didn't bother me that the only sounds the music empire

made here were the pearls clicking around the redhead's neck and the clinking ice in the glasses an anemic girl in a yellow microskirt outfit brought in behind me. She distributed the drinks and was gone.

"Sit down, Martin," said Ward. "Cheers."

At least four, maybe five, Wards drank their drinks in the bank of video monitors behind the original—profiles, rear shots (that included me, now sitting down, drink in hand), and three-quarters—their Adam's apples moving as they gulped, their lips smacking a little too much to be just tasting a cocktail. Other monitors showed views of the club, the street scene outside, rock videos, and a vintage gangster movie.

I tested my drink. Cape Cods are not my favorite beverage. Lorraine was staring at a corner of the room somewhere behind me.

The gun was no longer in sight.

"Have you decided to come work for me, then?" he said abruptly.

"If I did, I'd really get her?" I said. The video screen images danced behind him, and I scanned them for signs of Johnny. People partying, dim corpuscles awash in seas of light and phony and real smoke, the videos, the movies, the awful quietness around us, but no VJ named Johnny.

"Hey baby, what do you think? You want this dude?" He flicked his hand at her, limpwristed and silly. She was still poured in the chaise, sultry and silent.

"Martin," he said through curled lips, "since I get the coke now," shrugging, "I don't see why she'd want anything to do with you." Pause. I spotted Johnny in one of the screens. He had a VHS tape in one hand and a drink in the other. It looked like a Bloody Mary. He was wearing a headset and his Ray Bans, smoking a cigarette. A few feet away from him, a DJ was cueing up discs on a set of CD units. Ward said, "Speaking of it, let's have it."

I tripped the latches on the bass case at my feet, pulled out the big bag and tossed it on the desk where it landed with a light thud. It seemed like something that had caused so much trouble should make more noise. "There you go," I said. "Now where's the gun you plugged Bud Salvador with?"

He reached inside his jacket and put the gun down on the corner of the desk. "He got weird on me, Martin, OK? He said you implied that I was trying to put him in the hot seat when I used his corporation on the land deal."

"Too bad you didn't have my gun when you deleted the critics," I said. "That would have at least made everything consistent."

"I was in a rush then, Martin. Things came together rather suddenly and unexpectedly." He administered more of his drink, crunching more ice as he spoke. "But I think that it's worked out OK for everybody, considering. Lucky for me, Lorraine and I got together. I didn't see why I should have to be out the fourteen grand on the reunion gig and she didn't see why she had to lose the coke her old man ripped off from me. So we worked it out. You think that's funny, I bet."

"Not as funny as your suit. Go on."

"Always a sarcastic bastard, Martin," he crowed. "That's OK. Where has it gotten you? In a bad spot. Like those writers. Look man—they couldn't hold on to a simple deal I handed them on a silver platter, they didn't deserve the land deal, either. Maybe I'm too aggressive but the way I see it, Jake would have taken care of them anyway, and by getting it over with, I was able to scoop up the option on Noon Street and keep my investors off my back. Bruce Springsteen and Prince cost me almost three million bucks, Martin. They're greedy, man. Adding those dates wiped me out. I couldn't just let my ticket operation go down the tubes and it's a dog eat dog world, Martin. And I'm a hungry dog, right babe?"

He winked at the redhead. She looked tired. Her nose was red, her cheeks puffy like an infant's. She crossed her legs, then put them back the way they'd been. Drank some of her drink, got more lipstick on the glass.

"You're a swell guy, Ward," I said. "I can see why she goes for you."

"Hey," he said, "I'm not that bad, OK? You know those

guys totally bullshitted me? Said they needed ten grand for a little real estate deal. Didn't say anything about their little secret—about how they knew the city council was going to make the land worth a couple of hundred times the original value by rezoning it. But do I hold a grudge? I actually offered them a sweet deal. I said, keep the kilo, OK, just let me have the land option and I'll give you ten grand on top of that when I make a deal. And they said—you know what they said?—they said screw yourself. *Screw yourself.* Can you believe it? Ha!" He laughed hard, the noise a dry, choking sound. "It's a good setup, Martin. All I've got arc investors, hundreds of them. Now I need a new corporation, with Bud being dead and all. Victim of a drug war, right? Nothing ties me to it and that's important if I'm going to keep the scene flowing around here."

He spun around in his swivel chair, grinning at the monitors. "Look at them. Christ, it's beautiful," he said. "Suckers, god I love them. Investors in *me.* All those years running those dives, those pissholes, dodging the TABC, the IRS, putting up with musicians' egos and critics' full-of-shitness. *Fuck* them. Fuck them *all.* Every *one* of those cockroaches down there is giving me a money transfusion every day. Fuck everybody!"

"Ward."

"Fuck everybody. I love it. Fuck you, too. You might wanna wash that gun off before you stick it in your pants. It's got pussy juice on it." He spun around and leered at the redhead. "Right, babe? She says it's the best thing you got."

I held myself back no longer. I slammed the tire iron down on the glass desk top, shattering it into a million chunks and shards and pieces as beautiful to me as diamonds. The noise was good. I liked it. The birds of paradise were scattered on the floor now, the Beretta lying ineffectual on the charcoal carpet, the cocaine bag and everything around him showered with broken glass. The redhead had dropped her drink.

The clubowner's skinny legs twitched, looking sick and vulnerable now that he sat behind a desk that was no longer there, just a slim black framework that was less than a shell. His drink was still in his hand, but it couldn't seem to find his lips.

"What the hell's wrong with you, Martin? I can't fucking believe you."

"You've got nothing, Ward." I waved my steel wand in front of his face. "Your little kingdom is going down the toilet. You needed that five million dollars to cover one day's losses, the way I figure it. If you can make a million on one concert in one city and all of a sudden you get dates added the next day, your tickets are nothing but a liability, right? Unless you buy up the next date, too. So the way I figure it, you needed five million so bad that it didn't even make a dent in your problems. Or a dent in your greed. You're a tick full of blood, Ward. You don't even know when to stop sucking. That's why you wanted the coke so bad. You couldn't stand to see somebody get it for free."

"Wrong, Martin," he snorted, jerking his head at the girl. "She wanted it. She figures her old man owned it when he started jamming with the maggots and she needs it. So I promised I'd get it for her to show what an ineffectual faggot you really are. She thought you were some kind of perpetual hard-on there for awhile." He crossed the spasmodic legs and tugged on his jacket and said, "And both of us had a problem with Johnny. But he's not gonna be a problem any longer. Take your damn gun and bass and get out of here, OK."

She opened her mouth and started to speak. "Martin, I . . ."

"Get out of here before I turn the security monitors back on, Martin."

"Have you told her yet that you can't even afford to let her have this kilo? Have you told her that the drink she just spilled was catered by Alamo catering because you don't even have the cash for the deposit on your liquor license?"

"*Fuck* you, man. Just get out of here."

And she, she was looking more and more uneasy. Her elbows weren't holding her up as well as they'd been and she looked less like she'd been poured into that piece of furniture and more like she'd backed herself into it.

"And what's more, U-Haul is on your ass for not bringing that van back," I said.

"Fuck you, man, that's your pal Johnny's fuck-up. One of many, I might add."

"Let me finish. You might be glad to know that I'm willing to pay the bill on that, as part of our deal."

"What deal, Martin? You're out of here. You're history. You're some kind of maniac. You, well, you might as well know—"

"What, Ward? Go ahead. Go ahead and scare me to death."

"OK, Martin. You're carp food. You're walking around dead but you don't have the sense to lay down. I got boys at the bottom of the stairs. In case you get past them, there're guys at each bar, at all three exits. They're big fans of yours—they'd know you any day—but I'm the one who pays them."

"No, Ward. You don't pay anybody after tonight, except for a lawyer. This game show has just begun." I gave Johnny the thumb's up. He made the phone call to Ladonna's beeper. I went on, taking pleasure from the strange look on Ward's face. "Take a look at that video screen in the second row, showing the corner of the club at 6th and San Jacinto." Using the tire iron as a pointer, I had their attention, or the video screen did, anyway. Ladonna was standing at the back of the rental van, seductively pointing out the curves and features of the vehicle, shiny as a nickel-plated gun under the street light. Like a hostess on a game show, she had dressed for the part—silver lamé miniskirt, go-go boots, and sequined stretch top. Her hair was in a pony tail, and big thick bangs framed her big brown eyes.

"How about it, Ward?" I said. "What a deal. I know it's a rental, probably got over a hundred thousand hard miles on it. It's knee-deep in rubber though, and I've got the keys."

"Fuck you, Martin," he said. "What's your problem?"

"Well, I can't keep it a secret any longer. Remember that silly idea you had when you gobbled too many quaaludes, when you made the critics steal something before they'd get this coke?" Ladonna fingered the door handle, smiling coyly.

"But wait, there's more," I said breathily. I quickly lit a cigarette as my assistant down on the street unlocked the doors and let them swing open wide.

The domelight was on inside, shining down on the Texter-minator bug. One of the eye lights was broken, one of the glass wings cracked, and the yellow nylon rope was still fastened around him between the head and thorax, like a leash. He wasn't much the worse for wear. The same couldn't be said for Bud Salvador, astride the bug like a rodeo cowboy but slumped over in the saddle from too much Rebel Yell. The back of his undershirt was black with dried blood. Then he moved. He raised up his head, smiled a grotesque smile, and pointed his finger at the camera. *Gotcha,* he mouthed.

"Oh, you're sick, Fender," hissed the clubowner. "Oh god. A sick motherfucker, OK. Oh god. What's the idea?" he poked at rows of buttons underneath the monitors but the scene did not change.

"What's the idea planting my wallet in his car? I thought we were going to have a deal."

"You could explain your way out of that, you prick. I'll take care of Bud. Just tell me what you want, OK? Just tell me what you want."

"Oh, a fleet of Karmann Ghias. A dozen or more Fender Precisions, preferably pre-CBS, black, with maple necks. A rent-free, roach-free apartment. Fifty thousand bucks."

"Fifty thousand? Are you nuts? I'm only offering a hundred dollar bonus to the guy who bumps you off."

My drink was starting to taste better. I took a sip and puffed on my cigarette. "I'll be reasonable, though. You can give it to me in stock. Surely you've got some of those bond contracts lying around."

He nodded his head, mumbled something. Knocked his knees together as some pieces of glass fell off his pants, gobbled his drink, and set it down by the monitors without looking up at them. Too bad. The Wards in the video screens seemed to be talking to themselves as he opened a drawer in the wall and pulled out a folder, spun back around, and pulled out a form and began scratching on it with a gold pen.

There was a sound. Like a baby coughing, I thought at first. Then more like twigs being rubbed together. I looked at the redhead. She wasn't making any noise by chewing her nails and looking collapsed. It was the clubowner. He was laughing. He handed me the piece of paper.

I took it. It was what I wanted. A bond certificate issued by the Futura Corporation.

"You know, Martin, I almost like you. You're crazy. You're completely unhinged, man."

"I know." The tire iron was still a cold weight in my hand. I wondered how hard I would have to swing it to crush his skull.

"Really, Martin. That's good for ten thousand bucks now, fifty thousand in six months. I guess you deserve it. Now take it or leave it and get out of here and take that van and that cunt downstairs with it."

"You're such a charmer, Ward," I said. "You'd stick a shovel up your mother's ass if you thought there was some money in it. I just want you to understand that this doesn't make us partners."

"Of course it doesn't."

"I want to be your agent, is what I want."

"Quit clowning, Fender, before I send for my boys."

"I don't think they'd come, Ward. They're enjoying the show too much," I said, pointing to the monitors.

"Get outta here, I'm telling you," he said, glancing over his shoulder. On some of the screens, his images turned and looked back and looked over their shoulders. On others, customers down below stood in motionless clots on the dancefloor, as motionless as the CD players and the DJ, watching the drama unfold in the gun metal gray and dead pink office.

"What the fuck . . ." he stammered. Blinking his eyes. "What the fuck is going *on* around here?"

"Look down there, Ward. The last two screens in the corner," I said, indicating the bar on the top level, where, standing next to a couple of discount-suited stonefaces and a punk rocker with a crew cut, was a homicide detective with a beard and beer gut. Then his badge filled the screen, held up to the camera lens by a big hairy hand with a high school ring on it. The men next to Lasko, judging from their taste in suits and no-fun attitude, where from the all-powerful Texas Alcoholic Beverage Commission.

Some of the faces on the screens were laughing, others trying to figure out if it were a put-on show or real life. Others just watched with no expression at all.

Ward just shook his head, not saying anything, his mouth chewing on itself. He was looking at a monitor focused on Johnny, sitting in the VJ booth, grining ear-to-ear, holding up his Bloody Mary in one hand, using the celery garnish to point out a pair of video cassette recorders, their recording light indicators a precious red.

Soon the room was full of policemen. They scooped up the coke bag and cuffed Ward. Their utility belts and gruff voices clashed mercilessly with the pastels and high tech decor, their box-toed shoes crunched on the broken glass. They read him his rights and asked me to come downtown with them. Lasko alternately worked a cocktail straw around in his mouth and gave instructions to the officers. The video screens went dead.

They gradually cleared out. I told Alaska I'd be right down. He said there would be people waiting outside the door to make sure I didn't forget. Lorraine got slowly out of the lounge chair, came over to me and buried her head in my shoulder, chewing on my neck between whimpers.

35

"You must think I'm bad," she sobbed. "You must think I'm awful."

Her arms were squeezing hard, her breasts heavy, squashed up against me. The pearls hurt where they came between us. It was hot and wet where she breathed on my neck, repeating herself, waiting for me to say something.

"Don't cry," I said. "Get a hold on yourself. Here, have a cigarette." I gave her a Camel, but didn't try to light it. I put one between my lips, then asked if she had a match.

"I think there were some on the desk." She looked around on the floor, and among the scattered flowers and broken glass, found a box. "Here," she said, striking one.

I let her light both cigarettes before letting the third one fall out of the pack into my palm, with the firecracker fastened to it by a scrap of duct tape. "Here," I said, "one of your brand . . . three on a match. It's bad luck, you know. Just like that night." I took her hand and held the flame to it, got it going, and blew the smoke in her face.

"Martin, don't be weird. What's gotten into you?"

"You did, and that was the problem. The shot that killed KC, and the one you fired to get gunpowder on his hand are on Billy's tape. You crawled into bed with me to be sure I'd be awake and you told Billy to quit playing, went to your room to get those beers that had gotten warm and to set up this little time bomb, this little junior high school prank."

She didn't deny it. She puffed on the cigarette and pouted. "It was an accident."

"Both shots?" I was tempted to laugh.

"No. He wasn't going to do the gig. He was burned out. I asked him what he planned to do with himself then and he said he might as well just put his gun to his head and pull the trigger. I said, go ahead, you don't have the balls for it. We got in a fight. It was a bad one. Really disgusting. There's no way to win a fight like that. I shot him." Another puff on the cigarette. "He really pissed me off," she pouted.

"I suppose you and your new boyfriend thought it was pretty funny," I said, "watching me running around trying to find this kilo and all the while trying to slip a frame on me for the critics' kill. You were the only person who knew I was going to visit the critics so you called Ward and he beat me there, then waited at Neil's and knocked me on the head so the police would find me and pin it on me."

"I didn't know he took your wallet," she said.

"That doesn't really do a lot for me."

She slumped down in the chair in front of where the desk used to be and cupped her chin in her hand. The broken glass crunched under my feet as I moved around. I thought back on seeing her naked for the first time, and it sent a chill through me, but for different reasons that it did then.

"Why'd you do it?" I said. "How could you be so dumb as to show me parts of how you killed KC and then try to use them as clues so I could try to pin it on someone else?"

"Dumb? You're calling *me* dumb? Ha. That's a laugh. it worked for awhile, didn't it? I *liked* you, Martin. I really did. I guess you think I used you. You're right. At first I thought the coke would be easy to find. I figured KC just hid it under our bed at home, like he had at the ranch. He was usually so fucking predictable. Well, I was wrong. So I figured you'd want to help me, so you could get over your guilty conscience. I was right, and there's still no way you can prove I pulled KC's trigger."

"Oh, man . . ."

"You guys think you're so cool, with your hard-ons and your guitars, driving all over the country, letting little naive girls suck your cock, grinding their fuzzy young pussies in your face. You stay up all night and brag about this and that and drink till you fall down or get in a fight then the next day you're all swollen up and you look like shit and expect me to cook breakfast for you. Well I like the way coke makes me feel so cold and numb and tingly and, you know, I just don't give a damn. I wake up in the middle of the night and he's not there and I used to feel lonely but I got over that. You guys think you're so cool. KC wouldn't lick my pussy. He said it smelled bad. Well I found 345 guys in the last six years, not counting you, that thought it smelled just fine . . ."

The firecracker in my hand went off with a nasty little bang.

She jumped. My hand was one numb shaking thing on the end of my arm. I can't say I didn't let it happen on purpose. The heavy door swung open the rest of the way and the cops were back in the room.

"Oh, Jesus," I mumbled, to no one in particular.

"You bastards," she hissed. "You don't know what it's like to be a woman. You don't know what it's like to be alone."

They were gentle when they put the handcuffs on her.

There was a small crowd out on the sidewalk watching the goings-on. Lasko took Lorraine and helped her into the back of a blue and white. Then that car sped away and there was only the crowd, one of the blue and whites, and Ladonna DiMascio walking over to me next to Bud Salvador.

Ladonna put an arm around me and hugged. She looked at Bud and smiled a timid smile.

"How I do?" he asked.

"Great screen test," I said. "Ward thinks you play dead better than Robert Mitchum."

"Fenner, I been shot four times, twice by wives," he said. "I know when to dive, when to play dead. I hope this' the last." He was still wearing the blood-soaked undershirt.

I moved my head up and down. It was hard to believe it was over.

"One thing though, Fenner," he said. "Next time we do this

you're gonna have to put us up in a higher class motel. Walls are paper thin at the San José. Couple checked in next door this afternoon for a twenty dollar honeymoon—a-blowin' an' a-goin' for six hours' straight an' I never did get no sleep," he said, scratching his crotch.

"See you around, Bud. We're going to the police station, and I suppose you are, too." I watched him walk his splay-footed walk over to one of the policemen, then I turned to Ladonna. "You were good, too. Better than Vanna White."

"Martin . . ."

"Just kidding. Much better. Where's Johnny?"

"They took him away already, Martin. Conspiracy to distribute, some other charges, too."

36

It was Monday afternoon again. The weather people were predicting rain, and later they'd turn out to be right. Meanwhile, it was the worst of both worlds, because the unreleased moisture in the air weighted it down like a steaming blanket.

We were standing around the Tavern parking lot, across from the Texterminators International Pest Control building. Lasko, Ladonna, Michael, and I were looking at the bug, re-installed on his throne, making his counter-clockwise rounds. The drooping antennae, the blinking red eyes, the glass wings and stinger looked just like they always had.

"Well it's good to see him back up there," said Lasko, squinting behind a pair of shades. "You know, when I was in college, we used to do acid and come down here and hallucinate on him."

"Don't get Big Chill on us, Alaska," I said. "I have enough trouble remembering you're a cop, without being reminded you used to be a hippie."

"I was never a hippie, Fender," he protested. "You're such a right-wing cowboy. Ladonna, did you see this guy on that video? Looked like a cross between Perry Mason and Elvis Presley from *Kid Creole*."

She laughed. Sitting on one of the Ghia's fenders in her capri pants and tight pink T-shirt cut off ragged and short, showing off a perfect navel. Michael, wearing a brand new Bruce Springsteen souvenir T-shirt and miniature Ray Bans, leaned against her, using her knees as an armrest. "You're not having flashbacks, are you?" she asked.

"It's lucky for us," he said, "that the Feds and the Securities Exchange Commission are getting involved in this case, Martin. Selling unregistered bonds is very much against the law, you know, and that's the most solid thing we've got on the guy, but we got it on video. We had twenty more of his investors call since this morning. We figure he's in hock to the tune of well over ten mil. Maybe fifteen."

"It's so hard to believe," said Ladonna. "How could anybody act like they did, killing people, acting like that's the way you get things done? Like it was so normal that no one would suspect them or come after them."

"Skewed perspective," I said. "Lorraine lied to me so much my head was spinning. When you lie that much, you get good at it. Maybe even good enough to fool yourself. Ward was a pro, too, though he should have known better than to tell himself his house of cards hadn't been blown away. He probably just stayed up all night one too many times."

"That makes sense," said Lasko, watching the cars go by, not much tone or conviction in his voice.

"No, it doesn't," I said. "It's a load of crap."

"Then why'd you say it?" asked Ladonna.

But I didn't have to explain myself. A pink Cadillac Fleetwood coasted up and two men jumped out. Ladonna squeezed my arm as we realized it was Johnny and Jack, her little friend who'd been a big help at the secretary of state's office.

"You make bail already?" asked Lasko, incredulous. "I thought they wanted to keep you in the shade for awhile."

"No," beamed Johnny. He made the rounds, pumping hands and giving Ladonna a big hug. He and Michael went through a ritual soul brother grip. "I told them I wanted to get some sun today, go out and take a walk in my yard."

"What yard?" I said.

"The prison yard?" said Lasko.

"It's been a long day," said Jack. "But it's been very interesting." He was grinning, wearing a gimme cap and the wrap-around shades, his hands in the pockets of faded jeans. "You know, when Ladonna told me Johnny's real name it rang a bell. I spent all day Saturday at the Texas History Center and over at the State Archives. We just came back from a meeting with the state attorney general's office and the D.A."

"Well?"

"You see," he said, resting one tennis shoe on the bumper of my car, "there's this land that the state of Texas claims now, about fifteen hundred acres. A man named Sam Goucher patented it back when Texas was a republic, but some of the paperwork got messed up. By the time the title got straightened out in 1840, a big parcel of land that included Goucher's tract had been given away by the land office. But later on, a court ruled in his favor."

He looked around the group to see if we were following him. A busboy came out of the Tavern kitchen and dumped some trash in the dumpster.

I made a guess: "So Johnny inherited some land?"

"Sort of," he said. He pushed the cap back on his head, wiping his eyes with a bandana. "Damn it's hot."

"It ain't the heat," said Johnny, strutting around with a new importance beyond just getting sprung from jail, "it's the humidity. Go on, Jack."

Jack cleared his throat. "So Goucher had legal title, but most of his family were killed in an Indian raid in 1838. Three family members came forward later and said they'd only been kidnapped. One of them sold his share of the claim, but two of the surviving daughters never did anything about theirs."

He pushed the cap back again, this time completely off his head, fanning it to dry the sweat. He winked at Johnny, who looked like he was about to explode. He wanted to be the one to tell us, but Jack had the floor. "One of those daughters was Johnny's great-great grandmother. Some legal authorities contend that Johnny's claim would be void at this point in time, but there are plenty of others who could argue that Johnny has a real valid claim."

"Well, where is it? Is there a house on it? Is it Barton Springs, Pemberton Heights?" I wanted to know. Maybe Johnny owned a shopping mall.

He chuckled. "Some of U.T. was built on the land, and that pink granite building over there with the double dome and the ugly lady holding the star."

Nobody said anything. For a second, even the traffic and the planes overhead seemed to come to a halt.

"Johnny owns the Capitol?" shrieked my favorite Italian. "The Capitol of the state of Texas?"

"My Capitol," said Johnny, radiating pride. A grin as wide as Congress Avenue, as cool as Town Lake.

"You gotta be kidding," said Lasko. "You gotta be bullshitting."

Jack was certain. And smug. He didn't even have to nod his head, which he'd smashed the cap back down on.

"Does that mean you can pay me back the twenty you owe me?" I asked. They laughed.

"Now just hold on a damn minute," said Johnny. "All this means is that we got some special consideration for my case. Certain parties agreed to ignore certain things, to overlook things that are coming out of the Ward investigation."

"Like trafficking cocaine?" said Lasko.

Johnny shrugged, but yes was the intended message.

"You're damn lucky," I said.

"The police are lucky, the way I see it," said Jack. "Johnny was so willing to cooperate, he started spilling his guts before they got a chance to read him his rights."

"Miranda luck," said Lasko.

"Lucky my ass," bellowed Johnny. "If my great-great grandmother or anybody after her would've done something about it a long time ago, I'd probably have grown up in Pemberton Heights or Westover or maybe even Paris, France. I might be governor. I might have a street or two named after me, be Old Money."

"Instead of Owed Money," I added.

"Come on, gimme a break," he pleaded. "I could be going

to prison instead of being out here sweating my ass off with you guys who're just being a pain in the ass." He pulled his sunglasses off, shaking his head and squinting at us in mock disgust.

"Oh, that reminds me," said Lasko. "Fender, here's your wallet." He tossed it to me. "Better keep better tabs on it from now on."

"Thanks," I said. I gave Ladonna a squeeze and walked around to the passenger side of my car and opened her door for her and her son, saying, "Dinner?"

Michael ran around to the side and hopped in the back seat. Ladonna slid off the fender, kissed Johnny, Jack, and Lasko on their cheeks, and got in. I gave the men the thumbs up sign, and they winked at me. Things were working out.

"Martin," she said, squeezing my arm, about to say something that was meant only for me.

"Save it," I said. "Make it last."

"Till morning?" she said.

"Why put a time limit on it?" I said. She liked that. "Where do you two want to go—Basil's, the Vogue, Green Pastures? Somewhere nice, with candles on the tables, waiters who unfold your napkin for you, and all that?"

"Oh, Martin, are you sure you can afford it? You spent an awful lot of money last night."

"Don't worry, darlin'," I said. "I've got a three thousand dollar check coming from the Texterminator people, and I should have George Garret's two hundred dollars here in my . . ." I stopped in mid-sentence as I opened my wallet. Inside was a lone twenty and an I.O.U. for two hundred.

Lasko came over and put his hand on my shoulder. "I'm sorry, pal," he said. "But, man, the other night I palmed those c-notes. I didn't feel too good about taking them but I was pissed at you."

"I hope you feel lots better now."

"Don't be that way, Fender. I still wanna talk to you about giving me some bass lessons. I'll pay you back on payday, and we can talk about it." We shook hands, two men who owed each other. He went back to the other two and continued a heated discussion over where to go for margaritas.

"I can't believe it," I said. I fired up the car and pulled up to the intersection, waiting for a break in the traffic. The bug maintained slow surveillance with blinking eyes and unchanging expression. "Is this how the world goes around, everybody borrowing the same money from each other? People get killed that way."

"You're externalizing your feelings on the situation, Martin," she said. Her voice was calm, her tone resonant with logic. "It isn't that big of a deal, and Lasko isn't crazy. That's the difference."

"People who wear shirts like that aren't normal," I said, turning down the night blinder on the rear view mirror so I didn't have to see Lasko's brilliant day-glo Hawaiian tent. Michael caught my eye and I winked at him. Cars kept lurching by, bumper to bumper, like frogs in heat. I offered her a Camel, stuck another one in my mouth and pushed in the dash lighter. "I don't suppose you'd settle for an OT Special and an order of onion rings at Dirty's."

"Let's go someplace nice, Martin. We deserve it. We'll go out to eat then back to my place and, you know, like last night, after the barbecue? That was fun. And you can leave your bass in its case until your finger heals."

"I can't do that," I said. "But I promise not to let it get in the way. I'll keep it under the bed."

"Maybe you'll write some songs," she said.

"Maybe. Sure you won't settle for a cheeseburger?"

"Can I have a cheeseburger, Mom?" said Michael.

"No, you guys. We deserve something special. And Martin— you, of all people, should know that Dirty's is closed on Mondays."

"I know, but . . ."

"Don't worry, I'll buy," she said. "You guys can drive and open my doors and light my cigarettes."

"Lucky," I said. And she knew I meant it.

The lighter popped out on cue, smelling like burned flesh. She wrinkled her nose as I lit our cigarettes.

I popped the clutch and we were on our way.

"I'll get a new lighter," I said.

But I never did.

FREE FROM DELL

with purchase plus postage and handling

Congratulations! You have just purchased one or more titles featured in Dell's Mystery 1990 Promotion. Our goal is to provide you with quality reading and entertainment, so we are pleased to extend to you a limited offer to receive a selected Dell mystery title(s) *free* (plus $1.00 postage and handling per title) for each mystery title purchased. Please read and follow all instructions carefully to avoid delays in your order.

1) Fill in your name and address on the coupon printed below. No facsimiles or copies of the coupon allowed.

2) The Dell Mystery books are the only books featured in Dell's Mystery 1990 Promotion. No other Dell titles are eligible for this offer.

3) Enclose your original cash register receipt with the price of the book(s) circled plus $1.00 **per book** for postage and handling, payable in check or money order to: Dell Mystery 1990 Offer. Please do not send cash in the mail.
Canadian customers: Enclose your original cash register receipt with the price of the book(s) circled plus $1.00 **per book** for postage and handling in U.S. funds.

4) This offer is only in effect until April 29, 1991. Free Dell Mystery requests postmarked after April 22, 1991 will not be honored, but your check for postage and handling will be returned.

5) Please allow 6-8 weeks for processing. Void where taxed or prohibited.

Mail to: Dell Mystery 1990 Offer
        P.O. Box 2081
        Young America, MN 55399-2081

NAME_____

ADDRESS_____

CITY_____STATE_____ZIP_____

BOOKS PURCHASED AT_____

AGE_____

(Continued)

Book(s) purchased:_____

_____

_____

I understand I may choose one free book for each Dell Mystery book purchased (plus applicable postage and handling). Please send me the following:

(Write the number of copies of each title selected next to that title.)

BLOOD SHOT
Sara Paretsky
V.I. Warshawski is back—this time a missing person assignment turns into a murder investigation that puts her more than knee-deep in a deadly mixture of big business corruption and chemical waste.

FIRE LAKE
Jonathan Valin
In this Harry Stoner mystery, the Cincinnati private eye enters the seamy and dangerous world of drugs when a figure from his past involves him in a plot that forces him to come to terms with himself.

THE HIT MAN COMETH
Robert J. Ray
When a professional hit man who has his sights set on a TV evangelist wounds Detective Branko's partner instead, Newport Beach's hottest detective finds himself with a list of suspects that is as bizarre as it is long.

THE NANTUCKET DIET MURDERS
Virginia Rich
A handsome new diet doctor has won over Nantucket's richest widows with his weight-loss secrets—and very personal attention. But when murder becomes part of the menu, Mrs. Potter stirs the pot to come up with a clever culinary killer.

A NOVENA FOR MURDER
Sister Carol Anne O'Marie
"Move over, Miss Marple, here comes supersleuth Sister Mary Helen, a nun with an unusual habit of solving murders."
                    —San Francisco Sunday Examiner
                    & Chronicle

SHATTERED MOON
Kate Green
When a young woman gets involved with the L.A.P.D. and a missing person case, her most precious gift—her healing vision—becomes her most dangerous enemy, filling every moment with mounting menace. . . and turning the secrets of her past murderously against her.

TOO CLOSE TO THE EDGE
Susan Dunlap
Jill Smith, a street-smart, savvy detective, finds herself trapped within a murder victim's intricate network of perilous connections.

A NICE CLASS OF CORPSE
Simon Brett
When the sixty-seven-year-old Mrs. Pargeter checks into a seaside hotel for some peace and quiet, what she finds instead is a corpse in the lobby and a murder to snoop into on the dark side of the upper crust.

POLITICAL SUICIDE
Robert Barnard
A member of Parliament meets an untimely—and suspicious—demise.

THE OLD FOX DECEIV'D
Martha Grimes
When the body of a mysterious woman is found murdered, Inspector Richard Jury of Scotland Yard finds himself tracking a very foxy killer.

DEATH OF A PERFECT MOTHER
Robert Barnard
Everyone had a motive to kill her. . . so Chief Inspector Dominic McHale finds himself stumped on his very first homicide case—puzzled by a lengthy list of suspects and a very clever killer.

THE DIRTY DUCK
Martha Grimes
In addition to the murders being staged nightly at the Royal Shakespeare Theatre, a real one has been committed not too far away, and the killer has left a fragment of Elizabethan verse behind as a clue.

TOTAL NUMBER OF FREE BOOKS SELECTED ____ X $1.00
= $_____ (Amount Enclosed)

Dell has other great books in print by these authors. If you enjoy them, check your local book outlets for other titles.